MW00965266

VINLAND

THE RAGNARÖK

R.G. JOHNSTON

This is a work of fiction based loosely on the Vinland Sagas. Names, characters, and places are products of the author's imagination or are used fictitiously. Any resemblance to actual events or locales or persons, living or dead, is entirely coincidental.

Robert Johnston, P.O. Box 1713, Belleville, Ontario. K8N 5J2

www.vinlandragnarok.ca

National Library of Canada Cataloguing In Publication
Johnston, Robert

Vinland: The Ragnarök / Robert Johnston
ISBN: 978-0-9782978-1-7

1. Historical Fantasy. 2.Viking. 3.Vinland

To my mother,

Marion

At the end of the gods and the world, as it is said in *Völuspá*

Surtur from the south
wielding fire
The gods' swords shine in the darkness,
like stars in the night
Mountains collapse into rubble
And fiends shall fall
Man walks the road to ruin
as the sky splits in two

12

Gudrid was not altogether happy with her long-time friend's choice of husband. She tried to keep the displeasure from her face as she stood with Freydis before Thorfinn, but her thoughts were far from neutral. *The man brings nothing to the union—no family and no lands to speak of!* But the main reason for Gudrid's displeasure was her belief that Freydis's marriage was a reaction to seeing her husband Ari again, only to watch him die in the treasure cave.

Movement on the ocean distracted Gudrid and she looked out to sea, seeing only the pewter sky that rolled always into Vinland She couldn't remember the last time she'd seen a sunrise that wasn't obscured by the grey haze. She thought she saw a figure riding on a knarr, obscured by the mist of the water or the mist of her mind, she couldn't tell which; either way, she knew that the vision was real.

She knew that Freydis was still in love with Ari, her sight didn't have to tell her that. She also saw a difference in her friend that she couldn't quite put her finger on, but Freydis was abrasive and solitary. She assumed it was the shock of having to face repressed feelings that she'd closely guarded for decades. Ari had never been good for Freydis, and recent events didn't help; they'd brought to the surface bad memories that best remained buried.

"Since we landed on this great land," Thorfinn said, "we've been witnesses to many adventures. None are as adventurous as the union between a man and a woman. It is a great day in the life of a community when one can say that he—or she—has invested heart and mind in continuing the community at large."

Gudrid's eyes strayed back to her friend. Only weeks had passed since Freydis and Ari had met again for the last time. Freydis should have taken months to recover from that experience, not weeks. And there was her unsettled stomach—a clear sign to Gudrid that this marriage would not turn out well for anyone involved.

Her eyes slid to the groom. She didn't know Thorvald very well, but during the pre-ceremony interview, Thorfinn had learned that Thorvald's birth had been illegitimate and unplanned. His mother had been given to the Arab Ibn Fadlan as a concubine by the Rus, a group of traders of Swedish origin accompanying the embassy sent by the caliph of Bagdad to the king of the Bulgars. When Thorvald's mother realized that she was pregnant and that Ibn was not going to support the baby, she escaped, eventually making her way to Iceland and then following the other settlers to Grœnlandia, along with Eirik the Red.

As far as Gudrid could see, Thorvald was in the marriage for the money and the position that a socially affluent family like Eirik's could bestow upon him. For Freydis and her family, this union didn't ally her with any family of equal status. There were no lands to be gained. She felt, and hoped, that Eirik would not look favourably on the marriage, just as she didn't.

In the absence of Eirik, Thorfinn acted as the representative for Freydis's family. He received the mundr, the bride-price to be held in trust till the day that they returned to Grœnlandia. Thorvald had paid the absolute minimum mundr—eight ounces of silver in the form of a loan of Freydis's jewellery. Yet another embarrassing arrangement that wasn't favourable in Gudrid's eyes.

Gudrid wondered if the assembled settlers standing around the couple knew that the silver Thorfinn held in his hand was actually Freydis's. She didn't look, but she suspected that the smiling faces would contain a hint of disapproval, if they knew.

Thorfinn dipped a leafy branch into a bowl full of animal

blood, the tapered green tips of the pinnates becoming ruddy as he swished them around in the liquid. Lifting the branch, he sprinkled blood over the couple in the sign of the hluat-teinn, the shape of the hammer. The swaying branch flicked blood over the couple, Gudrid, and those of the congregation standing nearby; they closed their eyes as the warm droplets struck their faces, slipped tongues out to taste what landed on their lips.

The couple exchanged rings and swords. The witnesses looked on in silence as they said their vows.

"Freydis, from the day that I gazed upon you, I knew that I wanted to be yours. We are warriors of the heart and mind. The only thing that I can offer to this marriage is me; I ask nothing in return. I betroth myself to you."

"Thorvald, my love, I offer you myself. We will begin our life here, on Vinland, and live out the greatest adventure that two people can. I betroth myself to you."

Strange, Gudrid thought, that death and renewal always were married to one another. It was not so long ago that the battle between the natives and her people had occurred; only viknatals earlier, in fact. She looked beyond the crowd at the killing field, stained with the blood of their kin. So many brave warriors had died in that battle; so many hopes and dreams had been crushed as both armies clashed at the centre of the field—but more tragically, at the centre of their being.

Thorfinn had hoped to settle this bountiful land, to use its resources and the resources of nearby Markland to help his people. Grœnlandia was a dying community, Thorfinn had said, its resources unable to sustain its immigrant population. Which was why Thorfinn and Gudrid and many of the adventurers in the group had left the relative safety of their home to find new places to live—especially places where they could prosper.

Once the three native chiefs had decided that the Norse could no longer remain on Vinland, the natives proved more helpful than the group could imagine. They left the Norse alone so the group could rebuild their destroyed knarr. But there was always a scouting parting walking along the edge of the forest, usually on a daily basis, ensuring that Tostig and his men continued their work on the knarr.

Gudrid could feel their presence even when they didn't show

themselves. It was as if she could see the outlines of their bodies through the foliage in her mind, smell their sweat and hear their whispers. She didn't feel threatened by them, but then again, she didn't tell anyone of her visions, not even Thorfinn. That was best for all, Gudrid decided; let the natives keep their vigil to satisfy the native leaders and let the Norse remain ignorant of the native scouts so that fear didn't escalate into another battle.

Day by day, Gudrid's sight deepened and her visions changed from foggy, dream-like impressions to images of eyewitness clarity. She knew, by this same insight, that the life growing within her fed her improved perception of inner and outer reality, just as Gudrid's body nourished the growing infant inside her womb.

Thorfinn wrapped the hustrulinet around the couple's intertwined hands. "In front of these witnesses and by your own words, I now pronounce you husband and wife." He unwrapped the garter and placed it over the crown of Freydis's head.

Stepping forward, Gudrid pinned the cloth to Freydis's hair as the congregation cheered and clapped the traditional close of the ceremony. She stepped back and presented the happy couple to the audience, but all the while, her thoughts were elsewhere. She clapped and smiled autonomously, not taking any notice of events.

There was a thought riding on the offshore wind, as strong and pungent as its salty smell. Even though the autumn day was warm and sunny, a foreboding chill permeated Gudrid's body. It penetrated her heart and soul; she felt it as far down as her stomach, and in the womb where her unborn son lay. Her head snapped toward the open water as if drawn by something in her peripheral vision, but it didn't move into her line of sight; she swore that she saw a ship, but she knew that the vision originated in her mind rather than her eyes. Before the image escaped she glimpsed an old man standing alone at the centre of the deck, in front of the mast. Its blue sail ballooned above him as the knarr was guided to shore by an unseen hand.

"Gudrid, my sister, are you not happy for me?" Freydis squealed, as if she were a young girl in love for the first time.

"Of course I am," she said, hoping that her empty smile and hug were enough to convince Freydis. "I'm so happy for you." But Gudrid's eyes remained on the empty horizon visible over Freydis's left shoulder, half expecting the ship in her vision to reappear at any moment.

But, Gudrid reminded herself, ever since their ship crashed on the shore of Vinland and then drifted out to sea, Gudrid looked to the horizon, hoping to see some sign of a ship that would carry them back home again. She expected a ship to come and she assumed that it would come from Grœnlandia.

The original intention that brought Gudrid back to the shore of Vinland and Markland—to return her husband's body to Grœnlandia and to open the treasure cave—was gone. That dream had collapsed with the destruction of the cave and the loss of the treasure. The only riches she'd found were their lives, preserved through their narrow escape.

Other well-wishers pulled Freydis from Gudrid's caring grasp, handling her like royalty as they eagerly held her hands and admired the intricate designs on her hustrulinet. Gudrid was being pulled away as well, but in a less than social direction. As the sea wind blew across her face and murmured in her ears, the feeling of something riding on the wind returned, much stronger this time. She closed her eyes, trying to hold onto it as if she could grab the wind and squeeze it between her fingers.

The images reshaped in her mind and she saw a figure with one eye staring back at her . . . and then heard a whisper: " . . . *Gudrid . . .*"

"Gudrid!"

She opened her eyes, startled by a touch and the word shouted in her ear. "Thorfinn," she exclaimed, "don't ever do that again!"

"I'm sorry," he said, placing a hand on her stomach, worried about the baby. "Was it another waking dream?"

Gudrid nodded, unable to speak till air returned to her lungs.

"You've been having quite a few of those lately," Thorfinn continued. "Was it about the baby again?"

"No. I saw a man on a ship. He wore a robe . . . No, not a robe . . . a hooded cloak . . ." Gudrid struggled to reclaim the vision. "A blue . . . hooded cloak."

"Was he headed to Vinland?" Thorfinn asked, looking out to sea.

"Why would you say that?"

"Well, it seems your visions usually impact on us in some way. I just thought that—"

"Yes, I see what you mean." She grinned.

Thorfinn grinned back, immediately recognizing this as one of those moments when he and Gudrid could share the humour in what they said to one another. Their first year together was one of magic and adventure; neither one had time to become discontented or bored with the other.

"I must speak with Grimhild," Gudrid said, her tone as urgent as her body language. "She will know what this vision means."

Thorfinn nodded, knowing the legend of the völva, Grimhild. Her followers sought the wisdom she was able to draw from visions, delivering it verbally to some and to others by transmutation. Others feared Grimhild as a strange and demented being, or as one of the Jötunn, a race of nature spirits.

Gudrid gave Thorfinn a quick kiss on the cheek and walked back to the settlement. She caught up with the wedding procession and followed the yelling and laughing crowd toward the Great Hall. They passed wicker baskets strewn across the field, left half full when the harvesting had stopped for the ceremony. Much of the wild wheat that grew in abundance here had been stained with human blood; it blackened the earth and stained the hearts of the community. The fertile fields of Vinland had become an alien and harsh world littered with broken spears and splintered shields; they felt as unwelcome as a hungry child being pushed away from its mother's breast.

Much had been lost in the fight, and very little gained. They had fought a battle that they didn't fully understand and couldn't win. Mounds dotted the field beyond where bodies of the fallen lay, all less one small body part that would be carried back to Grœnlandia to be buried in home soil. It was a grotesque job to amputate a finger or a toe, but as every Norse knew, it had to be done; the return of an explorer, either dead or alive, was paramount for the psychological well-being of the community. To know that the physical remains of a loved one were back at home settled the mind and eased the pain of the loss.

The line separating the field of death and the beginning of the community garden was impossible to see. Each served a different purpose in the community. Gudrid hoped that the graves would serve as sustenance for their souls, just as the harvested wheat would be sustenance for their bodies.

Beyond the battlefield animal hide flapped, loosed here and there from its frame of wood by the wind—Grimhild's tent, where she lived alone, pushed away from the community because her visions and possessions were too frightening and too disruptive. She channelled the power of the gods, who gave her glimpses of the future and insight into the past accompanied by violent shaking, spasmodic tics, and full collapse to the ground, where she'd roll around until she either passed out or opened her eyes and instantly regained lucid consciousness.

The settlers saw Grimhild many nights, wandering through the field of the dead, gathering the bloodied spires of wheat and body parts. Today she sat in front of her tent, shaking the contents of a bowl as Gudrid approached. Chalky white bones bobbed in a pot of pink-tinged boiling water hung over the fire; Gudrid heard the clack of more bones against the side of the bowl. Grimhild tipped the bowl and human hand bones fell into the dirt at her feet. She muttered a few incomprehensible syllables, then gathered a fistful of bones and dirt into the bowl, and repeated the process again.

"Loki shape-shifts and Odin comes," Grimhild muttered, and cackled, not noticing Gudrid. Then suddenly Grimhild screamed and began wiping her eyes, as if she were trying to wipe an image away.

Gudrid grabbed her shoulders. "Grimhild, what do you see?"

"I see . . . I see the end," she answered, her eyes peering into Gudrid's; they were so wide, Gudrid saw her reflection in them. "It's the end of all of us . . ." Grimhild touched Gudrid's enlarged belly. "The child is stillborn. All of our children are stillborn. We will not conceive because the gods are impotent."

Grimhild leaned back, screaming and wailing as her body swayed from side to side. Then she looked up to the heavens and wailed to the stars, "Who will save us from ourselves? The land is full of death." She raised herself to her knees. "The land is stained with our blood and the blood of our future."

Leaning forward, she reached out to the bloody outlines of bodies still visible on the trampled grass. "This is a land of death; the disease will come . . . it will drag our limp bodies to our graves, where we'll rot and not rise again. The gods will not save us because they are the hunted. The land rises up against us and the world serpent, Jörmungandr, will kill us with a final swoosh from his tail; the oceans will be on the land . . . I've seen this before and I see this now—he comes!"

Grimhild collapsed in a muddy pool of her own urine as she released control of her body to absorb more and more of the vision that she was forced to endure. She rolled around in the mud, her feet kicking and stamping on the ground, her face contorted, the skin sagging to the back of her head. She looked up at Gudrid with a cadaverous stare and stretched her arms toward her. "I've seen the end." Tortured tears rolled down her cheeks. "This marriage is a union of destruction!" Grimhild spat the last out angrily before she collapsed into unconsciousness.

Gudrid stood over Grimhild's still body, frozen by shock and fear. She felt pulled apart inside; had the völva confirmed a truth that Gudrid experienced inside herself? She reached down and tentatively touched Grimhild's chest, making sure that the völva still breathed. Then she backed away and sat down on the grass, touching her stomach and taking long, relaxing breaths.

Grimhild's abilities were controversial at best; some saw her as a true seer while others believed that she was dangerous and mad. A matter of opinion, Gudrid thought. Some could see Gudrid's gift of sight as delusional, but Gudrid knew that what she possessed was a gift; something that was given to her by her mother, Hallveig, and something that, like her mother, she had to share with her community.

Gudrid's sight, too, was every bit as important as Leif Eiriksson's deeds; this was Gudrid's legacy and she hoped that it would continue down her family line.

She looked up to the sky and noticed grey clouds moving in from the ocean; the air had become heavy, making Gudrid feel as if she were carrying a barrel of grain on her back. Her breathing grew laboured and she shifted uncomfortably; it felt as if a pole were being pushed into the small of her back. She stood, thinking of the dream that she'd had, the last two nights.

In her dream, she heard Snorri crying but couldn't find him in the thick fog that rolled across the land. As the mist cleared she realized that she stood on a stony shore lapped by waves. A ship approached through rough waters, pushed before a rolling pewter sky split by cracks of fiery orange light. And on the ship's deck stood a tall figure draped in a grey cloak . . .

ꟹ ꟹ

Elsu walked through the thick underbrush toward the clearing. Since the visitors, whom he now knew and referred to as Grœnlanders, had been ordered to leave their island, Elsu had been charged with watching them as well as communicating with them. The chieftain council that made that decision, in their wisdom, felt that keeping the lines of communication open with the white faces would avoid raising suspicion between the two groups. But the patience of the leading chiefs was wearing thin; omen or no omen, if the Grœnlanders showed the slightest sign of aggression, they were to be eliminated.

Elsu travelled alone for fear of a repeat of his previous visit, when a member of his party had picked up one of their shiny weapons to admire it. When he'd waved the weapon in the air, the white faces had misinterpreted the action as an attack, and killed him. Elsu sighed. Kiche had always been reckless as a youth, and that behaviour had followed him into his adulthood. He had lost his leg as a young man when a bear attacked him. Warned by the elders to stay away from the bear cave because the mother would defend her young, Kiche hadn't listened; losing his leg was a small price to pay for escaping with his life.

Elsu saw the hull of the Grœnlanders' new ship as he cleared the forest perimeter. It stood prominent on the horizon, men on scaffolding hammering nails into its wooden sides. The shipbuilders never stopped the hammering. It echoed into the forest all day and into the early evening.

He touched the metal nail hanging around his neck, a memento of his last visit. It was truly a miraculous act, he thought, that something as hard as a stone could be worked by the Grœnlanders. They mined the metal from the bog next to their camp and melted it down, then poured it into a mold chiselled into a rock and let it cool. One man sitting at the kiln all day made hundreds of them. He hoped that they would teach him this magic.

Even though Elsu was not wonder-struck by this method of creating, for his people also manipulated the wood that they used to build arrows and such, he was fascinated by the Grœnlanders' ability to take the shiny rock from the water of the bog and bend and twist it into anything that they wanted. He had not seen this done with any other rock before.

The Grœnlanders were used to Elsu dropping by. Initially they all stopped whatever they were doing to watch him, but lately they pretty much ignored him. He felt as expected as the morning sun or the next ocean wave.

೩ ೪

Thorfinn saw Elsu approaching and decided that he'd talk to him about what was on the minds of his leaders—more out of curiosity than any fear-based motivation. He had come to respect this native in so many ways, from his questions about building large ships that travelled vast distances across the water to stories of the gods of Asgard—Thorfinn had been feeding him bits and pieces of the stories he had learned as a boy. During their sometimes long conversations, Thorfinn had discovered that their beliefs were similar in many ways. They both had a family of gods and goddesses who lived in a realm beyond Earth.

But Thorfinn couldn't forget that he and the rest of his group were on borrowed time. He hoped that his willingness to allow Elsu into the affairs of the Norse who occupied Vinland would show the chiefs of the three tribes that Thorfinn and his people could be trusted to honour their agreement to one day leave this land.

"Thor-a-finn, are you well today?" Elsu asked, struggling with the pronunciation of the Norse name.

"Yes, I am. Is there any news from your elders?"

"Yes. Some still want to attack and drive you off our land. But the chiefs are not ready to risk the lives of our people. They still honour your agreement with us."

"Good," Thorfinn said. "We also honour the agreement." He beckoned for Elsu to follow him to the knarr construction site, to the hull that rose almost two storeys high from the beach. It was flatter and its angle much more gradual than the *Mimir's* hull; this design improved stability and gave the deck more room. The inside of the hull was also larger, the ceiling high enough for a full-grown man to stand up while walking below deck.

The dwarf Tostig was the first that Thorfinn noticed staring at Elsu. The rhythm of the hammers dwindled to sparse taps as the others quickly followed suit. Thorfinn knew what they were thinking: would today be the day that he reported back to his leaders that it was time to drive the Norse from Vinland? Thorfinn could almost feel Elsu's distress washing over him like the constant wind blowing cold from the ocean.

"Tostig, how goes the building?" Thorfinn called up.

Tostig began the slow descent down the scaffolding. "Get back to work!" he yelled to his men.

"We are working as fast as we can," Tostig told Thorfinn when he reached the ground, glaring askance at Elsu. "I thought we had until your son was born, Thorfinn. Are the natives changing our agreement?"

"No, Tostig. Elsu is doing his job. It's his opinion that will influence and appease the elders of the three tribes."

Tostig's aggressive stare softened, but the stress of the unrealistic timeline still showed on his face. There were shadows as dark as the sky overhead around his eyes, and the flesh below them was puffed into ashen bags. His movements were tight and edgy, as if the slightest thing would set him off.

It's as if I'm looking at my own reflection in a still pond, Thorfinn thought. Work on the knarr was proceeding at double the pace they'd originally intended, and Thorfinn feared it was more than they could handle, that a major detail would be overlooked, perhaps something that wouldn't be discovered till they were at sea, when it would be too late. Making repairs at sea was always riskier than on land. He feared a repeat of the incidents that had led to the sinking of the *Mimir*. And with Thorfinn's intention of returning with cargo, a fatality on the water was a certainty.

"I hope to have the ship completed by the time Snorri is born," Tostig answered.

Every time Thorfinn heard that name, fear shuddered from his head to his chest. The idea of progeny was both frightening and exciting. A child completed the cycle of life. His mind spun with the questions and absurdities of being responsible for another living being. Snorri was a part of him, and in turn Thorfinn was a part of Snorri.

Stop! his mind yelled back. *The future will happen when*

it happens; all in due time. He was needed in the present, for Gudrid. He felt almost embarrassed about his irrational fear. Here Gudrid was, vomiting almost every dægur, trying to be present for Freydis on her wedding day, sewing her wedding dress from whatever pieces of cloth they could find. And the only thing he could think about was the awesome responsibility of a son.

"Yes, that's good," Thorfinn said, returning to the moment.

Without a word, Tostig returned to work. Elsu and Thorfinn walked away from the hammering.

Elsu stopped, and Thorfinn paused to look at him. "Thor-a-finn, I would like to ask you something. Do you have people who see things that have not yet come to pass?"

"Yes, my wife Gudrid has that ability."

"We have a seer as well. She has seen things, including a white-face with child. Is Gudrid with child?"

"Yes, she is."

"Then she must come to our camp and share thoughts with our seer, Bantam."

Thorfinn saw this as a chance to turn the strained and tenuous relationship with the natives into what he'd hoped for from the very beginning of the voyage: a working and healthy alliance. With some work and merchant savvy he might, in fact, be able to replace the suspicion and fear with a new union of hope and understanding. "I will ask her," Thorfinn said.

"We are linked, Thor-a-finn—your people and mine," Elsu said as they resumed walking. "I saw that when my dead wife, Yakima, showed herself to your wife. I always knew that my wife walked with me; there were brief moments when I felt her presence, though she did not choose to reveal herself to me. I now know that when she came to Gudrid on that day, it was a sign that the lives of your people and mine were intertwined, as the roots are with the earth. Now I see that it is larger than you and me, Thor-a-finn; it is your people and my people, just as we both breathe the same air and walk on the same land."

Thorfinn couldn't help but appreciate the intelligence and eloquence of Elsu's words. This was the language and the passion of a like-minded individual who saw beyond the everyday and the physical world. He appreciated that same characteristic in Gudrid.

A creak made Thorfinn turn as the door behind him opened,

and Gudrid walked out with a basket in her arms, its bottom resting on her stomach. Her hair showed the morning's work—strands that had escaped her bun blew in the wind. He saw the same tired, strained look on her face shared by every member of the community as they worked to finish what needed to be done before their departure from Vinland.

"Gudrid," Thorfinn called, and she looked up.

"Good morning, my love . . . good morning, Elsu," she said, trying to smile through her fatigue.

"Greetings," Elsu replied.

"Elsu has invited you to meet with his seer," Thorfinn said.

"Yes, Gud-rid. She has had a vision of you and she seeks understanding."

Gudrid stopped, looking intrigued. "I will be happy to consult with your seer," she said. "I seek clarification about my visions, as well. When do we leave?"

"I will return in two days," Elsu said. "We will arrange to meet in the great forest, beyond the meadow."

"We'll be ready," Thorfinn told him.

Elsu turned and left Thorfinn and Gudrid, who watched him leave the settlement and cross the meadow toward the forest. Although he trusted Elsu's good intentions, Thorfinn was a little nervous to enter the native camp. "Do you have enough strength to make the journey, Gudrid?" he asked.

"Oh yes, I'll be fine. My visions are becoming much stronger. They're infiltrating my days." She hesitated. "Thorfinn, I'm afraid that I'm going a little mad."

"Maybe it's because you're with a child. I've seen it change the emotions of women."

Gudrid's face froze in a stare.

"Gudrid . . . Gudrid?"

"Early of ages when nothing was; there was neither sand nor sea nor cold waves. The earth was not found nor the sky above; Ginnungagap was there, but grass nowhere."

Seconds later Gudrid blinked and looked into Thorfinn's confused face. "Was I in another place?" she asked.

"You were quoting something—a passage from a song that I've heard before, but one that I can't place right now. Do you know what you were saying?"

"No . . . I don't know what I was saying."

"You were saying something about Ginnungagap."

"Ginnungagap . . . the void preceding the creation of the world?" She frowned in thought. "For the last few viknatal I've had a vision of an energy source coming . . . riding the waves of the ocean. And I've seen us falling into a black, bottomless void. Thorfinn," she looked into his eyes, "the world will end just as it began: ice from the north and fire from the south and in between, the world swallowed up by the Ginnungagap."

Thorfinn took the basket from Gudrid and set it down at their feet. He hugged her, trying to protect her from a vision that he could neither control nor understand.

"I feel something is on the horizon, Thorfinn," Gudrid said, burying her head against Thorfinn's chest. "It will shift the landscape of our lives."

Gudrid squeezed Thorfinn tighter, then escaped his embrace.

11

Adam sat on a bench in the Great Hall, preferring the solace of the building for prayer and meditation away from the rest of the Vinlanders. The building was used occasionally for administrative meetings as well as celebrations and gatherings, both official and unofficial, but now he sought solitude, and so sat alone.

He'd done this for weeks, listening to the howling wind outside as he searched for an answer to why he'd thrown away one of the most sacred artifacts in Christendom, the holy lance. He'd had it in his grasp; he'd only had to hold onto it until he returned to his leaders in Europe. With their wisdom and experience, they'd know what to do with it. At the time, he thought it was the best course of action; the power of the lance was too powerful in the hands of humanity. Now he wasn't so sure that his decision to throw the head of the lance into the abyss was the correct one. Its tempting power still shouted to him from its final resting place.

The lance could have benefited the world in so many ways. The Church could've demonstrated the full power of the faith through an object that was otherwise used to kill; it was a clear and present demonstration of how violence could be changed to peace.

Adam no longer felt that he was part of the Vinland

community. They were too different. Now that their common goal was gone, nothing allied him with them. Their religious differences resurfaced and Adam felt trapped; he couldn't bend himself far enough to accept the Norse world, even though it surrounded him daily.

The miles that separated him from the fellowship of the Church also distanced him from his faith; killing Ari had added to that feeling, the mortal sin leaving his mind in turmoil. Killing Ari had been more a betrayal of his beliefs than the right and just thing to do. He couldn't reconcile the act of a mortal sin with the act of destroying evil. What if Ari could have been converted to the faith? Killing him hadn't allowed him the chance to atone for what he had done.

But the real question taunting Adam was, *Is destroying evil a sin?* Was he, a representative of the Church, justified in taking life to protect the Church?

It was all too late to change. He had to come to terms with the fact that his mortal soul was doomed for all eternity; he was damned to wander through the sulphur caves and boiling oceans of hell.

Adam closed his prayer book; today, it didn't provide its usual solace. There was no restitution for murderers.

The wind rattled the door and disturbed the low-burning fire in the centre of the room as the door blew open. He was about to get up to shut it when he saw a bulky shadow that preceded Gudrid's entrance into the hall. She slowly pulled the door shut, swirling a few autumn leaves that had blown in with her. Then she turned and jumped when she saw Adam.

"Adam! You startled me." Her eyes fell to the prayer book in his hand. "I hope I'm not disturbing you."

"No, you're not," he said. "How is the baby?"

"A little too restless for my liking, but we're getting through it."

"I know this is your third marriage. Is it your first child?" Adam asked, wondering if a woman of Gudrid's years would be giving birth for the first time.

"Yes, it is," Gudrid answered, rubbing her stomach. "I was told by a seer that I could not bear children. So I look on this birth as a blessing."

"Yes, all births are a blessing."

Gudrid's eyes fixed on Adam's robe. "Adam, I would like to ask you . . . Please explain the Christian concept of providence."

Adam sat up and removed his finger from his prayer book. "That is a big question, Gudrid. It covers a large area. But I think if I had to give you a quick, all-encompassing answer, it would be that our heavenly Father has laid out a plan for all of us, both collectively and individually. Unlike us, God has foresight and foreknowledge of things to come."

"Oh." Gudrid nodded. "What about my sight? I am able to see events that haven't happened yet, without prior knowledge of what will come to pass."

"Maybe you only think that you know these events. Is it possible that it's a coincidence, what you think you see and what actually happens? Does everything you see come to pass, Gudrid?"

"Well, I've been pretty accurate so far, Adam."

"Yes, your prophetic abilities have been proven time and time again. Gudrid, have you considered that your abilities have been given to you by God, rather than by Odin and the Norse gods?"

"Lately, that question has been on my mind," she replied. "The Norns control our fate; I do know that I'm a descendant of one of those sisters—Skuld, a valkyrie who determines the future of our fallen warriors; her name literally means 'future.' We believe that fate has power over the physical world, but not over the human spirit."

"Gudrid, what if your power comes from God and not from Skuld, as you believe?"

Gudrid looked at him, her brows pinched together. "I don't understand your question, Adam."

"Perhaps you having the power of sight is part of God's divine plan for you, and not part of your Norse plan."

"Because you see your god as more powerful than my gods?" Gudrid asked.

"Yes. Why else would your king become a Christian and decree that your nations convert to Christianity?"

ഌ ര

Gudrid thought that Adam had a point. Following the

Christian god had made Midgard a much tamer place in which to live. She felt more in control of her life and much more in control of determining her destiny, maybe even in instigating change in her life.

If she openly declared her thoughts of conversion to Thorfinn, though, he would never understand. How was she to reconcile her beliefs and her life to her husband? Was Thorfinn holding her back? Like the rest of the realm, would she eventually have to convert to remain a part of the community? Even Thorfinn wore the Christian symbol around his neck when he did business with the countries of Europe. Did this one action put his integrity into question?

She almost felt that Thorfinn, in a way, was holding her back from exploring the path that her mind wanted to understand. Unlike Thorfinn, Gudrid felt that this path for her people was inevitable, chiselled in the stone history of Adam's providence.

"Are you joining the expedition to the native camp?" Adam asked, changing the subject.

"Yes, their seer has requested my presence to discuss and hopefully use our combined power and abilities to see our collective futures."

"Perhaps if you had a little bit more faith," Adam suggested, "you wouldn't need to see the future . . . or the future would be something that you'd want to actively participate in. Providence has much to do with our active participation, as it involves believing that events will unfold for the best possible good, as they should."

Adam does have a point, Gudrid thought. She looked out the window and noticed for the first time since beginning her conversation with Adam that rain flowed over the fascia of the grass roof in a translucent sheet of water. She was stunned that she hadn't heard or noticed it earlier. They were so involved in their discussion that even the elements were a little beyond her immediate comprehension.

ꟾ ꟾ

Gudrid hastily put a few things together in a knapsack for their half-day trip to the native camp. She didn't exactly know what she would need other than food and several herbs, thin sheets of birch bark, and some binding as a makeshift first aid kit.

One of the fortunate things about living so close to a people who relied heavily on the land as a source of nourishment and sustenance was that she quickly learned about healing plants that would enhance her skill as a shaman, as the natives were beginning to call her. She did feel uncomfortable with such a title, but she decided it was wise not to question their hosts while the treaty remained on such shaky ground.

This afternoon, Snorri was unusually active, as if he were trying to kick his way through her womb wall and out into the air. She knew that her delivery would not be long; Snorri's head was beginning to turn.

She wondered if this was the reason that Bantam had asked for her specifically to visit their camp. The native seer seemed to be in constant contact with the community of Norse. By what means, Gudrid was never told; she assumed it was through a combination of Elsu's reports and heresy among the scouting parties who kept a constant vigil on Leifsbúrðir.

The door creaked and a moment later Thorfinn stepped inside the longhouse. "Are you almost ready?"

"Yes, but I'm afraid that I may be forgetting something. Well," she sighed, "we'll just have to make do en route." She slung the strap over her head and adjusted the pouch to rest snugly on her hip. "Okay, let's go."

The early autumn air had a bit of a bite; the wind smelled of an approaching winter to end all winters. Gudrid felt a sense of déjà vu in the breeze. It was not so long ago that she faced her destiny in Markland; a twenty year journey that began with the wind pushing them across the North Atlantic.

Today they would travel farther inland to Elsu and his people's camp, a place that no Norse had seen. Gudrid—and the rest of the party, for that matter—would have to place all of their trust in Elsu for their safety. She trusted him; the visit from his dead wife, Yakima, months earlier had established a link. Gudrid knew that the destinies of both their peoples were intertwined, grounded in the earth, somehow. She had felt it for the past few weeks—for that matter, since they arrived on Vinland. How else could she explain her vision of the native female counterpart and the outcome of their last battle with the natives? They were two sides of the same coin; each playing a part in the whole. She wondered if Grimhild saw this as well.

As the small band left Leifsbúrður, all eyes looked up from their tasks to watch Thorfinn, Gudrid, and Elsu walk through the field where so many of their comrades had fallen. Gudrid couldn't look at the bloodstained earth. She focused on their destination, the tree line of the forest ahead. From this distance, the pine and spruce trees were so straight that they looked like soldiers guarding the land beyond, a first line of defence against any intruders.

She could see smaller dots among the branches of the trees—watchers. They'd probably been watched from the very first day that they landed on Vinland. Gudrid tried to look upon this situation with distant objectivity. They were natives sitting in their natural watchtowers, monitoring any and all travellers to their camp. Thorfinn had ordered similar sentry activity to guard their camp. Gudrid knew it was unnecessary for such guarded vigilance on either side; their chief's omen would be obeyed and honoured.

Gudrid wasn't sure what her role was in the drama in which she was destined to participate. She suspected that once she talked to Bantam, all would be revealed.

Their silent journey through the trees spoke of tension. No one spoke. Even Elsu, with his friendly, diplomatic style, seemed a little uncomfortable; she suspected that the constant reminder of his deceased wife accompanied him. Gudrid herself was preoccupied with their surroundings; her senses were registering an underlying current—they were being followed.

They were like black cats in the night, consciously stepping through the underbrush and using the natural surroundings just as a garter snake uses foliage to mask its presence. Gudrid saw them, not with her eyes so much as with her outstretched senses. It was as if she was the prey stalking the stalkers, following them, anticipating their movements . . .

Assassins!

"Get down!" she screamed.

Gudrid ducked behind a large maple and crouched there, her cheek pressed so snugly against the bark that she could almost feel the sap pulsing through the tree's veins. She instinctively looked toward the treetops and saw a small dart falling through the air like a raindrop marking the beginning of a storm. She crawled behind a fern, her stomach dragging along the ground. She didn't know where Thorfinn and Elsu had landed, but she hoped they were safe.

Another dart whistled through the air. She crawled as fast and as far as her arms and legs could carry her.

"Gudrid, where are you?" Thorfinn called from somewhere ahead.

"The darts . . . poisoned," Elsu yelled.

Gudrid noticed the underbrush moving up ahead. "Thorfinn, I'm here."

The bushes stopped shaking and she glimpsed Thorfinn through the foliage between them, moving toward her. He stopped next to her and instinctively shielded her body from the intermittent darts thwacking the large leaves of plants lining the forest floor. "Elsu is just up ahead," he said.

Gudrid looked up; she could see just a thin line of his animal hide tunic behind a large maple tree. The tree she and Thorfinn hid behind was at best a temporary barrier. Soon the assailants would reposition themselves so they could more effectively continue the barrage of poisoned darts.

"Follow me," Thorfinn said. Pushing to his feet, he ran in line with the tree trunk, concealing himself from their attackers. Gudrid also made use of the tree trunk barrier to get away. When they were in range, Elsu assisted Thorfinn in getting Gudrid out of danger.

"Gudrid, you are hit," Elsu yelled in a voice high with panic, pulling the almost invisible, needle-thin dart from her arm. He quickly pushed up her sleeve and began sucking on the small, black-stained wound, spitting periodically.

Gudrid began to panic as she felt the poison trickling through her veins. Her arm began to go numb; she felt off-balance, and the world took on a fluid quality—any slight movement on her part threw Gudrid against Thorfinn or Elsu. She gripped them while she searched for her equilibrium.

Elsu stopped and pulled lips stained purple from her arm. He examined the blood tricking from the wound to ensure that the blue tinge of the poison was gone. "I think I got most of the poison," he said in his broken Icelandic, but Gudrid knew the truth: he hadn't gotten all of it in time.

"I . . . I'm feeling a little tired; I want to lie down."

"No, Gudrid. You must keep moving—for your life."

Each grabbing an arm, Thorfinn and Elsu supported Gudrid as they ran, using whatever natural cover they could to blend into their surroundings. Gudrid stumbled and her head occasionally wobbled as the poison took effect. Their getaway was successful, but Thorfinn looked worried and kept glancing over his shoulder, as if expecting that the next dart would be the one that ended Gudrid's rescue.

Gudrid felt herself rapidly losing consciousness; running on the forest floor felt like running across the bobbing deck of a knarr. The air ahead shimmered, as if she were looking through the rising heat from a firepit—she couldn't focus.

Fears of losing Snorri pulsated through her mind and she doubted that her visions of his birth were true. But beyond the fear, she felt something powerfully threatening; for some reason, she knew that her power of sight had diminished in some way. It was like knowing there was sun shining on the other side of closed shutters, but she was unable to open them to feel the warmth on her face.

A single word came to her as if carried on a breath of the wind: *Ragnarök.* In a flash she saw everything: the end of her people and her race; Midgard forever changed; a tunnel of light and the beginning of the battle that would end all battles, between the Jötunn and the gods.

Her last memory before she lapsed into unconsciousness was Thorfinn picking her up and cradling her in his arms. Perhaps, she thought, this feeling of total dependence was what it was like for Snorri.

ഌ ଓ

Gudrid dreamt of an ocean voyage. She stood above deck, looking out at the setting sun. She thought she was on the *Mimir*, but she couldn't be on the *Mimir* because she was married to Thorstein, not Thorfinn. *Where is Thorstein?* she thought. She looked to the stern of the ship and through the mist she saw sixteen coffins, stacked one on top of the other. *Thorstein is dead,* Gudrid remembered.

She turned back and saw the outline of a figure, partially concealed in the mist. She cautiously approached, wondering who it was and why they were the only two on deck; where were the rowers, and who was steering the knarr?

"I am Gudrid," she said, "daughter of Thorbjorn Vifilsson."

"I know who you are," the man said, not taking his eyes off of the horizon. "I am here to take you with me."

"Where are you taking me?" she asked, feeling both fear and hope.

"Back to Iceland," he answered.

"Shouldn't I return to Vinland? My husband, Thorstein, is waiting for me there."

The figure turned his hooded head.

"Why have you come to take me back to Iceland?" she asked.

"You know why. Have you forgotten what the prophetess told you, that you will mother a great family line?"

"Yes, I know." Gudrid touched her enlarged belly, feeling its roundness, its smoothness. "But I must return to Vinland; I have so much more left to do."

She was alone on the silent knarr with only the rush of the ocean waves and the roar of the wind. Fear slowly overtook her. Would she never see her comrades or her husband again?

"You already expelled yourself from that place," the hooded man said, "when you met yourself in the longhouse and subsequently told by the chiefs to leave Vinland and never return."

"I was trying to prevent my people from being annihilated. I talked to the chiefs to stop the war."

"Yes, and in so doing, you put into motion a sequence of events. Do you remember what was foretold? 'And over your progeny there shall shine a bright light.' Gudrid, look up to the heavens."

The mist cleared in front of Gudrid's eyes; she touched a presence with her mind.

The ocean wind whipped around the knarr—Gudrid knew that she was on the *Hringhorni*. She looked to the sky and saw the pewter clouds moving with the ship; for even the most experienced sailor, that was the worst possible condition for travelling. But for the lone blue-cloaked figure who stood on the deck, traversing the wind and the beating rain was as easy as a leisurely stroll on a calm day.

Gudrid knew that it was Thor's magic that kept Odin and *Hringhorni* protected from the ravages of Ægir; his beer-muddled hand gestures as he commanded the waves and wind threatened Odin's attempts to fulfill his final quest. Thor's spells could not be relied upon to fully protect Odin. Like all the gods, in the twilight of the world, his power was fading. No longer was the tree Yggdrasil supplying them with the continuous life force that pulsated from its roots to its branches, supplying and recirculating the power to and from the nine worlds. Odin's powers, though great, and his wisdom, though far-reaching through time and space, narrowed slightly with each passing day. It took the gods longer to regenerate, and they disobeyed the decision to spare the use of their magic unless necessary. They were truly victims of their own greatness, unable to live without the abilities bestowed upon them by their birth.

Gudrid reached out to Odin with her mind. He lifted the patch covering the hole where, so long ago—*or was it yesterday?*—he'd sacrificed his eye for *Mimir's* wisdom. The wind blowing through her mind was an odd sensation. Gudrid saw many images on the wind, ones that she was aware of but had not given much attention. She heard human whispers, voices of those that were gone, all waiting for Odin to usher in the end. She immediately silenced the voices and focused her thoughts on his destination: Vinland, the island where the beginning of the end would take place. The Vinland settlement reflected in the empty orifice in the same manner as it would in a human pupil. They'd arrive at Vinland soon.

Gudrid could feel Odin's shame in the light of his setting powers. He'd decided to guard that secret when he walked among humans. He didn't fear them because Odin knew that even without his magic, the humans would still follow him, treat him as their leader. If he was to save them, then he desperately needed their cooperation.

ꙮ ꙮ

The announcement of Ragnarök would be a shock to the Vinland humans. Odin didn't know if they would respond violently toward him or if the news could totally incapacitate the humans to the point of abject despair. He hadn't quite decided how he would tell them.

Odin suddenly heard a name on the wind, a name that he hadn't heard in a long time: " . . . Grimhild."

෴ ෴

Gudrid woke screaming, more from the shock of not knowing what was happening than the excruciating pain that was shooting through her belly.

She was surrounded by unfamiliar native faces. "Where's my husband?" she screamed. "What are you doing to me?"

Gudrid's legs were in the air, her dress pulled above her waist. She found it hard to take a breath; there was an incredible weight on her stomach and an overpowering urge to push down. She soon realized that her stomach muscles were involuntarily contracting. She blinked away the sweat dripping into her eyes and noticed that the natives around her were all female; some were attending to her, while the others chanted in the background.

Another contraction, then more pain, and suddenly she realized that she was having her baby. That truth lifted her veil of fear. She felt the cool cloth on her forehead, heard the soothing humming of those nearby, felt the warmth of another hand holding hers; she saw the two women at her feet, waiting to see the child's head.

Gudrid was almost panting; she slowed her breath into a rhythmic pattern, anticipating her next contraction, the memory of the pain of the previous one still fresh. All the sensations she felt were integrating into one impression of the birth of her first child: the physical sensation of Snorri's birth, the fear of an experience described to her as joyful pain, and the unfamiliarity of her surroundings and the women assisting in the birth.

Another tightening of the muscles around her womb—

Through the pain, both within and separate from it, she became more and more agitated. It was a reaction that she'd witnessed many times, but until now hadn't understood its reason.

Gudrid now knew that it was Snorri's life force pushing itself free from her body.

This child is ripping me apart, she silently screamed.

The final contraction hit Gudrid like a well-aimed kick. She felt part of her insides move, being pushed through the opening between her legs. It was like an outside force pushing down on her stomach and a force inside pushing out. Then a flood of anxiety washed over her, the cold clearness of it bubbling and frothing over her body before being pulled out to sea by the vast strength of the ocean. Only glistening grains remained on the beach, sparkling in the sun. Gudrid felt nothing else but that rush of joy.

Gudrid suddenly felt heavy; the only things still moving were the frantic thoughts in her head, until they were interrupted by a single screaming voice, and the flames of her thoughts faded to rising wisps of smoke disappearing into the night sky.

༄ ༄

Gudrid opened her eyes to flashes of light pulsating through slits that she barely managed to see through; a distant, arrhythmic beating echoed in her head. Her chest heaved irregularly; she struggled to steal a meagre breath. Her body quickened and shook as her mind swam, not unlike a ship on the ocean—waves and waves of endless ocean, rushing toward her until her body could no longer stay on the surface.

I see valkyries: Skuld who bears a shield, Skögul, Gunnr, Hildr, Göndul, and Geirskögul with her spear . . . they ride to the gods.

What sort of dream is that, Odin? I dreamt I rose up before dawn to clear up Val-hall for slain people. I aroused the Einheriar, bade them get up to strew the benches, clean the beer-cups; bade the valkyries serve wine for the arrival of a prince.

Gudrid's words were lost in the feverish pitch of her unconscious mind.

Suddenly a baby's cries tore through the thin web between her worlds. Gudrid woke. The cries morphed into screaming, high-pitched chants and beating drums outside, their timbre infiltrating the hide walls and slowly rising above her with the wisps of smoke from the burning sweet grass. The smell made her sick to her stomach. It took over her beating heart, the drum's hysteric timbre matching her heartbeats. Her hand accidentally hit the pot of smouldering grass, as if she were reaching out for the water's surface . . . reaching out for air. She didn't know where she was but she needed to escape, needed to get out.

Her world was a dark veil rippling and swelling in the storm. And then it became still. Gudrid's hands touched her belly, a soft caress across her torso that changed to a frantic groping for her son beneath her skin and muscle. She arched her back sharply and tilted her head back to scream to the heavens for the return of her baby. She inhaled deeply, as if the power and strength of her screams, once released, could be sucked back down to the centre of her soul.

A native woman with wiry grey hair entered the wigwam. Gudrid silenced her screams and expressed her fear in erratic breathing. "Shh," the woman whispered.

"Where is my baby?" Gudrid gasped.

"Your baby is fine," the woman said. "He is with our ancestors."

Gudrid couldn't approach the horror in her soul. It was too unfathomable to feel, like staring up into the heavens to look at all the bright lights at once and describing every emotion in her heart. *Where is Thorfinn?* her voice screamed in her brain. "Where is my husband?" she wheezed. "Find Thorfinn," she yelled, not knowing whether the women standing in a semicircle at the end of the bloodied furs where she lay, out of reach of Gudrid's angry arms, understood her.

Expecting to see her husband, Gudrid looked past them, through the wigwam's open doorway, where a golden light flooded in, as if the light of Baldur bathed the interior in a warm summer evening glow. Her tears welled up again, then ceased with a strangled choke—walking out of the light was Yakima, the native who had walked into her longhouse viknatals earlier.

The ghostly figure raised her finger to her lips, as if to request silence so the other women in the wigwam wouldn't notice her.

Calm descended over Gudrid, her hysteria suddenly transformed into peace. She felt as if another part of her had walked into the structure. As the woman approached, Gudrid realized that the familiarity was more than just a passing knowing;

she stared into the face of a mirror image of herself.

Gudrid touched her stomach. She grabbed a fistful of skin and held it so tightly that it reddened. She had hoped the valkyries had taken Snorri to a place where he would grow into a powerful warrior, but now she prayed that wherever Snorri was, he was happy and being well cared for.

ꟸ ꟸ

Uneasiness crept up Thorfinn's throat—a tightness he couldn't clear, its grip almost choking him as he looked at the warriors surrounding him; his heartbeat raced, then slowed, then raced again. Their leaders' wish to end bloodshed was not unanimously supported within the tribe; tradition and sentiment demanded revenge for the slaying of the first delegation to the Norse camp. Thorfinn was the focal point for the tribe's hatred. He knew, looking around at their tense postures, that if given the order to attack, the tribe would instantly act. He found it ironic that he put all his faith in Elsu's protection, a man half his size.

A scream fired through the centre of the group, igniting Thorfinn's uneasiness into cold, burning fear. "Gudrid," he whispered, meeting Elsu's wide eyes before bolting in the direction of Gudrid's screams.

In the absence of hard fact concerning the safety of his wife and baby, Thorfinn hit head-on all the fear that his imagination could conjure. The tension receding behind him couldn't distract him from instinct: rescue Gudrid and save his son. From the corner of his eye, Thorfinn saw Elsu moving beside him, and knew that he could never hate the natives on Vinland, because of the caring of one man.

They crashed through the doorway almost simultaneously, nearly taking the frame with them. The four native women surrounding Gudrid turned to stare anxiously at Thorfinn and Elsu. Gudrid's hysterical expression slowly softened into a trance-like calm that Thorfinn couldn't decide whether to be happy about or fear. "Let me though," he commanded, and the women parted, not due to the meaning of his words but his tone and body language.

As Thorfinn grabbed Gudrid's cold and clammy hands, he noticed that blood stained the pelt underneath and around her. As if moving through a body of cold, clear water, his gaze slowly moved down to Gudrid's stomach and back up to her face. "Where . . . where is our son—where is Snorri?" he asked in an almost pleading tone, choking on his son's name.

Gudrid silently stared at nothing, as if lacking the will to answer. Thorfinn gripped her shoulders and squeezed gently, trying to coax the answer from her despite her fragile state. "Gudrid, where is . . . our son?" he repeated, fighting back tears of fear.

Tears flowed down Gudrid's cheeks. Thorfinn stared back at her, matching her blank expression. He didn't know what to feel or what to do. A hand touched his arm.

"Let our seer, Bantam, tend to Gudrid. She will be able to help." Elsu wrapped his hand around Thorfinn's bicep and gently tugged at him to step away from Gudrid.

Initially Thorfinn resisted, but finally he relented, not knowing what else to do. He knew that standing around reliving the torture of his dead son couldn't help either of them. "Where is my son, Gudrid?" he pleaded as Elsu led him to the door. "Where is my son!"

He stumbled from the wigwam, his eyes still on Gudrid. In the fresh air, Thorfinn gasped for breath, almost strangled by the burden of losing his son. The strength required for movement left him, as if his body wanted only to sleep. "Elsu," he whispered, turning to his friend, "how do we find those who committed this crime?"

"That will be hard. We are one people among many. I don't know whether our chiefs will risk reprisal from other tribes over an act against one woman, member of a people who were neither invited here nor welcomed."

The line is drawn, Thorfinn thought. He stood alone with his anger and thoughts of revenge. There was no universal right or wrong between cultures that must be honoured. They didn't have an alliance, after all, just an understanding that both cultures would acknowledge and honour the other for as long as necessary.

ꙮ ꙮ

"Come in," the woman within shouted calmly in response

to Elsu's banging of the hollow sticks by the wigwam's entrance.

The two men stepped inside and Bantam directed them to sit. "Do not speak," she instructed, and closed her eyes, as if resuming a state interrupted by their arrival. After a moment she opened her eyes and asked, "Where is the woman who is without child, the child of the daughter of Thorbjörn?"

"She is ill and is lying in another wigwam, being tended by some of your women," Thorfinn answered, fearing the power of the woman across from him; her very presence demanded respect and attention. His natural impulse was to leap forward and grab the seer, demanding she reveal the whereabouts of his son. Instead he stared intensely at Bantam, almost afraid to look away.

Bantam looked at Elsu. "I must speak with Thorfinn."

Bantam uncrossed her legs as Elsu left, and lit a central hearth of sweet grass. As the grass caught and crackled and smoke trickled into their noses, Bantam leaned forward and blew out the small flame. The grass continued to smoulder and the tendrils of smoke twined to form a swirling cloud that filled the empty space between them.

"Thorfinn, I have seen a great figure," she said from beyond the hanging smoke. "Your alfather . . . he is here, trying to communicate with me. I've been trying to converse with him, but we have been unable to meet on equitable ground, unable to understand one another. His images have a different meaning to me, and my images to him are having the same effect."

"I'm almost afraid to speak his name." Thorfinn quivered like a child looking up at his overbearing father. "We aspire to be him."

Bantam's eyes turned up to the smoke at the top of the wigwam. It swirled like a cyclone, picking up speed. Her expression grew fearful, tense, then she slowly composed herself and her expression calmed. "He is here with the wanderer . . . he walks on the land, also. One who some call the Heyókȟa: the one that tricks and deceives . . . They've been here for some time . . ."

Bantam's head dropped as if the retreating vision had pulled all the muscles in her neck with it. She thrust her arms up, pushing against the empty air as if trying to keep the image from touching her again; she sat in silence for a moment. Finally she exhaled. "That is all."

The red haze of the embers in the firepit changed to calm grey.

Thorfinn felt as if his head were being cooled by a damp cloth dipped into an icy stream; a fog bank moved past his consciousness and slowly dissipated as it reached the back of his mind.

10

Thorfinn stared at Gudrid, lying on the bed in the setting light of the day. There was no separation from the bloodied bed coverings and the bottom of her dress. Her hair, normally pulled back into a meticulously woven bun, was now wiry and wild, the errant hairs as twisted as the emotional torment inside of her. Her face held a grey pallor.

It was Gudrid's eyes that disturbed Thorfinn the most. What were previously full of life, emotion, and vitality were reduced to still, murky pools that reflected back nothing, instead swallowing and damping all of the energy of those who stared into them. The life force that grew inside Gudrid, absorbing and taking everything with it, took her life as well; Snorri was gone and Gudrid with him.

Thorfinn didn't know how long he stood at the end of her bed, waiting for any sign from her that she knew he was there—a blink of awareness, anything that would indicate to him that he hadn't lost his beloved along with his son. Thorfinn kept telling himself that if he waited long enough, she would eventually give him a sign of life and they could start the long climb to recovering from the loss of Snorri. But Gudrid couldn't or wasn't willing to give that sign.

Thorfinn turned away and was about to walk into the waning day when he heard a rustling—Gudrid's foot moving under the bloodied blankets.

"Thorfinn," she whispered, her voice laboured, "I want . . . to go . . . home. Please . . . take me home."

Thorfinn blinked away a tear and opened his mouth to speak, then stopped and nodded. He walked to her bedside and slowly peeled away the bloodied furs and blankets. He gently cradled her shoulders as he would a newborn baby, then pulled her forward and slid his arm down to wrap it around her back; she slowly and carefully pulled her feet from the covers and slipped them over the side of the cot.

Kneeling, Thorfinn slowly raised her dress past her knees. He fished into a water-filled clay bowl next to the bed and wrung out a cloth. Then he gently wiped the caked blood from Gudrid's legs and feet. He looked at Gudrid's face. She didn't flinch as the cloth touched the inside of her thigh. He continued washing up the length of her leg to her vaginal area, rubbing and wiping gently so he wouldn't irritate the already sensitive area.

Gudrid pushed her dress down, pushing Thorfinn's hand and the cloth away. She silently extended her arms as a young child would, to indicate that she wanted help up off the cot. Thorfinn dropped the bloodied cloth into the bowl and supported Gudrid as she stood.

"Gudrid, do you want to wait till morning before we head back to the camp?" he asked.

She shook her head and for the first time looked directly into his face. "Take me home," she muttered.

Thorfinn helped Gudrid on with her outer garments and escorted her out into the night. The still, cold air was a welcome contrast to the stuffy wigwam. Thorfinn felt invigorated, pleased that he was taking his wife back to their own people.

The native camp was dark, fires scattered throughout the camp either burning down to glowing embers or already wisping smoke from grey hearths. A distant drumbeat indicated a gathering on the other side of the camp, obscured by trees and wigwams. Thorfinn was relieved; he didn't need the added stress of leaving under the weight of suspicious stares. Only the bright stars witnessed their journey back to their people, guided by the protective voices of the valkyries whispering on the wind.

He hugged Gudrid to him and quickly guided her to the forest's edge. The last thing Thorfinn wanted was to be seen by someone who would alert the camp to their departure; he didn't want to risk reprisal, or another sniper attack.

On the camp's perimeter Thorfinn stopped and turned toward approaching footsteps, taking a defensive posture until he recognized Elsu.

"Thor-finn, here is your and Gud-rid's packs. You are leaving?" Elsu asked.

"Yes, I'm taking Gudrid home. It's time that we complete our ship and leave Vinland for good. Gudrid needs to be with her family."

Elsu nodded. "I understand. I'm coming with you."

"We can find our way home," Thorfinn said, trying not to sound too defensive.

"I know a shortcut along the river that will get us back to your camp much faster; the journey will be much easier on Gudrid—it's mostly downhill."

"Thanks, Elsu," Thorfinn said, relaxing.

The trio walked out of the native camp into the dark silence of the forest.

Now that the activity of the previous day was behind them, Thorfinn wondered why Bantam had wanted them to visit her. Even though Thorfinn trusted Elsu, he was unsure of Bantam's motive in requesting Gudrid's presence in their camp. Even after everything that had happened, why hadn't Bantam wanted to talk to Gudrid, which was the primary reason for their trip to the camp? The entire sequence of events seemed to suggest plans within plans.

As they headed toward the river, Thorfinn clutched Gudrid tighter, happy to have her safely next to him. The crescent moon peeked over the western horizon, faintly lighting their path ahead as they walked toward the sound of the rushing river. The moonlight cast the hill in an ashen grey glow, giving the landscape an otherworldly hue. Thorfinn felt as if he were walking through a dream. The shapes and forms in the forest had a strange vividness that imprinted themselves on his mind for recollection in years to come.

The sounds of the forest were somehow subdued, as if the animals realized there was magic at work, forces that were not altogether aligned with the Vinlanders' intentions of returning home. There was a tension in the air, tugging at expectations and trying to change present conditions to suit those other needs.

Thorfinn felt Gudrid's discomfort, something that went beyond the loss of Snorri. She didn't speak, but he sensed what her instincts relayed. "Gudrid, what is it?" he asked as she resisted moving forward.

"There's someone here," she answered in a feeble voice.

"Where's here?" Thorfinn asked, cocking his head like a morning rooster ready to crow.

Gudrid raised her arm toward a densely wooded area. Thorfinn almost automatically walked in the direction Gudrid indicated.

"Thor-finn . . . Gud-rid, you're walking in the wrong direction," Elsu said.

"There's something over here that we'd like to investigate first," Thorfinn replied.

Elsu didn't argue but followed them in silence as Thorfinn pushed aside boughs tinged silver by the moon; they walked farther and farther into the forest, crossing pools of moonlight and long black shadows cast by the pine and birch trees above them.

Thorfinn sensed that there was something at the centre of the trees; he felt pulled into a place where an intelligence waited that could explain worlds that were beyond human thought and reason. With each step there was an unceasing expectation that they'd find the answer—not on the level of human consciousness, but a feeling that their journey was at an end; it grew stronger and stronger, the closer they came to it.

"Why are we headed in this direction?" Elsu whispered.

"Gudrid sensed a presence that we're going to investigate."

"Who do you think is there?"

"We don't know yet, Elsu."

"Thorfinn, if we're headed into an unknown situation, shouldn't we prepare ourselves in case we're walking into an ambush?"

"I understand that that's one of the risks, Elsu. But I'm not worried about that right now."

"You should consider it. Remember the first attack on us? My people won't stop. They will make another attempt."

"Will you two shut up?" Gudrid snapped. "I can hardly hear myself think."

Thorfinn grinned at Elsu, unable to contain his joy at this small spark of Gudrid's usual self.

As they walked deeper and deeper into the forest, Thorfinn noticed a familiar glow, illuminating what looked like a clearing up ahead. The glow reflected up the bark of the tall trees, rising above the treetops into the night sky, filling the already starry heavens with floating embers carried by waves of heat; wisps of smoke intermittently obscured the heavens.

Thorfinn heard a frail voice, but one that held the power of creation in its words and the authority to capture life and mold it in whatever way it saw fit. It was a mature and soothing voice that could manipulate and control the human realm, a voice filled with timeless wisdom that had neither beginning nor end. "Do not be startled," it said. "I will not hurt you. Like you, I would not knowingly hurt my own children."

Thorfinn pushed a prickly evergreen branch aside and peered at a face lit by the glow of firelight; shadows danced and morphed across his face. "Who are you?" he asked.

"I'm a wanderer," he answered.

"Did you come from the Culdee community?" Thorfinn asked, thinking the old man's cloak looked similar to the cloaks described by Adam.

"No, but I know of the community of which you speak. They're on Markland. I've met them; they asked me to join their brood but I declined, telling them that it was against the rules of *my order.*" He smiled. "There is one thing that I seek," he said, looking at Thorfinn, who noticed that his right eye was missing. "I seek the return of my eye."

"How did you lose it?" Thorfinn asked.

"In an exchange," he answered. "A drink from a well when I was thirsty."

Silence followed the old man's reply, broken only by the

crackling of the fire and the sounds of the night.

"Can we sit with you for a while?" Thorfinn asked.

"Of course," the old man answered, staring into the flames. "I'm happy to share the warmth of my fire."

"Are you sure you don't want to be left alone?" Gudrid asked uncertainly as she moved closer to him.

"I can be deep in thought and converse as well."

A raven squawked from a tree branch overhead.

"You look familiar," Thorfinn said, hoping that the old man would reveal more about himself.

"Oh? Who do you think I look like?"

Thorfinn stared back without answering. He didn't want to get into a verbal tug-of-war with the man. He wanted the old man to voluntarily disclose his identity. He hoped that the words coming out of the old man's mouth were those of the alfather, the supreme being of gods and men. "I don't know," he lied, certain that there was another layer to this person waiting to be peeled away and examined.

"Where are you travellers headed to?" the old man asked, dodging the issue.

Thorfinn was too preoccupied with the old man's features to answer his question immediately. He couldn't decide if his features were Norse. He tried to imagine the colour of the wanderer's hair before it went grey.

"Back to our camp; after the tragic death of . . . my baby," Gudrid choked out.

"I'm sorry for your loss, my child. The hardest thing for a parent is to lose a child. We don't plan on a child dying before us; it's a disruption of the natural order of us as a species. Our reason for procreation is to give our existence a sense of continuity and therefore a purpose in our otherwise multifaceted but corporeal existence. Was he your first child?"

Gudrid managed a nod, taken aback that the old man knew her baby's gender without being told.

The old man closed his eyes and tilted his head to the heavens, as if he were saying a short prayer. When he opened them he looked at Elsu. "I don't recognize you. You are not one of us."

"No, I'm one of the people that inhabits this land," Elsu said. "I'm here as a representative of my people as well as Thorfinn and Gudrid's escort."

Thorfinn noticed that the old man said "one of us." He interpreted that as meaning that he was Norse.

"Yes, I see a heroic person in you," the man said to Elsu. "You are all welcome to stay with me for the night. I've had a long day and an arduous journey; I must rest."

"Thank you; we will," Thorfinn said.

As Gudrid and Elsu lay down, preparing their earthly beds for the night, Thorfinn had a burning desire to ask the old man who he was. But he wasn't sure he could muster up the courage to ask. The stature of the wanderer was similar to that of a warrior chief whose presence commanded the respect of his men as he led them into battle. Thorfinn wasn't sure whether he looked into the face of the warrior chief or whether it was a shadow from long ago. Either way, there was no denying the powerful posture of the individual lying down on the other side of the fire.

Thorfinn lay down and closed his eyes. As his thoughts began to close in on themselves, the fire warmed his face and set shadowy flames dancing across the inside of his eyelids.

ဢ ထ

"Damn you, Fenrir! Damn you, Loki!"

Thorfinn recognized the old man's voice. Though the words were belligerent, his tone sounded as if he were yielding.

"How have we come to this?" the voice continued. "My death is a concept totally alien to my very nature—I commanded the giants to construct Asgard and Midgard!"

His voice softened. "Thorfinn, from my first thought, I knew that I'd die; it was as much a part of my existence as my self-awareness. But I somehow thought that I was wrong. Sadly, gods are never wrong."

Fenrir planted his body firmly atop the old man's torso, his back claws digging into his groin. The wolf's pearly black eyes never left his as the creature focused for his first strike.

"It's hard to face your own death, even harder to come to terms with it," the old man continued, unperturbed by Fenrir's penetrating gaze. "Dying is easy—a dagger's blade across the throat, a broadsword through the heart—but accepting death . . .

therein lies the pain. The mind's struggle for life is at odds with the body's submission."

Fenrir raised his snout high into the air as if looking through the window in the sky, up to Asgard. He directed an ear-piercing howl toward the heavens, but Thorfinn knew that the worst would come when it dropped to a growl, when the razor teeth sank into his victim's larynx and esophagus.

Thorfinn closed his eyes as the wolf ripped the first bloodied chunk from the old man's throat, his head recoiling as it silenced his power once and for all.

But the voice continued. "Beginnings and endings are not the way of gods. I remember being born from my parents, Bestla and Borr—an interesting experience. Birth is not the same for us as for humans, who do not exist prior to this event; we are always present, waiting for conscious thought to give us form and power.

"There are things that are not talked about among us twelve: creation and destruction, responsibility for our creations, and most importantly, our dwindling power and influence over the races of Midgard. Some say it is a mistake to create such imperfect and corporeal beings. I say that it is what it is. Once in Midgard, the laws that affect linear time must be obeyed. What was created in the past cannot be uncreated; the only course is the cycle of destruction.

"Entering a realm with a past, a present, and a future, I feel like a fish jumping out of the water for the first time . . . what an odd feeling. I've been here many times before, but my foot was only in the stream, so to speak; I did not feel the sensations of heat and cold on my skin, or the air blowing around me, or the sensation of inhaling that same air into my corporeal body. But now I am standing in the stream, its numbing, frigid water flowing past me.

"I never mastered the current of time; its absence is like walking through locked doors: a boundless step into the next room. When I'm caught in time, it's like an ant crawling up a tree trunk and getting caught in the tree sap. Without time, I walk upstream while the current flows in the opposite direction.

"Out of the nine worlds, this world is the most confusing. Unlike the harmony that exists among the Æsir, here, one decision, one thought, will alter the proceeding timeline—so much so that it

is hard to see what lies beyond the portal of the present moment. I find myself having to will the next moment, and the next.

"Who can a god turn to when faced with the destruction of his physical form? Aren't gods forever? That's what we thought, in action more than in reality. We lived like gods and now we die like humans.

"I blame no one but myself for my feelings. I saw Ragnarök; even if I didn't know it in my being at the moment of my creation, the moment I tore apart Ymir to create Midgard, it was as if I was destroying Midgard as well. By creating Midgard, I created Ragnarök.

"Midgard has changed me and there's nothing I can do about it. I'm trapped by the flow of time; it flows like the blood flowing from the ripped flesh in my neck. This is the stream in which I now flow."

ꟸ ꟹ

Thorfinn woke with a start as the sun broke through the clouds, slicing a blue swath through the overcast. He rolled over, away from the sunlight, and noticed that the old man wasn't lying as he'd been the previous night, on the other side of the hearth. Lifting his head, Thorfinn looked around the clearing for him, but he was nowhere in sight. He raised himself on one elbow to get a better view of the surrounding forest. He still couldn't see the old man.

Thorfinn rolled over and slowly stood, pausing until his muscles finally cooperated with what his mind wanted them to do; then he flexed and contorted his arms, hips, and torso, trying to remove the stiffness left by a cold, damp night spent sleeping on the ground.

He looked around for footprints leading off into the forest or down the forest track, anything to indicate the direction the old man might've taken. Maybe he just left them and continued on his journey, Thorfinn thought. But he wasn't willing to detach himself from the old man just yet. Finding footprints into the forest, he glanced back at Gudrid and Elsu to make sure they were still sleeping, then followed the trail into the lush, green forest, where the air still hung damp from the night.

As he brushed against low-lying boughs in the coniferous forest, the needles released droplets of water onto his already damp clothes. His feet sank into the loam, hidden beneath a vapour that rose from the ground and hung over the understory plants; as the sun hit them, they glistened with dew. The forest was waking to another day. Unseen birds chirped in the trees, crickets creaked in the fading darkness. In one dramatic infusion of light, the forest was transformed into a living thing.

Thorfinn's thoughts kept returning to their first meeting with the old man, and his suspicions of who he really was. He was sure the old man was the alfather who wandered through Midgard, and stubbornly held to that conviction even though he had few and controversial pieces of evidence to identify the wanderer. Odin must have a good reason to keep his identity hidden.

Walking through the forest, Thorfinn felt as if he were walking further and further into early evening, and not breaking dawn. The foliage became so dense that it walled the spaces between the trees and blocked out more and more light; it trapped the moisture, preventing it from dissipating, so that instead it settled into a thick white carpet that swirled and dispersed as Thorfinn moved through it. It also confused his senses; Thorfinn felt as if he were swimming in a lake, stirring up more and more mud, clouding the water. His footsteps echoed in an oddly asynchronous manner, falling on his ears from somewhere above. The sounds of the forest moved into the background, muffled by the mist.

In the swirling confusion of the mist, Thorfinn heard the old man's voice; it sounded as if he was talking to someone, but Thorfinn couldn't hear anyone else, only the wind rustling the treetops. *Maybe he's talking to himself*, Thorfinn thought, *like some elderly people do.*

The mist thinned slightly and Thorfinn walked into an alien forest of towering trees and ancient root systems that pushed through the surface of the ground to crawl across the forest floor in a criss-crossing maze. He walked around waist-high outgrowths and human-high boulders, descending into a deep and mossy gully.

"Yes," Thorfinn heard. "Do you really think it wise to keep this information from them?" A pause.

"But how will they prepare for their survival? Who will they turn to for help? I can't say that I agree with your wisdom on this matter." The old man's voice sounded disapproving. "The humans have a right to know their destiny. By denying them knowledge of the future, we'll be partly responsible for causing their destruction."

Thorfinn spied the wanderer during another, longer pause. The old man jerked his head from side to side, as if he knew that he was being watched. "Who's there?" he yelled. "Show yourself or I will do it for you."

Thorfinn backed into the fog, then whirled as he felt something brushing against him—a stream of light whizzed past. It caught up some of the fog in its path and pulled it around Thorfinn's body. Another stream of light joined the first, whirling around Thorfinn's legs; he tried kicking it away, but the movement threw him off balance and he stumbled backward. He lifted his arms to push the streams away, but they always returned and resumed their twining, quickly winding up and down his torso. He felt as if he were being pushed by some unseen hand and struggled—and failed—to regain his balance.

Thorfinn stumbled out of the fog and onto the ground. He looked up into Odin's eyes like a child who'd been caught with his hand in the fruit basket.

"What are you doing here?" the wanderer demanded.

"I was looking for you."

"Were you spying on me?"

"No! I . . . uh, just arrived here. But who were you talking to just now?"

"I despise being questioned and watched," the wanderer snapped. "You should've made yourself known to me as soon as you saw me."

"I know." Thorfinn hung his head. "I meant no disrespect to you."

"If we are to have a continuing relationship, there must be total trust between us."

"Oh, yes," Thorfinn said, trying to play along. "Does this mean that you want to return with us to our camp?"

"Yes, I think that we can help one another," the wanderer mused, then changed the subject. "How much did you hear?"

"I heard you say that by not telling us, you'd be partly responsible for our destruction," Thorfinn said, looking up. "What were you talking about?"

"I can't tell you . . . not just yet," he replied, his abrasive tone softening. "I need to seek some answers before I can reveal anything to you. Will you trust me that much?"

Thorfinn forced a nod, still unsure on what to base his trust. "I know nothing about you or where you came from," he ventured. "Yet you ask me to be patient and to have faith in you. Despite my apprehension, there is something about you that I feel I can trust. You have an authority that transcends your appearance. Your words seem powerful. Just as I feel that I must protect my people, I know that you have that same feeling, that you want to protect not only me, but us as well. So I will give you time to seek your answers."

The wanderer looked at Thorfinn and grinned, as if acknowledging that he'd received the answer he sought.

"We should leave and return home to my camp," Thorfinn suggested as he stood.

They passed through the fog and returned to the camp where Thorfinn had left Gudrid and Elsu. They walked into the camp area as the native and Gudrid were gathering up their packs for the trip back to Leifsbúrðir.

"Thorfinn, we decided to wait and eat back at the camp; it's such a short distance," Elsu said. When Thorfinn nodded, Elsu led the group down to the river.

They journeyed in silence. Thorfinn thought about Gudrid. He'd noticed that she was able to groom herself before they left the camp. He took this as a good sign that her depression wasn't as deep as it appeared. He glanced behind him and saw her trailing behind them, her expression blank, the blanket brought from the wigwam clutched tightly around her body. Her eyes gazed straight ahead, and she stumbled over the uneven ground. He hoped that she wasn't blaming herself for Snorri's death.

Thorfinn looked forward and noticed a raven flying overhead, shadowing them. "It must be following us," he said to no one in particular, pointing at it.

"I understand that you're returning to Grœnlandia," the wanderer said.

"Yes; once we complete the knarr, we'll be going home."

"Might I suggest that, before you make the voyage home, you travel suðr to Hóp to gather resources, so your peers back home don't consider your trip a failure."

Thorfinn stopped and looked at the man suspiciously. The raven squawked overhead.

ꝏ ꝏ

Gudrid's face seemed to brighten a little as they cleared the forest and she saw the fenced perimeter of the Leifsbúrðir settlement. Thorfinn felt as if he'd been away for a viknatal.

The knarr towered over the roofs of the settlement's sod houses. Thorfinn was happy that it was in the final stages of completion. Even he looked forward to returning to the open sea and leaving Vinland behind them.

A figure waved to them from the other side of the field; as it ran toward them, Thorfinn recognized Tostig. "Thorfinn," Tostig yelled before pausing to pant for breath. "Something has happened."

"What?" Thorfinn asked, not sure how much more bad news he could take.

"It's a ship . . . another ship has drifted into the fjord."

"Is it the *Mimir*? Has the *Mimir* somehow returned to us?" Thorfinn asked.

"No, it's a completely different vessel," Tostig replied. "We now have two knarrs to take us home."

"It would be a complete waste of the other ship if you don't travel to Hóp to gather more resources," the old man interjected.

Thorfinn shot the wanderer an amazed glance as he tried to figure out the synchronicity of events. The raven, circling overhead, squawked.

Tostig looked at Gudrid; she returned his stare with blank eyes. "Thorfinn, the baby?" Tostig asked, unable to take his eyes off of her.

Thorfinn caught Tostig's eye and wordlessly shook his head: *Lost her son*. Thorfinn again wondered if, on some level, Gudrid blamed herself for the death of their son. If they used words like "lost," it would put the responsibility of the baby's death on her.

It wasn't that they needed someone to blame; the words they used created the blame. He wished that he could find some blameless words, something that would take her pain away. He was able to alleviate his own pain over Snorri's loss by focusing on Gudrid and trying to ease her pain. And the task of getting the Vinlanders back home to Grœnlandia.

"Did you board the ship?" Thorfinn asked. "Was there any indication where it came from?"

"Yes, we boarded her, but we found nothing—no evidence of a crew, no oars, no gear . . . nothing to indicate that the knarr carried anyone. As far as we can see, it's a ghost ship."

"Is she seaworthy?" Thorfinn asked, becoming more and more excited at the prospect of returning home with another ship.

"Yes, a far as I can tell," Tostig answered.

Thorfinn rubbed his hands together. "What a good turn of events."

As they crossed the field, more and more Vinlanders stopped their work to witness Thorfinn and Gudrid's return. The women set their baskets down in the vegetable garden and stood wiping their soiled hands on their work dresses. The rhythmic thud of hammers banging nails into the side of the knarr dwindled to occasional blows as the builders diverted their attention to those returning. Men climbed down off the knarr and joined the women, almost unconsciously, as if using their numbers to welcome Gudrid and Thorfinn back into the fold.

Adam stepped out of the Great Hall to stand in the open doorway, a curiously judgemental look on his face. A shadow fell over Adam's face as the raven swooped down, almost hitting Adam in the forehead; his arms immediately flew up to protect his head and wave the bird away.

Thorfinn looked at the old man, and saw a hint of amusement on his lips. What was the relationship between the old man and the raven, Thorfinn wondered; they appeared to be companions, one following the other in an unspoken bond. The raven appeared to be the old man's eyes in the sky, scouting across the landscape, keeping watch.

Thorfinn felt as if he was walking through a field of statues as they walked into the group of Vinlanders waiting at the gate. They reminded him of the onlookers at a procession in his own country, standing in still reverence; part curiosity and part respect. The old man held their focus as he walked through them.

"Freydis," Thorfinn called, looking for her in the crowd.

"Yes," she replied, pushing through the people toward him.

"Could you take Gudrid back to the house?"

"Yes, of course."

Thorfinn turned and walked down to the beach. He found the salvaged knarr tethered to the rocks, floating in the water. He couldn't believe that it was in such great condition; it looked as if it had just been built—there was no waterline marking the outer hull, the sail wasn't bleached by the sun. He assumed that the deck was in the same condition.

He thought of the old man's suggestion that they sail suðr, to harvest more resources before their return to Grœnlandia. It was tempting, to recoup their losses on the voyage. He couldn't see why they shouldn't make the trip. With all the setbacks, the community needed a victory to take them home with their heads held high. Their kin back home expected stories of heroic deeds and how enterprising and profitable the trip across the ocean was.

Thorfinn felt that he owed at least that much to his people; he wasn't going to deny them one final chance to acquire wealth on this trip. He slapped the side of the hull and turned back to the settlement, practising in his head his announcement that they would sail to Hóp in three dægur.

9

Thorfinn walked into the Great Hall and quickly scanned the assembled group. Most of the camp's members were present, lining the walls of the sod building or seated near the fire that burned brightly in the central hearth. This hall wasn't a permanent structure like their wooden hall at home, a palace by comparison, for a building constructed of wood was reserved for upper clan members and members of the royal family bloodline. This one did serve its purpose; despite its humbleness, the building echoed the affluence of the Eiriksson family.

His eyes touched on Eirik's family shield, hanging proudly on the austr wall of the longhouse as a constant reminder that when anyone looked at it, they were also looking in the direction of home. It symbolized the prowess and the bravery of the Eiriksson family in traversing the norðr waters to claim this land . . . and it was also a constant reminder of the power of the Eiriksson family and how their presence dominated this part of Midgard.

It was advantageous to align myself with such a powerful and wealthy family, Thorfinn thought. When families like the

Eirikssons expanded their domains, new opportunities and markets opened up. Soon Thorfinn's travels would be limited to his home country; he'd invest in vessels and crews to explore on his behalf while he focused his efforts on taking advantage of opportunities that opened up closer to home.

Thorfinn walked to the front of the room and stood next to Freydis. As a direct member of the Eiriksson family, her status was high in the community and therefore she was a member of its first council.

Despite outward appearances, he knew of the growing rift between Gudrid and Freydis. Thorfinn wasn't privy to the full details of their disagreement, but he noticed that they weren't talking to one another and Freydis remained distant toward both of them. Even before Gudrid mentioned Freydis's odd behaviour, Thorfinn had noticed her distant and at times argumentative posturing with other members of the camp. Many stories fell onto Thorfinn's ears, of how demanding and unreasonable Freydis was becoming. She threw her weight around, and Thorfinn suspected that she was also undermining his authority in covert ways. He wondered if it had anything to do with her marriage; perhaps she was regretting her choice of a husband.

Thorvald was often distant and unsociable, rarely smiling or speaking in public; he seemed to prefer being on his own. He was happy to remain in his wife's shadow. Thorvald did do his share of the work and bore his share of the burden of responsibility, which Thorfinn respected.

Perhaps Freydis had adopted some of Thorvald's behaviours, as some spouses do, but Thorfinn suspected something beyond that. It was as if she were possessed by something that slowly controlled more and more of her thoughts and actions.

There was another issue that concerned Thorfinn; Freydis had been put in change of part of the group as an agent for her brother and father, in order to secure half of the resources for the Eiriksson family. That was a part of Thorfinn's agreement with Eirik and Leif. But Thorfinn worried that her authority, however rightfully given, was being abused or misused by her and Thorvald.

Thorfinn searched his feelings for what really bothered him. It was the fact that despite his agreement with Eirik and

Leif, Freydis, in her present state, was capable of anything. And if she did organize a coup d'état, then her position could subvert his authority, thereby splintering the camp and giving rise to a mutiny, either on land or perhaps at sea.

Thorfinn wasn't convinced that his mere presence would prevent a breakdown of the power structure in the community. Authority sometimes needed enforcement; his influence was no longer enough to peacefully quell an uprising or subversive action against his position and authority. Thorfinn had to tread lightly but still remain a strong leader, because any seed of discontent would threaten his leadership.

And indeed, the structure of the community was breaking down, not from any pragmatic reason but rather by some underlying force that pulled at people's patience and their wills. The arrival of the old man seemed to coincide with this, but Thorfinn couldn't see how they were connected.

He knew that it was time for them to return to profitable work. A common goal seemed to cement the community together. The knarr's near completion gave them the means to return home, but it couldn't quench the disappointment felt throughout the camp that the profits on the trip so far were negligible to nonexistent. He feared that Gudrid's failed quest to recover the treasure from the cave would be seen as a failure on Thorfinn's part, and would call into question his leadership abilities.

Previously, the camp had worked together. Where equanimity and cooperation had prevailed, now disharmony, fear, and suspicion were rampant throughout the community, always unpredictable as the weather. It was as if the Vinlanders had a preset notion in their minds to confirm their beliefs against one another, as if their minds sought evidence for what they perceived as the truth. Human fear wasn't based on what actually was real in the world, Thorfinn realized as he reflected on the situation; it was how the mind judged what was out in the world and what it feared about the world.

As he stood patiently waiting for individual discussions to fall silent, Thorfinn knew the enemy wasn't the unknown; the real enemy was how an individual interpreted what the eyes and the mind perceived. He wondered why it had taken him so long to realize this truth. Perhaps the people he led had taught him something about himself.

When he faced only a quiet murmuring and a few shifting bodies, Thorfinn began. "Tostig has informed me that the construction of the knarrs is complete. There are just a few finishing touches to be done, once the vessels are in the water." He looked to Tostig for a confirming nod. "We sail for Leif's southern settlement at Hóp in three dægur. With two knarrs, we can double up on our load to take back to Grœnlandia."

"Who is this old man that sits in my father's Great Hall?" Freydis demanded, pointing to the old man as if redirecting her anger at Thorfinn to someone else.

"He's our guest," Thorfinn replied.

"*Your* guest," she shot back.

"I'm a traveller. Is the threshold of your home so barricaded with suspicion and fear that you don't invite guests in?" the old man asked.

Freydis whirled on him. "Who are you to question me in that manner?"

"Have you not heard the stories? Has no one told you about the figure with one eye who roams Midgard? You do not know who you're talking to, child. I go by many names; you know me as your alfather, Odin."

The assembly rose in a great uproar—some, like Freydis, shouting in angry voices fuelled by fear and doubt for validation; others turning to one another in silent awe before exploding into cheers and reverential clapping as their suspicions were confirmed. Still others remained still, immobilized by indecision.

"If you are the alfather," Freydis yelled above the cacophony, "then prove it to us; do something a god would do! How about taking us home?"

"I've already brought you a knarr," he replied in the sudden calm. "It's tethered at the water's edge."

"How do we know that was your doing?"

"You don't know that I *didn't* do it. I think I know what you're asking. You want me to perform like a harnessed ox plowing a field," Odin sneered.

The room remained still, only the howl of the blowing wind stirring the expectant silence.

Odin pushed himself to his feet with the help of his staff and shuffled over to the raised platform. He stepped up beside Freydis, dwarfed by her size, and gestured for her to tilt her ear closer to his mouth. He began whispering in her ear, and her expression changed from the clenched jaw of doubtful curiosity to wide-eyed concern, even fear. The wind outside seemed to increase in strength. Those watching grasped the power in his words to Freydis, even though they couldn't hear what he was saying.

As Odin pulled back, Freydis lowered her eyelids and pouted, doubt masking her face. "You could've found that out by talking to anyone," she said, her attitude making it impossible for her to hold onto the words that he'd spoken.

Odin turned and quietly shuffled back to his seat. "That is a matter of your faith," he said as he sat down. "More will be revealed at the proper time."

Freydis's doubt that Odin was the actual alfather wasn't based in any truth as Thorfinn saw it; it had to do with Freydis's unwillingness to bow down before anyone. The old man she saw didn't have the might that came with the stories humans invented about the gods. Freydis was showing her true stripes; she seemed drunk with power, confirming Thorfinn's suspicions about her lust to splinter the community and take control.

Perhaps that was the full limitation of all self-aware beings. At some point the belief in an omniscient being would be so incomprehensible and awe-inspiring that the imagination doubted its existence.

Thorfinn shook himself from such thoughts and looked out over the crowd. "We're leaving Vinland in three dægur," he said again. "Tostig, can you complete the knarr in that time?"

"Yes," the dwarf answered. "We're about to move her into the water."

"I'm splitting the community into three groups. Freydis, you will lead one; Tostig, you will lead the other; I will take the third. We're travelling to Leif's suðr camp; once we've gathered as many resources as our knarrs can carry from Hóp, we sail back to Grœnlandia."

Thorfinn scanned faces. "The next day or two will be hard on all of us. We've had many challenges on this trip already." He glanced at Gudrid. "The blood running through our veins may be from different families, but it now pumps in the veins of one family."

As the group broke up, Thorfinn joined Odin, who sat with his head in his hand, his fingers massaging his forehead as if working thoughts across the expanse of his cranium, activating dormant, rarely used parts of his mind.

"I've felt the presence of Loki . . . here, in Midgard," Odin finally said, his eye still shut.

"How is that possible?" Thorfinn asked.

"The wall around Asgard was never finished. I suspect that he escaped that way."

"How do you know that he's here?"

"He is my brother, after all. I or any other member of our family would have felt his presence. It's just the nature of the Jötunn. We live in symbiosis with them, just as the four elements of Midgard make up the world. It's rare, when one thing affects another, that it will pass us by without our notice."

"Do you know what he could be up to?" Thorfinn asked, unsure whether he really wanted to know more.

"He could be up to many things; shape-shifting most likely. It's hard to say what he wants, though I do have my suspicions. I will have to see which way the wind blows, so to speak. The wind of time will carry us in whichever direction it's headed; like knarrs scattered on the water, it will take us all to one convergence, whether we want to arrive there or not," Odin concluded with a chuckle.

Thorfinn reacted by looking quickly around the empty hall. Odin again chuckled wryly. "You look like a man who expects to catch the damage before or as it is happening. I can assure you that it will be done before you can see it. I suspect that he's now planting the seeds of his plan in members of the community. If I can't see it immediately, I don't think you will be able to, either."

"Where do we go from here?" Thorfinn asked.

"To Hóp," Odin answered.

The alfather's truth didn't comfort Thorfinn, but he didn't think that he'd meant it to.

Without a word, Odin rose from the bench and walked to the door of the hall, Thorfinn following. As they stepped into the midday overcast, Odin stared into the ashen sky with a concerned expression. The sun hung in the haze like an ant caught in flowing yellow tree sap, its light too feeble to break free. People stood huddled in small groups as if viewing a rare event.

As they headed for his house, Thorfinn noticed that the vegetables still unpicked in the garden, plump and vibrantly coloured only dægur ago, were beginning to whither and die; the tomatoes and cucumbers had stopped ripening and their skins looked bruised, in some cases beginning to turn black.

Beyond, the grassy battlefield was oddly illuminated, as if the soil beneath the grass had slowly changed from blood red to a fiery orange; waves of rising heat distorted the cool air above it. Thorfinn realized that the blood-laden grass, bent under the weight of so many dead warriors and natives, had begun to grow again, pushing its bent stalks toward the muted light of the sky. The undamaged part of the field, in contrast, shimmered as the wind blew across the top of the blades in waves, undulating like the surface of the ocean, bowing as Odin walked past.

Thorfinn couldn't help thinking that Odin's influence on the human mind was as powerful and invisible as the wind. He held them spellbound. But unlike the wind over the field of wild wheat and grass, when fear travelled through the human imagination, it imprinted itself on the mind, gaining in strength and making itself real.

"I'd like to sit outside," Odin said.

Thorfinn led the alfather to a worn stump that had been used over the years as a stool. Its ringed surface was now shiny and smooth. He left the old man there, deciding to use his free time to check up on Gudrid.

ꙮ ꙮ

Grimhild slowly approached Odin, sitting so still on the stump, her old eyes narrowed in curiosity. She stopped a short distance away and extended a craggy index finger toward him, her bland expression shifting to one of surprised recognition.

"Good day to you, Grimhild," Odin said without opening his eye. "I wondered when we would meet in the cold light of day."

"You again!" she gasped in awed familiarity, stumbling backward. "I thought I'd never see you again. And I never wanted to see you, after what you did to me the last time we met."

"You ungrateful old toad!" Odin yelled. "I gave you the past and the future, something that I wouldn't even give to my own brother."

"You gave me madness," she spat. "Since I gazed into your eye socket, I cannot control the visions. When they come, they consume my body. I've been banished to the fringes of my community. I'm a monster to my people because they don't understand. You forbade me to give the memories vocal form."

"I gave you what you asked for, Grimhild. All wisdom comes at a price." He pointed at his eye patch.

"You gave it to me, but you didn't tell me what it would do to me. Look at me!"

Odin sighed, knowing that she spoke the truth.

"Odin, it's the end that you seek, and knowledge of what the new beginning will hold," she said. Her body jerked and quivered; she stumbled back, then fell to the ground.

"Don't fight the energy that's flowing through you," Odin instructed.

Grimhild began pulling at her clothes, as if trying to tear them from her frail body.

"Resisting will do nothing for you," he yelled, his face stern.

Grimhild writhed and arched her back, pointing her index finger at Odin. "Yggdrasil quakes where it stands," she shrieked; "a serpent chews on its roots. Jörmungandr writhes, whipping the waves to froth. Valkyries are in the air." She reached toward the sky, then covered her face as if she saw them swooping down at her.

"I see death and destruction; the serpent suckling on cadavers . . . new babes. The sun grows dim and Midgard sinks; the sparkling stars fall from the firmament. Odin meets with the wolf!" she shrieked, sitting up and looking at Odin.

Grimhild collapsed as her vision concluded. Her chest heaved as it struggled to take in air. She raised one bent finger toward him. "Odin, I know your question," she gasped. "I know the fate of the gods; come closer," she murmured, as if enticing a lover to her side.

As if he'd awaited that answer, Odin scrambled to his feet; when his frail body dropped to the ground, he crawled to the trembling Grimhild's side. Grimhild raised her arms and grabbed both sides of Odin's skull. She pulled his ear closer to her grinning, trembling lips. Like old lovers, they froze in anticipation.

"Odin . . . the end—"

Suddenly the sky split and a thunderous boom shook the earth. The raven flew along the length of the shrieking lightning that arced through the sky until the bolt struck the bird, sending it plummeting to the ground. The air reverberated.

"A baby cries for . . . its mother," Grimhild whispered before she collapsed into unconsciousness.

Odin remained over Grimhild as her hands dropped to the ground. He stared into her sleeping face, at the peacefulness lying below the thinning skin stretched over her skull. Her lips parted slightly, revealing broken and yellowed teeth, dark gaps where others were missing; the stench of a rotting bog rose from her throat.

Odin settled back on his haunches and gently touched her chin to close her mouth, then kissed her forehead as a father would kiss his daughter. He stood and shuffled to the ocean's edge, leaving Grimhild where she lay.

Odin closed his eye and allowed the breeze to blow his hood back off his face. He felt the wind touch his skin and move its fingertips across his beard, tickling his nostrils with his moustache. It blew through his thinning hair and down the back of his neck. He welcomed this new sensation just as he welcomed the other new and strange sensations he'd experienced since arriving on Vinland. It was just another way for him to experience his humanity.

Being alive felt so different, like a rebirth, but it came with its own challenges; it also came with subtle nuances that he'd known about but couldn't experience before he took human form. He had to focus and be present to experience the differences, or he found that he missed them. It was like being accustomed to your own surroundings: it was easy to miss something unless you focused on it.

The wind always travelled, as the humans travelled across

the land and water, and the birds flew through the sky. It blew strange shadows across the wheat field as it travelled to an unknown destination. It carried the thoughts and the fears of the people of the settlement through the camp to the crews building the ships, and beyond, through all of Vinland.

Odin thought he heard chimes blowing as the wind brushed the beard of the wheat spire in its travels across the surface of the land. It teased the long grasses, almost enticing them to join in a dance with it, then left them and the field and the stalks behind, leaving no evidence of its existence.

The wind carved the features out of the rocks and propelled humans on their ships across the water, sending them to the other side of Midgard. The wind brought the rain that watered the crops and devastated the habitats and the ships as it pushed the vessels and homes without thought across the rock or raging water. It brought life and destruction wherever it went and it was looked upon with both contempt and gratitude. It created permanent rises and hollows in the physical landscape just as thought changed the landscape of the mind.

Though the wind created permanent shapes in the earth and the rock, its light touch didn't leave a trace of its passage on the field. For all of its power and strength, it couldn't leave the same permanent changes in the living landscape; that was humankind's legacy—to do what they could to permanently alter the landscape into how they wanted it to be; it was how they created their future. But Odin couldn't envision that future. Their world would cease to exist in one climactic shift, with one human thought that travelled around the world on the wind currents, touching everything, sometimes leaving its mark and sometimes taking with it all evidence that it really was there.

As Odin drifted further and further into the place between breaths, he heard the far-off sounds of something that was carried by the internal currents. It began as a tense silence that he felt but couldn't hear, then grew into an intensity that hissed of life and finally into a growing rumble. That trailed off, then suddenly built in waves as it reached another peak. He felt a quivering within himself. It was as if Midgard moved beneath his feet; the sensation was unmistakable, a quake that shifted everything.

He felt heat on his face, as if the sun warmed his cheek or

he sat too close to a blazing fire. The smell of sulphur hung in the air, an acrid odour that penetrated the lining of his nose and pushed itself into his mind.

The earth pushed up fiery liquid rock. It was the time when all would permanently change, when fire both destroyed and purified. It was as it was at the beginning of time, a cycle repeating itself over and over again to the end of time. It offered Midgard the opportunity of continual renewal.

The mind and the heart kept the timing of creation and destruction in one thought, emotionally separating it but paradoxically joining the two states into one. The human mind created it and the human heart gave it substance; it was a matter of where one's consciousness was placed.

Odin spent much of his time thinking about the human mind and whether it needed to survive; he spent much of his time thinking about whether it served its original purpose. It was designed to comprehend and witness the majesty of Midgard and to rise above its surface to imagine and wonder at the gods of Asgard. Odin remained undecided.

Humans were instilled with the ability to create their world in the human consciousness and to keep it real, but in so doing it could capture everything, both negative and positive, and hold onto it. As a problem-solving mechanism there it was unsurpassed, but even when there wasn't a puzzle to solve or a problem to resolve, the mind, like the wind, swept everything up in its path and blew every thought with the same emotional intensity. It created problems, even where there weren't any, just so it could fulfill its purpose.

Emotions were difficult to control and their frenetic characteristics created inner worlds of fear and mania. Rather than the mind focusing on the gods, the mind used the gods to fear the Jötunn. As it continued its revolt, it created its world in fear, then forced itself to live in that fear.

It was a world where the dawn light reflecting off a wisp of fog created apparitions in the mind, not in the air. The heart generally trusted the mind, not the other way around. Odin often wondered what would happen if he created humans the way he wanted to create them, with the heart as the only governing force. That was out of his frame of power.

Humans created their world, but creation was far different from control—humans created and controlled what they created; gods created for the pleasure of creating. That was the difference between gods and humans; for them, the control was part and parcel of the creative process. When humans learned this small but valuable lesson, then their minds could touch the far reaches of his mind.

He missed the simple days of wandering across Midgard, travelling along the energy meridians of the planet's surface. The farther he walked, the more he felt the primordial energy that created Midgard pumping through his veins.

Odin looked at *Hringhorni* and hoped that the knarr still had its power to save the humans. They would need its protection as it took them to Hóp.

The future needed the humans to exist, and Odin needed to know that there would be a future to save.

8

Tostig stepped back into the ranks of his men, his eyes glued to the naked beauty towering in front of him. It was magnificent, perhaps the most magnificent thing he had seen in his life. It stood tall and statuesque in the daylight. A shiver ran along Tostig's spine, radiating out to fill his torso. It brought back the distant memory of being bitten on the back of his neck; of being surrounded by full, moist lips. He couldn't help but fall in love with his creation.

His crew stood patiently waiting for his self-indulgent love to subside, for Tostig to bark out his next order. They had laid felled logs to roll the knarr down to the lagoon, where they would anchor it until they could test, rig, load, and finally launch it on their voyage to Hóp.

Tostig looked around, noticing that more and more people were noticing the activity and joining them. They all shared in the building of the vessel, most by actually hammering the nails into the planks, but also those who mined the iron from the bog, the smiths who melted and shaped the metal into hardware, the weavers who wove the sheep's wool for the sails and those who donated scraps of clothing and other fabrics to be patched together into a sail. And there were those who tended the gardens and harvested the food for the voyage home.

In the coming days, during the inspection of the vessels, they'd probably find more and more work to be done, but there was nothing like the mind's first look and the heart's first acknowledgement of what the mind saw.

Unable to fathom the full majesty of his creation, Tostig took several more steps back, surveying her as a secret lover from afar. Tostig had specifically designed her based on some of the *Mimir's* weaknesses. The planks that reinforced this knarr's hull were much thicker than those of the previous ship, and there were twelve more places for oarsmen, enabling the knarr to travel closer to shore and through inland waterways.

Tostig walked forward and ran his hand along one of the planks of the ship's hull. The tar seal along the seam where the planks joined was still warm to the touch. *This is what makes my people strong*, he thought, *the skill to construct powerful vessels to sail the serpent's back.*

In times past, a similar design made his people feared; to see the shape of such a longship on the horizon or the ghostly outline of the ship emerging from a cloaking fog sent their adversaries running. The stories of such events began the reunions of Norse men and women from all over the norðr world, told and retold to children so they could take pride in their heritage and pass that piece of history on to their children and grandchildren, the tales forever growing in the hearts and minds of the people, as a culture and as a race.

The ship in front of Tostig was not for battle or conquest. It was for returning his people along with their resources safely back home. That was Tostig's only intention: to get his people home with the wealth that they voyaged to Vinland for in the first place.

Part of Tostig felt the ocean tugging at him and calling him back to the sea, as it had many times before. It was the only place where he felt truly alive. Where others saw the ocean as a temporary place that connected the continents, he looked upon it as his home. He had no memories of family prior to his adoptive mother and father, and they hadn't had information about Tostig's real family. The only story that Tostig remembered was that he'd been found as a young child, playing on a beach around water caves.

Tostig assumed that his birth family had abandoned him—if he'd been lost and his family was actively looking for him, then why hadn't they found him? He took their failure to find him as a decision to not look for him. Perhaps his family believed that they'd given birth to a dark elf. They may have seen him as a punishment for something that they had done, and getting rid of Tostig meant that they could remove the curse hanging over their heads.

Tostig had accepted his new family because they were kind and generous to him and accepted him as theirs without question. He remembered his father defending Tostig from prejudice because he was so different from the other young adults around him. It was then that he decided that his home would have to be a place of no home, a life of wandering.

Tostig suspected that being abandoned and his inability to overcome his feelings of inadequacy were the crux of his undaunted drive as well as the answer to his resolution. He knew that the pursuit of wealth and power would not totally give him what he sought, yet he couldn't help but pursue these things that represented value to him and made him feel valuable. He felt the drive to have a better life, to chase dream after dream because facing the end couldn't fully satisfy him.

Tostig wasn't sure whether he needed to know his past to find his future, but he did need to know who he was to find his place in the world. He needed to know what home was.

"Men, take a break," he ordered. "Go get yourselves something to eat and meet back here."

Following the men back to the settlement, Tostig smelled the pot of rabbit stew simmering over the open fire and looked forward to pulling a dipper full of potatoes and white carrots and tender meat from the steaming pot. But as the aroma pulled him closer and closer to the dinner pot, he glimpsed the cloak of the alfather as the old man disappeared behind one of the longhouses. With the burning question of his identity still fresh in his mind, he decided to satiate his mind rather than his stomach.

Stopping at the end of the longhouse where he'd last seen Odin, Tostig peered around the corner. Odin sat on a log bench in front of a burning firepit, staring into the flames. The firelight bathed Odin's face, but it appeared that more light than that radiating from the fire shone from the old man. Tostig hesitated, watching the alfather with fear and admiration. His questions weren't so pertinent that he dared insult Odin and risk experiencing the power that Odin carried in his oddly shaped staff.

Still, there sat all the knowledge and experience of an eternal brain; the force that could create Midgard from flesh and blood, the mind that possessed the strength to watch it end, when that time came. There waited Tostig's answers. He crept forward and crouched behind a bush, peering at the alfather through the thin screen of branches.

"You can approach me," Odin yelled. "I can see you over there; I'm blind only in one eye."

Feeling like a child being called to his father's side, Tostig skirted around the bush, rustling its dried leaves. He shuffled forward, almost unwilling to approach out of fear but compelled to obey for fear of repercussions.

"Sit," Odin snapped, then, as if exerting the last of his patience, he added more gently, "Tostig, you have nothing to fear from me."

As Tostig lowered himself hesitantly onto the bench, Odin dug his finger underneath his patch and rubbed his eye socket. He picked up a handful of dirt and threw it into the fire. Flames and small lights danced up into the cold air and whirled above their heads, caught by the wind.

"What do you see, Alfather?" Tostig asked.

"I see nothing. I just like watching the dancing firelight and the sparks rising into the air."

Tostig lowered his eyes, chastised.

"Tostig, you have many questions, some questions dependent upon the answers to previous questions. But there is one question that rises above all others," he said, watching the rising lights disappearing one by one.

Tostig stared intently at Odin, tracking his every word.

"You want to know who your family is and where they are." Odin replaced his eye patch and peered at Tostig with his good eye. "As if this information will validate you as a person."

Unable to organize the words in his head and form them on

his lips, Tostig managed a nod.

"This is a difficult question," Odin said. "It is one that I know, but one that I cannot answer."

Within the span of five syllables, Tostig's hope turned to despair and rage.

Odin noticed his expression. "Tostig, you are from a race of beings that are not under my influence, or my authority. I cannot direct the course of my vision because I have no knowledge or direct influence over your race."

Tostig frowned, perplexed. "What race am I a part of?"

"You are a Jötunn, a race of beings who use the elements of our universe to create themselves and to create the nine worlds."

"I was not born here, in Midgard?"

Odin shook his head. "But you are a member of the human race, just as they are a member of your race; one of your parents is human." Odin shrugged. "What does it matter? we are all created from the elemental forces of the universe and that is where we will all return. You, my child, are as unique and as special as the rest of us."

"But what of my own kind; how will I find members of my own kind?" Tostig asked.

"I cannot answer that question for you."

"You cannot, or you will not?"

Odin turned his head to glare at Tostig, his brow furrowed.

"I meant no disrespect, Alfather, but I must know who I am," Tostig pleaded.

Odin looked away and heaved a sigh. "I cannot understand this race's compulsion to find out where they came from." He looked back at Tostig. "You descended from us, isn't that all you need to know?"

"Alfather, the Christian, Adam, says that he has descended from another race of beings—"

"Yes, I know," Odin interrupted. "But he is not you; he is not from us or a part of us. Do you understand?"

Tostig looked down at the ground and moved his foot in the ashy dirt. Once again he felt like a child being taught by his father. Odin's tone was reminiscent of Tostig's adoptive father's as he tried to teach Tostig about the nine worlds connected by the great tree, Yggdrasil. "Yes, I do understand, Alfather."

"You understand it, but I sense that you do not accept it. Your heart is where it should be, Tostig, but I fear that your head has taken over and obscures everything that you're capable of seeing."

Again Odin sighed. "Tostig, if you could only see the world with your true eyes—what I can see with my one eye—your doubts and fears would dissipate into the sky like the smoke from this fire." Odin turned back to the flames. "I understand your limitations, here on Midgard. Since I arrived here my vision has been limited; there is something about this world that makes me feel as if I'm walking underwater. I see, but my field of vision is dramatically reduced; my movements are almost manacled. I now understand the human concept of imagination. If I were tethered to this world as you are, I would need my imagination. It's there that we create and recreate our existence, as well as all the things that you deem miracles—everyday occurrences for us because the imagination is limitless, not because we have superior abilities. It's as magical as fish breathing underwater."

"It's like my tracking skills," Tostig said in understanding. "Those who don't understand how I do it may see me as a völva."

"Yes," Odin replied. "Now you understand. It's the difference of being skilled in one area and unskilled in the ability that someone else possesses. That is why the Æsir works, because for all of our differences and independent thoughts, we know that each of us brings a special ability to our community as a whole. That is why our society works together; it's not too unlike your society working together, Tostig." Odin stroked his long beard in thought, his hand flipping the bottom of his beard. "Just as you bring a skill to your community, your community brings a needed skill to our community, as well."

"How?" Tostig asked.

"We exist because your thoughts brought us into existence."

"I thought it was the other way around—you created us."

"Well . . . yes, that is also true, but suffice it to say that, without you believing me into existence and I believing you into existence, there wouldn't be us standing in front of one another."

Tostig grimaced, a little confused.

"Don't try to think it," Odin advised as he picked up another log and threw it on the diminishing fire. "The risk of taking belief out of the human heart is the collapse of all that supports it. If you keep belief where it belongs, you will always have it. I will ask you one more question and then you must leave me. Before I arrived, how did you know that I existed?"

"I . . . uh . . . I suppose that I didn't know that you existed . . . but I felt it."

"*Never forget that, Tostig*. It's your feelings that are real; thinking is the illusion that we create from our feelings. It is never the opposite."

Odin's words hit Tostig like a backhand across his face; the impact of their meaning momentarily stunning him. His knees felt weak as he stood and he swayed, shaken.

Without another word, Tostig walked away from the alfather. His original question had expanded beyond anything that he would have thought to ask and the answer he received was beyond anything that he would have expected.

The alfather's wisdom was everything that he sought.

His thoughts returned to the knarr as he heard the work crew returning to the ships. He walked around the longhouse and saw their black figures backlit by the haze-covered sun as it slowly sank closer and closer to náttmál. As the bottom of its sphere touched the horizon far out on the ocean, it stained the pale sky the colour of fire. The backlit masts towered in the setting sun, an outward sign that the ships were close to completion. They sure are tall, he thought as Baldur gradually moved below the horizon, giving way to the dark and secretive night that would remove all evidence of the day's progress and replace one sense with the other—sight with sound—before finally silencing the land.

After speaking with Odin, Tostig felt that he could leap over the highest mast in just one leap, and brush his head against the wispy haze in the sky.

ꙮ ꙮ

"Men, let's get this beauty into the water and give the serpent the fight of his life when he tries to capsize her," Tostig bellowed to the men who had gathered like ants crawling out of anthills to stand around the base of a mighty oak. Six groups of men—two on her port, two on her steerboard, one group at her bow and the final group at her stern—had awaited his command. Now those concentrated at the front of the ship heaved the hull onto rounded logs carefully aligned on the ground from the scaffolding to the water's edge.

Tostig had designed a base to fit the prow that would provide stability for the knarr which, like a fish out of water, couldn't stand upright without being stabilized. The base kept the ship from tipping precariously from side to side as they moved her down to the water, the men's efforts aided by the logs and the downhill slope. As long as they kept her moving across the logs and each team provided proper measures of balance with counterbalance, momentum would carry the ship steadily toward the water. The offshore wind blew along the length of the knarr, providing a measure of resistance that helped the men control the knarr's speed as it approached the rocky beach.

During the course of construction, through experimentation, Tostig had come to realize that his men could exert a quarter of the amount of force if his pulley system used longer ropes. He'd installed a simple pulley system on the stern of the knarr; the men pulling at the rear of the ship were actually assisting the men at the front pulling the knarr forward, as well as helping to steady the ship. He realized that if he placed a pulley at the front of the ship, just as he did at the top of the scaffolding to more easily and quickly hoist materials up onto the ship during construction, he needed fewer men to help move the ship forward; or he could apply the same amount of force using half as many.

As the grade of the meadow levelled out, the system worked wonders, but it showed its true power as they heaved the knarr across the ramp that they'd built over the rocky shoreline, bridging the land to the water. As the men heaved the large wooden vessel across the makeshift bridge, Tostig sensed their drive to go home. If pulling the ship across the ocean would get them home faster, Tostig believed that they would. With each grunted exhalation and yell, the offshore wind provided the choral counterpoint for their homeward voyage.

"You're getting us closer to home," Tostig yelled, feeling the strength that his words provided; they were the final gale that pushed the knarr closer to the water and the men's hearts closer to home. Sweat and salt water left rivulets in the dirt and grime on vein-pulsing arms and legs that strained against the weight of the knarr as the men pulled. The boards of the makeshift bridge creaked and squealed in protest as the weight of the knarr spread itself across its expanse.

"Steady," Tostig warned as the men on the port and steerboard sides of the vessel stepped into the knee-deep water and waded against the force of the approaching waves. The men at the bow of the ship were moving to either side of the vessel to get out of her way.

With one final heave, they pulled the knarr over the apex of the ramp and allowed gravity and momentum to push her into the water. The front of the keel made its final descent over the logs and dove into the water just as a gust of wind caught the knarr and threatened to smash the hull against the rocky shoreline. The planks creaked and moaned as the knarr's weight momentarily focused at her bow. As she slid into the water, the mast yawed from port to steerboard until the ship balanced on the surface of the sea.

The ship settled into its element, pushed and pulled by the waves. They tethered the knarr to the rocks along the shoreline and underneath the water. As the ship settled, an exhausted calm descended over the sweat- and saltwater-soaked men. They managed to raise their aching arms into the air in a cheer that was quickly lost in the blowing wind.

"Excellent work, men," Tostig yelled as he walked toward the vessel. "Hoist me up," he asked two men standing knee-deep in water next to the ship.

Tostig jumped down onto the deck and like a squirrel scavenging for nuts, ran along the deck looking for fractures or damage that would allow water to enter the vessel. He looked down the port hole to the lower deck, but saw no signs of water. Satisfied, Tostig returned to the side of the ship and climbed into the arms of the men waiting to carry him to the shore.

Thorfinn's decision to explore farther down the coast of Vinland for more resources was a good one. It allowed them to start the knarr's trial runs closer to shore, working out any problems or issues with the ship's construction before an extended voyage home. If time didn't allow them to resolve all problems found before they departed for home, then they could work out any remaining issues en route. They would be minor.

Tostig, knowing all details of the construction of the ship—

what he saw as his responsibility—was confident that she would carry them safely home. "She will float!" he shouted.

The crew cheered again, then slowly lowered their aching bodies to the ground.

Tostig looked out across the whitecaps flowing over the great world serpent's blue back, and his brows pinched together. It looked as if a storm was brewing over Jörmungandr's realm; a storm like no other. It brought memory of a story his adopted father had told him as a child, when the thunder clapped so loud that it shook the walls of their house and his bed.

His father had run to his bedside, drawn by his crying. "Did I tell you the story of Thor battling the great world serpent, Jörmungandr?" he asked.

Tostig shook his head, tears still streaming down his cheeks.

"As Thor's hammer, Mjöllnir, came down to strike Jörmungandr, it missed—Jörmungandr writhed out of range of the heavy and slow-moving hammer. The hammer instead struck the top of the sky. That's why you hear that thunderclap; the bolt of light is the sky splitting in two from Mjöllnir's strike."

"Who won the battle?" Tostig asked, seizing on the story to distract him from the storm.

"That's an ending that is best saved for another day," his father answered, as he always did when asked to finish the story.

The tale his father spun put a heroic face on the unseen elements. Tostig still hid under the fur throws covering his bed, hoping that Thor had no reason to send a thunderbolt down upon him, but he noticed that his father wasn't scared, and emulating that behaviour helped Tostig fall asleep feeling safe and empowered.

ஐ ஐ

Tostig lay in the tall meadow grass and thought of Iceland as he looked at the clouds drifting overhead. In his mind's eye, he saw the mossy green cliffs that formed the gorge walls where crystal blue rivers rushed; he saw the waterfalls where water roared over high ledges to crash into rock basins and explode into misty clouds that rose into clear blue skies. He saw the networks of rivers and lakes formed as the water flowed ceaselessly everywhere, collecting in pools, working its way through human-size cracks and breaks in the cliff walls, flowing under rocks into and through hidden caves to be heated up by the fiery earth and pushed back above ground once again, or carving out new tunnels and passageways. It flowed into sapphire-blue pools and emerald green puddles, bringing nourishment to the volcanic soil. This was the magic of where Tostig wanted to be.

The clear rushing water fed the peoples' hearts and their souls just as it fed the land, infiltrating their senses with beauty and majesty as it infiltrated the cracks and crevices in the rocks. It was the waterfalls of Iceland that Tostig missed the most; they were everywhere. The rocky cliff faces, for all their majestic strength and dominance, could not move and change the land like the erosive power of the water flowing over and around and through them. Water always found a way to pass through barriers and seep into the small cracks and fissures of the mighty rocks that stood their ground. It was something that couldn't be captured. It pushed its way through the fingers as the hand closed into a fist, and disappeared.

His people farmed the fertile land, which fed and clothed them just as Vinland did. But Vinland couldn't, for all its beauty and potential, grab his heart and hold onto it like Iceland did as he travelled across the endless oceans of Midgard.

Tostig closed his eyes and relaxed his tired, sore muscles, sinking into the layers of meadow grass. It didn't matter where he was; he could only feel close to home, but never be home, not in the way that he envisioned home, or the sense of place within him that a home could foster. He knew that it was a place beyond himself; it is a place where tradition and culture and the art that bound these two identities defined its people.

7

Thorfinn stared into the night sky hanging over the cold ocean. There were few stars out; an undaunted haze blanketed the heavens, dimming all except the brightest objects.

A shimmering light just above the horizon caught his attention. He stood motionless, as if in a trance, staring at the iridescent curtain of light rippling in the night sky, the ghostly lights dancing across the dark night in mesmerizing and random patterns. It was as if he was looking at a reflection of the ocean on the ceiling of the heavens, the waves of light moving it as easily as the water moved across the surface of the world serpent. It was a ghostly light. Just like the ocean surface, it hid whatever was on the other side of it.

They'd stolen away in the night, Thorfinn wanting to avoid being seen by the Vinland natives. Still, Elsu had mentioned that there were night scouting parties, so their departure may still have been noted. They'd tried to load the two knarrs in secrecy as well, with the supplies and equipment needed for a short trip. Thorfinn had to leave much behind at Leifsbúrðir to make room for the supplies they'd need to gather before the long voyage home.

Leif had told Thorfinn about the settlement at Hóp. It wasn't as large as Leifsbúrðir, consisting of two main longhouses. A source of water flowed through the small settlement, but the harvesting season was short and there hadn't yet been a need to enlarge the camp. The suðr territory was largely unexplored; Leif planned future journeys to investigate more of the surrounding waterways going inland and a nearby cave system that provided additional shelter during the stormy season.

Leif hadn't mentioned the native population, so Thorfinn interpreted it as non-issue. He couldn't lose more men to battle; they'd already had to double their efforts to make up for the men lost in their first battle. A certain number lost was expected, of course, but not the loss incurred from all-out war. As Thorfinn always maintained, the voyage was one of exploration, commerce, and alliance-building, which was the crux of a profitable and successful voyage. Indeed, Thorfinn had plans of returning again and again. He saw this as a place to build his wealth over time. He needed a peaceful trading relationship with the people of the land to establish his own permanent base on Vinland.

Thorfinn wished Gudrid were standing next to him to share in the beauty of the night sky. He turned to see her huddled in the back of the knarr. She had been drifting in and out of sleep for the last three dægur and he didn't want to deprive her of any sleep, so needed, that she could find. Still, he thought seeing the beauty in the world would calm her mind. He'd watched her sink deeper and deeper into a sinkhole of grief that grew larger and larger by the dægur. He sometimes felt that he was caught in that hole of grief as well. For Gudrid's sake, he scrambled out of it so he could care for her.

He carried much on his back: the daily grind of the mission, his own feelings of loss for his son, and coping with Gudrid's guilt that somehow it was her fault because she agreed to travel to the native camp. As much as he tried, Thorfinn couldn't convince her that the attack, which had caused her early delivery, was not Gudrid's fault. There was no separation for Gudrid between what she controlled and what was out of her control. And the stress of caring for Gudrid, even though his love for her was without limits, just added more stress to his feelings of loss over his son, and the fact that he couldn't take his dead son back home with him.

Why don't I have his body to return to Grœnlandia? He

clutched the side of the knarr tighter, pushing the blood from his fingers, the pressure changing to pain. His heart pounded harder and faster, thudding against his ribcage as if trying to beat through to escape; his head spun and he had to rest it on the railing until the ocean and the sky stopped spinning.

He looked up to the sky once more and focused on the greens and yellows moving in waves, like the sail moving in the wind. The floor of Asgard fluttered, its fabric holding the remnants of the day's sunlight. A low crackling sound tickled his head, as if a swarm of flies buzzed around him. It reminded him of sitting next to a campfire, hearing the spitting and the crackling of the wood as the heat split it apart.

He thought of valkyries and didn't know why, though some said the lights and the accompanying sounds were the angels of the Norse pantheon, riding their horses over distant battlefields of bloodied and decapitated warriors, choosing the best for Valhalla. Some flew under their own power, riding the currents of air on huge raven wings, tails of light leaving a streak across the dark heavens. Others cried out for the winged guardians to hold them to their bosoms and whisper praises in their ears of valiant conquests on the field of battle.

Thorfinn looked out across the water at the other knarr. Since no one had any idea what its name had been, they'd chosen the name *Hringhorni* because it was obviously a gift from the gods. The swinging lamps hanging from her sides kept her visible, just as those on Thorfinn's ship, the *Mimir II*, made them visible. Thorfinn watched the ghostly figures of the night crew moving in and out of the shadows on the other ship, as they walked the deck their eyes on the light show above. He knew they were human but they could as easily have been apparitions travelling across the water.

There'd be no rest for the weary, he thought; they would have to work harder at harvesting wood and grapes to make up lost time before they sailed for home. Both the time they'd spent at Markland and the time it took them to build the *Mimir II* had played small parts in delaying them and fragmenting their resources.

Thorfinn sensed someone nearby and turned to see Adam in the lamplight, standing next to him. He also looked out across the water, eyes on the points of firelight dotting the Markland shoreline. "It's a beautiful night for sailing," Adam commented.

"Yes it is," Thorfinn replied, pulled back to the containment of the knarr. He had grown to respect Adam's monotheistic beliefs. His display of courage in the caves at Markland and his part in rescuing the group from destruction had earned him that respect. Thorfinn couldn't ignore Adam's important role in saving his country, and the rest of Europe, from collapse. If Adam ever decided to change professions, Thorfinn thought, he wouldn't hesitate to hire him for future voyages.

"How is Gudrid?" Adam asked with genuine concern.

"She's talking; I take that as a good sign."

"Thorfinn, I'd like to speak to her. I think I could be of some help."

Thorfinn nodded, knowing that Gudrid trusted Adam for the same reason that he trusted Adam: he had saved their lives by destroying Ari. He watched as Adam walked over to her.

ഇ ര

Sensing a presence, Gudrid moved around in the mass of furs and sat up, pushing stray hairs back from her face. She said nothing as Adam knelt on the deck near her.

"Gudrid, I don't know what you're experiencing," Adam began, speaking slowly, as if choosing his words carefully. "But I'm here to help you through this; feel free to talk to me about anything."

After a long silence, Gudrid finally sighed and said, "I'm angry, scared—I feel lost. And so alone. There is no woman I feel comfortable confiding in; Freydis and I have grown apart since her marriage. I can't turn to Thorfinn—"

"Why do you feel that you can't turn to him?" Adam interrupted.

"Because I blame him for losing our son as well as bringing us here," Gudrid whispered, staring at the silhouette of Thorfinn standing on the deck and feeling ashamed for vocalizing her thoughts.

"If I remember, Gudrid, you insisted on coming," Adam

replied. "And because you blame Thorfinn for losing Snorri, it's a good reason for you to talk to him."

Gudrid sighed again and picked absently at something clinging to one of the furs. "I know. I know it was my idea to come to Vinland. Even so, I still blame him and I can't resolve that . . . it's part of the turmoil I feel."

"As I see it, you're blaming yourself for the death of your son; that's what's causing these feelings. Can you see that blaming Thorfinn, Vinland, or yourself isn't dealing with the feelings of loss? You are transferring your feelings to situations that you do have control over."

Gudrid stared at him for several long moments, digesting that. Then she nodded. "I think I understand," she said slowly. "What do you think I should do?"

Adam smiled gently. "That was my next question to you. What will you do to stop feeling this way?"

Gudrid stared into Adam's face, contemplating options. Then her eyes shifted over his shoulder as a mist suddenly rose up from the ocean's surface, churning and growing till it obscured the horizon. She watched it rise higher and higher into the air, spreading to blanket the night sky.

The mist turned in on itself, twisting into tentacles that reached out to drift across the deck of the knarr. The wisps moved toward Gudrid as if reaching for her, wanting to pull her into the centre of the cloud out over the water. They crawled through the crew, flowed between the sleeping oarsmen, moved around and through the lanterns. The crewmembers on duty didn't appear to notice the fog swirling around them; they walked through it, their bodies pushing the tendrils out of the way as they carried on with their work as if nothing were happening. Gudrid quickly realized that she was the only one who saw the fog rolling across the deck.

She looked across the deck at Odin, who stared back at her with knowing eyes until he too disappeared in the fog. Now Gudrid stood alone on the deck. She was having a vision, she knew.

The wind immediately died; the knarr stopped bobbing and the deck ceased yawing. Gudrid felt safely wrapped in the still heavy mist. Then she sensed an unfamiliar presence. "Hello?" she called. "Is anyone there?"

Dead silence answered her.

Gudrid felt pregnant again; she knew that there was another human life growing inside of her. Suddenly she felt the baby kicking . . . and then she heard a baby crying.

"Snorri!" she screamed, bolting blindly into the fog.

A hand reached through the fog and grabbed her arm; the fog quickly dissipated and Gudrid found herself clutching the side of the ship, with Adam holding her back. "What hap . . . ?" Gudrid began, feeling disoriented and confused as, for a second, reality and dream were the same, the transition so seamless that she couldn't distinguish one from the other.

"Was I about to go overboard?" she asked, looking at Odin, who stood beside her.

"Yes. And you yelled out, 'Snorri.'"

"Yes, that's right," she said, her confusion turning to understanding and then to excitement. "I heard Snorri crying. He's alive, Adam; I know he's alive—I heard him and I felt his presence." She turned to fully face the old man. "Odin, you must help me; convince my husband to turn the ship around and drop me off at Vinland."

Odin only stared into her intense eyes. Adam stepped forward, frowning, clearly displeased that Gudrid chose the old man over him. "Gudrid, he will never agree to that," he said.

"What if you agree to return with me?" she pleaded. "I cannot do this alone."

Thorfinn sauntered over, curious about the building activity. Noticing Gudrid's sudden transformation, he stood silently, a relieved yet puzzled smile on his face. Gudrid stepped over and grabbed his coat. "Thorfinn, Snorri is alive," she said.

ꕤ ꕤ

Thorfinn opened his mouth to speak, but the words receded into shock and confusion as her statement moved through his brain, aggravating unhealed wounds. "Wha—" He felt the knarr spinning and a gust of air blew past him, too fast for him to inhale it.

"I heard him in a—"

Thorfinn raised his hand as if to push away her words—or perhaps to protect himself from further injury. He struggled to remain on his feet. His entire world had capsized and Thorfinn hadn't resurfaced yet; thousands of tiny bubbles brushed past his body, tickling his skin, pushing their way to the surface—or pushing him farther and farther under; he couldn't tell. He only knew that he had to keep kicking to remain where he was; he had to kick away from the darkness. He saw the light directly above him; he could almost touch it with his hand—if he could reach high enough, he'd break the water's surface and grab the sun from the sky and pull it down to him, pushing the darkness farther and farther beneath him.

It took Thorfinn several minutes to recover. Once his senses returned, he realized that Gudrid was steadying him with one arm and holding onto his hand with her other hand. "What did you say, Gudrid?" he asked.

"I said that I heard Snorri in a vision." Gudrid lowered her voice, treading lightly with her words as if tiptoeing barefoot across a stony beach.

"Do you know where he is?" He asked, finally able to raise his head.

"No, I don't. I just know that he's alive. When I awoke in the wigwam," she said, her gaze growing distant as she relived the experience, "I knew something wasn't right. But I was so overcome with grief because I couldn't see him. I knew that Snorri was gone, but I could feel his presence, as if he were still inside of me. I thought that it might've been an afterimage caused by grief, a memory of him still inside of me. I do get them occasionally, but not when someone dies; that should've been my first clue that Snorri is still alive."

Gudrid took a deep breath. "Thorfinn, my love, our son is still alive; I must return to Vinland to begin searching for him."

Thorfinn looked at Gudrid's lips. He saw them forming the words and heard them, but he struggled with their meaning. "But you don't know where he is," he finally managed to say, spitting out his reply as if it had stuck at the back of his throat like phlegm. If he allowed Gudrid to return to Vinland, he risked losing her; but if he didn't let her try, he would never get his son back.

Then, as her words sank in, Thorfinn pursed his lips and scowled. "No, Gudrid," he bellowed. "Absolutely not! It's too dangerous; I will not send my wife back there after losing my son."

"Odin and Adam have agreed to make the trip with me," she protested, glancing at them.

"Then they're as foolish as you are. You're sending yourselves back to your deaths." Thorfinn shook his head. "No, I will not allow it; it's a violation of our treaty with the natives."

Determined, Gudrid met Thorfinn's resolute stare with her own; their resolves struggled with one another for a moment. "I'm returning to Vinland even if I have to swim back there," she insisted.

"You are making a grave mistake, Gudrid. If Elsu's tribe catches you on Vinland, they will kill you on sight. Besides, where would you start looking?"

"Returning to Elsu's camp is a good place to start," she said lightly.

"You are crazy!" he yelled.

"Thorfinn," Gudrid said, her tone reasonable, "if you were convinced that Snorri was still alive, wouldn't you attempt to rescue him?"

Thorfinn exhaled a long, slow breath and stared into her eyes. He always seemed to find the right answer there. Gudrid had him caught in another one of her tightening nooses; the more he pulled, the more her point tightened around him. "If you're going back, then I'm going with you," he said.

Gudrid lifted her eyebrows. "What about Hóp?"

"Freydis and Tostig can take care of that. It's strictly coordination and gathering resources; they can do that on their own." He turned and yelled, "Tostig, signal the *Hringhorni*. Tell them to come alongside."

Tostig ran to the steerboard side of the ship, unhooked a lantern, and raised it into the air, signalling to the *Hringhorni's* lookout. As soon as the signal was acknowledged, Tostig changed his signal for the *Hringhorni* to come alongside.

The night oarsmen quickly responded to the command from Freydis, the port rowers lifting their oars from the water while the steerboard rowers dragged their oars on the top of the water, turning the ship. At Freydis's second signal, the port oarsmen rowed, turning the ship to converge with the *Mimir II*. To complete the maneuver, the port oarsmen dragged their oars along the surface of the water, moving the *Hringhorni* alongside the *Mimir II*.

As soon as the two knarrs matched speed, Tostig lifted the boarding planks and laid them across the gap, one near the bows and the other at the sterns, connecting both ships.

Thorfinn leaned over the hull. "Freydis, we're returning to Leifsbúrðir and will rejoin you at Hóp later. Begin setting up camp; Tostig will return with the *Mimir II* to join you shortly." When Freydis hesitated, clearly confused by the abrupt change in plan, Thorfinn continued. "It shouldn't put our schedule behind too much. We'll be able to catch up in time so that both ships are full for our trip home." Thorfinn didn't know what the next few dægur would hold, but he felt it was important to speak with confidence.

Tostig looked at Freydis, then back at Thorfinn, nodding in agreement. "Tostig," Thorfinn told him, "once we're unsecured from the *Hringhorni*, order the rowers to turn us around and take us back to Leifsbúrðir."

Thorfinn turned to Gudrid. After all that they'd been through, he was still crazy about her; he'd follow her anywhere.

"Gudrid," Freydis yelled, "I'm coming with you." Thorfinn's brows rose in wry surprise. She seemed eager to leave her newly wedded husband and join her sister for another adventure.

"No, sister," Gudrid said; "we will see each other at Hóp. Save a place for me at the hearth and I will tell you our tale. Besides, I will have the great Christian warrior, Adam of Breman, with me." Gudrid smirked at her joke.

"Then all evil be damned to Hel . . . or to Hell, in Adam's case," Freydis quipped.

"And don't forget our bond, sister," Gudrid said, serious again.

"I will see you again and I will never forget our bond," Freydis returned. She leaned forward and grabbed Gudrid's shoulders. "Bring my nephew home to me and we will celebrate, the likes of which the world will never see again." She dropped her hands and stepped back. "Safe travels."

As they stepped back, Thorfinn looked at Gudrid. "I don't know whether I should commend you for your heroism or your stupidity, Gudrid. We both want our son to be alive and home."

"I know he's alive, Thorfinn, as surely as I know you're standing in front of me. I've seen it. My previous visions showed Snorri in a longhouse with us where we're all standing around a fire, drinking and laughing. Don't worry, my husband; have faith that he will be with us again."

Thorfinn sighed as he saw the face of the woman he'd fallen in love with coming back to life. She looked like Baldur rising after a long sleep. The heroine returns and lives again. Hugging Gudrid, he looked over the *Mimir II*'s bow at the familiar black shape of *Hringhorni* as she sailed away toward the shimmering, emerald-green horizon.

Then Tostig's voice rang out as he ordered his oarsmen to turn the *Mimir II* and begin the journey back to Vinland.

The rower's arms undulated and their bodies heaved forward in unison, the heavy wooden oars rhythmically scooping and pulling at the ocean in time to Tostig's grunted cadence.

As the ship settled into its return course, Elsu walked across the deck to Thorfinn. "We are heading back, Thorfinn? Why?"

"Yes," Thorfinn answered, moving Elsu aside to talk to him in private. "Do you know what your people's reaction will be, seeing Gudrid and I return after we agreed to leave?"

Elsu's brows drew together as he thought. "It's hard to say, but they may not consider a few people a threat. Gudrid is known to my people; they may feel more curious than threatened."

"Will you come with us?" Thorfinn asked.

"Yes, I think that's a good idea, Thorfinn. I overheard; is your son alive?"

Thorfinn hesitated; how could he honestly answer a question that he kept asking himself? Did Gudrid have the ability to see the truth? And did he believe that Snorri could still be alive, or was all of this just for the love of his wife? "Yes, I do believe that my son is alive," he said. "And I believe that Gudrid has seen it as well."

Elsu nodded, understanding the dedication that Thorfinn had for his wife, the faith that went beyond a couple's physical and emotional connection. "I will do all that I can to help you and Gudrid on your journey; I will take both of you back in safety."

Thorfinn felt his kinship with Elsu strengthen. Gudrid had told him that she felt a kinship with Elsu's dead wife, Yakima, during their brief meeting. Elsu felt like a brother to Thorfinn, and the closest companion that he could ever have wanted on this trip.

As the shimmering lights in the sky faded and the *Hringhorni* disappeared into the waning darkness, the atmosphere on *Mimir II* changed from the flurry of onboard activity to the steady creaking of the deck and the dipping of oars into the cold ocean water. They'd lowered the sail and tied it to the mast for the return trip; only dark silhouettes moved across the deck.

The night air quickly changed to a stinging slap as it whipped past their exposed faces and around fur collars grasped tight within fists. Thorfinn's ears were numb when Gudrid walked up to him and wrapped her arms in a hug around his generous torso, nestling her cheek in his collar. "It's getting unseasonably cold," she said. "We're moving suðr, shouldn't it be getting warmer?"

"Yes," he replied, still engrossed in the norðr sky. "It's a strange season."

"I'm going to bed," Gudrid said. "Wake me when we arrive at Vinland."

Gudrid disappeared into the darkness of the stern, the corner of the ship that she'd arranged for herself where she felt most comfortable, away from the noise of running the ship.

Thorfinn returned his attention to the heavens until whispering among the crew distracted him. At first he thought that something was happening among the oarsmen, but when he followed their sight line, he noticed the shimmering of celestial lights once again. *Here we go again*, he thought, *another adventure or another distraction.*

6

The moon moved toward the trees lining the horizon, threatening to leave them in full darkness. The little light it did provide was enough to see their way off the ship and into the knee-deep water. Thorfinn hadn't dared bring the ship closer to the shore for fear that the keel would beach on the sandy bottom of the land shelf; he didn't have the men to pull the knarr free.

Gudrid pulled her dress up at the waist, hoping to keep the hem away from the lapping waves, then jumped over the side. The frigid water numbed her calves and knees, turning them cherry red from the cold as she waded toward shore. She scanned the land for signs of movement, hoping that their nocturnal landing wouldn't alert any of the native inhabitants. Thorfinn, Odin, Elsu, and Adam of Bremen followed close behind her with armfuls of equipment and supplies.

Despite her efforts, the soaked bottom of her dress slapped against the rocks as Gudrid climbed over them to the stony beach. Turning, she took some of the supplies from the men as they climbed after her, grabbing whatever she could and dropping it to the ground. Then she extended her arms to assist Odin over the rocks. His frail legs wobbled as he stepped onto their uneven surfaces, but Odin managed the obstacle quite easily. His last step, though, landed him on the beach with a thud, throwing him off balance; Gudrid managed to catch him before he toppled backward onto the jagged rocks.

"Thank you, my child," Odin said as he steadied himself. Gudrid smiled. The old man extended a frail hand toward Adam, behind him. "Adam, would you like a hand over the rocks as well?" he quipped. Adam glared back, not appreciating the joke.

Gudrid touched Odin's arm and took a few steps back from the boulders. Odin placed his hand over hers and turned to her. "Gudrid," he whispered, "I know the question on your mind; I'm sorry, but I can't answer it. I don't know where your son is."

Gudrid burst into tears. She had gotten used to what she called the "surprise onslaught of grief" that came without warning, like a sudden rainfall on a sunny day, but she preferred that it happened in private. Gudrid wiped her eyes and glanced apologetically at the others, whose eyes had turned her way.

"We should head into the Dark Forest," Elsu suggested. "Just in case my people have scouting parties roaming the field and your camp."

"Yes, Myrkwood Forest," Odin said, nodding. "I know it well."

They followed the edge of the field as they moved farther inland, glancing over at the dark shapes of Leifsbúrðir's empty buildings as they passed them.

"You've been quiet," Gudrid said, slowing to allow Adam to catch up with her.

"I have nothing to say," he replied.

"Your silence doesn't have to do with the presence of the alfather, does it? Do you feel threatened by him?"

Adam thought a moment before answering. "I don't believe that he's the alfather; he's just a crazy old man," he replied. "I think he's demented and confused."

"But where do you think he came from?" Gudrid asked.

Adam shrugged. "He could've come from anywhere; perhaps the Culdee colony in Markland."

Adam's assessment struck at a suspicion that Gudrid's thoughts had been revisiting since Odin's arrival. Odin had not displayed the slightest proof of being a supernatural being. In fact, he seemed to be teetering between senility and eccentricity, two characteristics that made him both interesting and frightening, but didn't qualify him as the leader of the Norse pantheon and the universe.

"What do you think, Gudrid?" Adam asked.

"I don't know. He's had some interesting insights. I can't believe that he can fool all of us, if he isn't the alfather."

"He hasn't fooled all of us," Adam interrupted. "He hasn't fooled me."

"I did have a vision of his arrival, riding on the back of the world serpent, Jörmungandr."

"Do you think he's your god, Odin?" Adam asked, his tone insinuating.

Gudrid thought for a moment, digging through her feelings over everything that had been happening to her during the last several viknatal. "I believe that he's the alfather," she replied. "Until he does something that changes my belief, I must believe in him."

Adam looked as if he felt a little betrayed by Gudrid's announcement; she suspected that he was trying to convert her over to Christianity. To do so, he was struggling to dig through a life of conditioning, beginning with beliefs instilled in Gudrid at an early age and reinforced on a daily basis throughout her lifetime.

"Are we really going to the native camp?" he asked, changing the subject.

"Yes, that's where it all began," Gudrid said with a sigh.

"Gudrid, you'll be walking into a lion's den," Adam warned. "How will you get in and out of the camp alive?"

"I have a plan," Gudrid said, lowering her voice as if there were eavesdroppers in the trees. "But, I need Elsu's help."

Odin stepped up beside her. "Can I talk to you, my daughter?" he asked, pulling Gudrid away from Adam.

"Yes," she answered, moving a few steps away with him.

"I'd like to know more about your vision. Do you know where Snorri is?"

Gudrid shook her head. "No, I didn't actually see anything. There was mist around me."

"Did you hear anything else, other than your baby crying?"

"No, nothing that I can remember."

Odin sighed. "That's unfortunate; I was hoping that my knowledge would be helpful to you."

"I must . . ." she stammered, pointing to Elsu.

"I know—talk to Elsu. He is wise. Don't worry, Gudrid, I have a feeling that you *will* see your son again."

Gudrid smiled, unsure whether Odin spoke words of support and encouragement or a revelation of something he had witnessed in the future-time; she wanted to think that they came from knowledge of future events. When Odin nodded and stepped away, Gudrid pushed forward to where Elsu and Thorfinn had stopped to scan the trees ahead for movement.

The two men jumped as Gudrid approached them from the dark, their senses still fully alert as they focused on the silent, grey shapes of the night. They relaxed and smiled when they recognized Gudrid.

"Elsu," Gudrid said, "I'd like your help to infiltrate your people's camp."

"No, out of the question!" Thorfinn hissed. "I agreed to return to search for Snorri; I didn't agree to walk straight to our deaths."

"I must agree with Thorfinn; they will see your presence as a breach of your agreement, and kill you on sight," Elsu said. Then he dropped his voice to add ominously, "Or they will torture you, force you to tell them where the rest of us are before putting you to death, and hunt us down with death squads."

"Not if I look like Yakima and walk into the camp with you, Elsu. Your people will look on it as the spirit of your wife returning and welcome me into the camp as a sign of good fortune."

"That is extremely risky," Thorfinn said.

"I agree," Elsu said. "They've seen you, Gudrid, so there will be skepticism."

After a moment's thought, Gudrid understood Elsu's reluctance. Her idea was unfair to him; she was asking him to figuratively dig up his dead wife and to walk with her into a deadly situation. Her intention was not to dishonour Yakima's memory for her own purpose. "Elsu, I understand how you feel—that I'd be dishonouring your wife's memory by involving her image in such a deceptive way. But Yakima did visit me; maybe it was a sign that she was willing to help."

Elsu nodded carefully. "I will have to think on this."

Gudrid was satisfied with that. She also nodded. "Do what you feel is right."

They walked side by side in silence. Gudrid couldn't—or chose not to—interpret what Elsu may be thinking or feeling. If Elsu decided not to help her, Gudrid didn't know what else she could do. All hope of finding her son would be lost.

They followed an unmarked path parallel to the water's edge; Gudrid hoped that the sound of the surf concealed the heavy rustling that five of them made through the tall wheat grass. She also realized that the tall grass and the sound of the surf could also cloak the approach of anyone heading in their direction.

She looked down at the water seeping across the ground, washing away all evidence of their passage. *But we've all left traces of our presence*, Gudrid thought. Even by walking on Midgard and even sailing on the great serpent's back, humans influenced their environment. Her feet sank ankle-deep into the sandy surface; granules of sand crept into her shoes and tickled her feet and toes on the way down to the toes of her shoes. She shook her foot in mid-step as she walked, and heard a few low chuckles at her waddling.

As the night wore into the very early hours of morning, Gudrid looked up and noticed that the trees were denser and much larger—they were entering Myrkwood, the Dark Forest. The huge trees reminded her of the ones back home. They towered above their heads like living mountains, branches extending so far out around them that they could block the sunlight and the rain from ever reaching the forest floor. Massive root systems pushed through the ground, heaving the earth up all around them. As she led the group into the forest, she was overcome more and more by not only the height of the trees but the size of their trunks and the extent of the branches. Walls of bark surrounded them and plumes of green extended to the sky above their heads. They were walking into a land of giants, where the landscape dwarfed human consciousness. And where they would all have to fight to survive.

Gudrid sensed a weight on Elsu's mind. Perhaps he felt responsible for the group, or perhaps he felt that he was betraying his people by returning to his home after making the decision to leave. Gudrid wondered if she had re-ignited his feelings of loss for Yakima when she suggested that she disguise herself as his deceased wife and walk back into the camp.

She was a little shocked at herself for not considering Elsu's feelings in this matter, or the possibility that he had his own fears, before she asked him to help her with her plot to find and rescue her son. The feeling so overwhelmed her that she thought of little else.

"The sun will rise soon," Elsu said. He shivered and crossed his arms over his chest, instinctively insulating himself from the cold night wind that blew over the waves, across the field and into Myrkwood Forest. "It's been colder this season; autumn has come early this year. Where you come from, Gudrid, have you noticed a change in your seasons?"

Gudrid thought for a moment; she had to admit that the growing season was always short in Grœnlandia, but: "I've noticed that there is a grey ash in the sky that blocks the sun."

"Yes, I've noticed that too," Elsu replied. He hesitated, then said, "Tomorrow will be a difficult day."

"Why?" Gudrid asked.

"Because I will be walking into my camp beside my long-deceased wife. That is, if you still want to go through with your plan?"

Gudrid stared into his dark eyes, then smiled.

"I suggest that we do it before the sun sets," he continued. "It will take me most of the day to gather enough materials to cover your face and skin. I'll need to find you clothes."

"What made you decide to help us?" Gudrid asked.

"I feel responsible for the disappearance of your baby, Gudrid."

"But you had nothing to do with it, Elsu."

He sighed. "Yes, I know. But it happened while you were my guests; I brought you to our camp and that makes me responsible."

"We don't blame you, Elsu," Gudrid told him. "There are forces that operate beyond our control. I don't know who or what to blame, until we find the person responsible for Snorri's abduction. I know that my son is alive, so I also know that I will get him back. It's just a matter of time."

As they pushed through gaps filled with large ferns and ducked low-hanging tree branches, she allowed her emotions to ride the wave of confidence she'd suddenly felt when speaking to Elsu. Snorri was out there and he was looking for his mother! It was just a matter of time before they found one another.

ℌ ℭ

As the others made camp for the night, Thorfinn noticed the alfather sitting on a fallen log, shifting uncomfortably and glancing around, as if agitated. "Alfather, are you alright?" he asked, walking over to Odin.

"I'll be fine," the old man answered with a sigh. "I'm finding it a little hard to keep up with you younger folk."

Thorfinn nodded. "We've had a busy two dægur."

"Yes, and I'm afraid the coming days will be harder," Odin whispered, looking past Thorfinn to the others.

The back of Thorfinn's neck prickled. "What do you mean, Alfather?"

"I haven't been totally honest with you, my son," Odin said. He beckoned Thorfinn to him. "We must talk."

Thorfinn took Odin by the arm and led him away from the others as they prepared to bed down for the night. He looked into the old man's face as they passed the small campfire. Odin looked haggard and tired. Dark rings circled his eyes and the skin on his face looked as if it was thinning—a skeleton hanging onto old skin.

"There is a reason that I'm on Midgard," Odin said when they stopped just beyond the firelight.

"Yes," Thorfinn said, unsurprised. "I've suspected that since we met you."

Odin sagged a bit and Thorfinn found himself supporting the old man by his arm. "There's no good way to tell you, so I'm going to just say it. It's the Ragnarök, my son; it's the ending of our reign."

The disparate pieces of Thorfinn's fears slid together into one terrifying truth. He'd wondered why cattle mysteriously died as if the air and ground were being poisoned, and worried over the grey haze in the sky that the sun couldn't fully penetrate. But that was as far as it had gone; they were all so consumed with their own lives that they couldn't or didn't want to lift the veil of darkness and see what was approaching them from the dark. What could they have done, even if they did see the end coming? It probably wouldn't have made a difference; they'd still go about doing the same things to survive, just as they did now. That's what humans did—the things that justified the beginning and defined the end.

The reins that Thorfinn had grasped so tightly were beginning to slacken and lose their influence over him. Where the many old and dying gods were separating the people, he saw the one God stepping forward to unite them under one heavenly purpose, preparing to destroy all other independent political and secular thought, leaving no room in the human soul for anything else to germinate and grow—one thought, one mind, one people.

Odin's coming was part of this and more; he was harbinger of the new consciousness that would change his people and their world. Thorfinn saw the alfather's life force dwindling, but his knowledge of the nine worlds gave him some advantages.

"My journey is coming to an end," Odin said without sadness or self-pity. "I'm being returned to the place where everything began. Don't look sad, Thorfinn; why do you lament for me?"

"I don't know where I'm headed."

"You are headed in the same direction you were always headed. Do you fear the future?"

Thorfinn stuttered and hesitated, unable to bring himself to answer the question.

"I will take that as your answer, Thorfinn," Odin replied, sinking onto a boulder. "Do not mistake the uncertainty of the future as a bad omen. The end has been ordained from the beginning; we've all known that it was coming."

"The end of us, Alfather, but not the end of you."

"You and I are both of Ginnungagap; we are both made from the same substance. I have an ending, just like you."

"What will happen to me when you're gone?" Thorfinn asked, almost whimpering.

The answer lost its meaning somewhere between "what" and "happen." These words were relevant to the present world. The Ragnarök was meaningless in the context of the post-apocalyptic world. There was nothing after the end that had its basis in the present world; it was only the hope in the minds of conscious beings that fabricated the world afterward. Time made no such plan in the new world; it wasn't able to stretch beyond its natural end. The post-apocalyptic world was the beginning that the human mind couldn't separate from the present; in such an alien dynamic, the cataclysmic change couldn't be real, because the human mind can only understand evolution and the awe of transformation.

Odin stared at him without saying a word, thinking, or hesitating—Thorfinn couldn't tell which. He tilted his head up to study the fragments of sky visible beyond the canopy. "It saddens me to say this to you, Thorfinn, but after the Ragnarök, I don't know what will happen."

Thorfinn blinked back a tear; Odin looked about to reach and wipe it away, as a caring father would do for his son, but Thorfinn turned away, trying to hide how deeply the truth hurt. He felt betrayed by life, first losing his son and now losing his alfather and his world. There was an unwritten agreement that was somehow being violated, and Thorfinn felt that he was the victim in the relationship.

"Much depends on the outcome of the final battle; if the Jötunn win, they may take over Midgard," Odin continued.

"I thought the battle was taking place in Asgard," Thorfinn said, trying to remember what his father had taught him.

"That part of the battle has already been decided. The Jötunn have taken Asgard. The barrier was never completed when the giants built it and Valhalla for us. That is how they infiltrated my world."

"Where does that leave us?" Thorfinn asked.

"That is why I'm here—to protect Midgard. This will be their next conquest; they will move through the rest of the nine worlds, taking them one by one."

"Where are the Vanir and the Æsir? I thought they would protect us."

Odin slowly shook his head. "The rest of the Vanir and the Æsir are gone. When the Jötunn invaded Asgard, we dispersed; they're spread throughout the nine worlds. I only know where a few are, not enough to challenge the Jötunn. I have no means of locating the rest, nor can I contact them. As we speak, Nidhogg is chewing at the root of Yggdrasil. If he reaches the base of the great tree, it will fall; the ground will open as it did in the beginning and all will return to the Ginnungagap, the chasm where life began; it will be the end to our way of life."

"What will happen to my people?" Thorfinn asked, not sure whether he really wanted to know the answer. "What will become of us?"

"That will be entirely up to you," Odin replied. "Your lives will go on, whether the Jötunn are in power or not. The manner in which you live is something that I cannot speak of; I don't have that power. I do understand that the Jötunn are monsters; they will undoubtedly rule with a savage hand. They lead a savage existence and because they hate themselves, they cannot help but hate everything and everyone."

A chill ran up Thorfinn's spine. "Will we become slaves, an inferior people?"

"If they have their way, you will live a life of servitude. You may find a place to live out your lives beyond their authority. But just as your lives are now, as long as you inhabit Midgard, you will not totally be free of their influence and power. You will have to fight for the rest of your lives to retain your humanity. It's a circumstance of living here that you will have to live with."

Odin's reality was a hard one to swallow, but humans had never been completely beyond the Jötunn's influence, as Odin said; the Jötunn controlled the environment around them. They influenced human life by the changes that Thorfinn and the camp experienced on a daily basis.

"I don't know if I want to live in a world like that," Thorfinn said with a resentful sigh. "To live on our knees in servitude is against everything that we believe in as a culture and as a people. It will kill us by first killing our spirit. The Jötunn won't have to kill us outright; the thought of living in a state of perpetual submission will destroy us."

Odin sat quietly listening to Thorfinn, nodding as if he'd heard the same fears voiced over and over throughout time; indeed, Thorfinn suspected, the basic fear remained the same—the imprisonment of the human spirit.

"Do you know why he's here?" Thorfinn asked uncertainly.

"He could be up to many things."

"I don't think we should tell the others," Thorfinn said, glancing back toward the dim glow of the campfire.

"I agree," Odin replied. "When the time comes, they will be told. For now, we need their calm obedience, not frantic impulsiveness."

Odin rose and shuffled back toward the others, saying, "I'm very tired. I must sleep." Thorfinn followed and watched the old man settle on his side, his cloak wrapped around him and his staff hugged in front of him—for its protection or perhaps guarding it, Thorfinn couldn't tell which.

He returned to Gudrid and lay down next to her. He didn't know how much sleep he'd be getting tonight, but he had to try. Odin was right, the coming days would be hard on all of them.

ꟼ ꝏ

The *Mimir II* approached the Hóp coast as the sun peeked over the austr horizon, its rays painting the hazy sky with colour that bled over the white, sandy beach.

Tostig tried to focus tired eyes. He'd made it his sworn duty to get the crew to Hóp and to have the camp set up before Thorfinn and Gudrid's arrival, not knowing exactly how much time they'd have to harvest the resources before their voyage home. Today would be a busy one, he thought, rubbing his eyes, but not too productive for his crew. Once they unloaded the knarrs and restored the longhouses—or rebuilt them altogether, depending on their condition—they would have to devote their remaining time to gathering resources.

Straumfjörðr—Fjord of Currents—was aptly named; the ocean current swirled and churned the water to a frothy white, then leapt the boulders and hit the shore with a crash, exploding into the air; even though the knarr was still far away from the beach, Tostig heard the sound of the surf hitting the rocks. According to Freydis, on Leif's previous trips to this southern settlement, Straumfjörðr quieted when the waters receded. Leif had told her that, in all of his travels, he'd never seen a land where the waters mysteriously left the land for part of the day, only to return, then recede again. Freydis had chuckled when she relayed Leif's comment that, the first time his men landed at Hóp, they had to race across the moist sands of the exposed sandbar to capture their ship before it drifted out to sea.

A cold chill crept down his spine as Tostig glanced at the ever-present haze that blanketed the sky; it partially obscured the last few stars, and would block the sun when it rose higher. Denied the sun's heat, the summer and now the autumn days were colder than he was used to, as well. As it was doing now, it sometimes created beautiful sunrises and sunsets, but at other times it frightened him, especially when the sky turned a fiery orange. He wondered if the hue of the sky originated in Ginnungagap, the fiery chasm where life began at the beginning of time. Tostig had a bad feeling—the world had begun in Ginnungagap; was something beginning, something ordained by Valhalla that involved the alfather?

Tostig shook his head clear of such thoughts and lifted his voice to command, "Take us in."

The crew pulled the sail down and the rowers turned the knarr toward shore, backs heaving as they pulled the ocean's water back, struggling against the current to beach the knarr. Tostig glanced over at the *Hringhorni*; they'd turned toward the shore and were following the *Mimir II* on a parallel course into shore.

As the knarrs approached land, Tostig thought he saw a large black wolf peering through the bushes at them. He squinted at the border of the coniferous forest, trying to see more clearly, but he wasn't sure. The branches tended to make shapes in the trees that the mind translated into whatever it wanted to see. He shuddered. Strange and magical events were taking place on Hóp, happenings that would affect future events. He couldn't quite place it, but there was something in the wind: a smell or a fear that blew out to sea and met him on the knarr.

The *Mimir II* was the first to hit the sandy shore, pushing the sand up the beach as it plowed up the sandy shelf. Freydis jumped over the side onto the shore and ran to the tree line, disappearing into the woods. Tostig thought her actions were strange—she had a knarr full of crew, just as Tostig had; going off alone didn't make any sense.

"Stay here; I want to check something," Tostig said, jumping over the side. He followed Freydis's footprints across the sand and into the woods.

The forest was strangely silent. Tostig debated whether to call out to Freydis or sneak up on her and try to catch her in whatever she was doing. He heard her breathing up ahead—she wasn't breathing as a human breathes, but panting like an animal. Maybe it wasn't Freydis. Tostig stopped and looked around to make sure he wasn't being the hunted, rather than the hunter. Satisfied, at least for the moment, he gingerly stepped into a clearing where Freydis stood with her back to him. Beyond her, the branches on the far side of the clearing shook, as if something that had just been there was running away.

"Freydis," Tostig said in a low voice, trying not to startle her into drawing her sword.

She whirled toward him. "Oh—Tostig. You just scared away a hare that I was about to capture for lunch."

Tostig looked at her suspiciously, then looked at a large indentation in the ground that he assumed was an animal print—too large to belong to a hare but too small to be a human footprint. The branches at the point where the bushes had rustled were broken—too far up to be an escaping hare; she was lying. He remembered the wolf he'd seen from the knarr. "I wondered why you left your people and your knarr," he said.

"Oh . . . uh, I wanted to make sure that this was the proper landing place on Hóp," she said. Then she added, with no hint of emotion, "Tostig, I don't want you to set up camp with us."

"What are you saying? I thought we were in this together," Tostig replied, bridling.

She squared her shoulders. "This is *my* family's settlement and you're not welcome to set up camp with my crew."

Tostig crossed his arms. "I wonder what Thorfinn will have to say about this."

"Thorfinn isn't here," Freydis shot back. "I am the only direct relation to the Eiriksson family, so I expect you to do as I say."

"Your brother loaned the camps to—"

"He loaned Leifsbúrðir to Thorfinn; Leif said nothing about loaning Hóp to him," she said. "Hóp still remains under my family's direct control and because I'm the only blood relative to my brother on Hóp, it is under my control."

Tostig looked at her, stunned into silence by her words. Freydis was trying to justify her betrayal of the group by drawing fences around Vinland! Their agreement had been to return and split equal portions of the profits from the trip, once the costs were deducted and the investors back home were paid. "This betrayal will not go unnoticed or unchecked," he finally managed. "You will have to explain yourself to our elders when we return home."

"There's a lake just beyond the Hóp camp," Freydis said calmly, ignoring Tostig's threat. "You and your people can set up camp there."

Tostig stormed off, suspecting what was going to happen next. She would use the time that he and his group wasted in setting up camp rather than gathering resources with Freydis's crew against them; she'd fight for more of the profits because her people did more of the work.

"Grab your gear," Tostig yelled out to his crew as he grabbed a rope thrown to him and tethered the knarr to a large tree. "Follow me."

As Tostig walked through the woods with as much gear as he could carry, he wondered why Freydis was trying to take over the expedition in Thorfinn and Gudrid's absence. Had she always had an overblown sense of entitlement, and just kept it under check in their presence, waiting for the moment when she could exercise it? He shook his head, but he couldn't get her glazed stare out of his mind; Freydis's eyes had looked lifeless.

In all the years that he'd known her, Tostig couldn't remember a time when he felt that she couldn't be trusted; they'd been partners on so many expeditions that he had lost count. And not once had she acted in a way that put her honesty in question. He'd felt like he was staring into the eyes of a stranger—or even worse, into the eyes of an enemy.

Tostig scowled. Their unified group was fracturing into smaller groups separated by belief, politics, money, and kinship. Those who once looked out for one another now looked at those same people with suspicion; those who had once stood together were now at each other's throat, ready to squeeze at the first opportunity.

He wondered if they were regressing back to the madness of their Viking past, where nothing was so holy as to fight and kill, then move on to fight and kill some more, always taking more and never feeling that there was enough. If their history had taught them anything, it was that they couldn't sustain themselves as a culture and as a society by killing and taking.

Perhaps he had travelled on the sea for too long, Tostig thought. Maybe it was time to settle down and let younger men and women take over exploring new lands and living for the glory of battle, risking it all to be able to say that they lived.

His thoughts turned back to Freydis. Tostig wasn't going to let her get the upper hand and drive him into retirement. She expected too much already; the last thing that Tostig was going to do was allow her to take more. He didn't care that her father owned the settlements; that alone didn't entitle her to take from the rest of them. Regardless of what Freydis said and thought, their agreement still stood.

Leif was the first member of the Eiriksson family who had tried to repair their family's reputation of being killers; Freydis's parents and grandparents had killed. Leif had tried to return the family to their noble and dignified beginnings. Freydis, with one betrayal, was unravelling everything that Leif had tried to mend with his voyages to the new world. Any respectability regained for the Eiriksson family by Leif's accomplishments was being undermined by Freydis's actions on this one trip. If Leif was determined to change the reputation of his family with the Vinland voyages, then Freydis's actions on the trip would not go unnoticed by Leif, back home.

Many thought she was too much like her father: quick with the axe and far too slow with the justice. Tostig had to agree, but he also realized that until now, when she used her talents and skills for the group, it hadn't been an issue. It became a problem when she used it against them for her personal gain. Perhaps Freydis had intended profiteering all along.

As Tostig walked up the forest gully, he glimpsed the lake beyond the trees and momentarily forgot Freydis's betrayal. The distant mountains served as a fitting backdrop for the sapphire waters of the lake. The light glistened across the surface, dancing from one end to the other, stirring memories. Lately, Tostig longed for the lands that he once called home, even though he'd been travelling for such a long time that he'd forgotten what a home felt like. Dropping his gear, he focused on the beauty in front of him, and the ugliness of the moment with Freydis faded away, if only for a moment.

"Tostig, where do you want us to set up camp?" Snorri asked, his long, curly blond hair blowing in the wind off the lake.

"Right here looks good," he answered, looking around.

"We're close to the water; we can cast a line in and start fishing from here." Tostig wondered how Thorfinn and Gudrid were getting on; he hoped that they were safe and getting close to finding their Snorri.

ꟷ ꟷ

Even in the morning sun, Myrkwood Forest was dark; the sun's rays couldn't fully penetrate its dense growth. Large ferns and towering conifers struggled toward the sunlight filtering through the overhead haze. Myrkwood was also a strange and frightening place. Its huge trees intimidated; their root systems dominated the forest floor as far as the eye could see.

It was like that with explorers, Thorfinn thought as he lay on the ground and stared up at the treetops and the azure sky beyond. They pushed their crews and bodies to their limit so they could be first on the ocean, first in newly discovered lands, and first to harvest the resources of those new lands, not only at the expense of their health but usually at the expense of the native inhabitants—and ultimately at the cost of their lives when the toxic seeds that they sowed earned a backlash from the peoples that they encountered.

The air was heavy with moisture that clung to the damp ground, concealing the landscape like a blanket, crawling along the forest floor, swirling around the bases of the trees and writhing up the trunks until shafts of orange sunlight beaming into the forest dissipated the tendrils; Thorfinn watched as one swirled and curled in a shaft of light before disappearing. Then he rolled over carefully so as not to wake Gudrid, and paused to look at her sleeping face. Her blonde eyelashes fluttered—she was dreaming.

He hoped that the dream was pleasant, filled with good thoughts about Snorri, just as Thorfinn always hoped for himself. He hoped that the gods were watching over their boy, wherever he was; that, wherever Snorri was, he was looking at the rising sun with new eyes, feeling the cool mist condensing on his face and hands, perhaps raising chubby fingers to touch the shafts of light in the air over his head.

Stirring behind him made Thorfinn roll over to see Odin rising stiffly from his earthen bed, using his staff to hoist himself to his feet. Odin was showing the effects of time much more than the rest of them. Thorfinn guessed that the effects of Midgard were all that much more jarring on a being that wasn't used to living in a time-based world. *It must be like the effect that a cold lake has on a warm body*, he mused.

"I'm tired of Vinland," Adam grumbled as he jumped to his feet and kicked a snake away from him. "My mission is over; I should be back in Europe."

"Quiet, Adam," Thorfinn scolded, noticing the same frantic, manic look in Adam's eyes as had been in Ari's eyes; it was the look of madness that was sought after in the pursuit of power. *So it begins*, he thought, seeing signs of the madness and havoc that the Ragnarök elicited even in the non-believers. The madness that was the precursor to the end was already showing up in many places.

"That old man is a charlatan," Adam said, nodding toward Odin.

"Keep your voices down," Gudrid scolded, rolling over and looking at both of them.

"I don't fear him or respect him," Adam continued.

"Try thinking of him as a king," Gudrid suggested, pushing to her feet. "Offer him the same respect that you would to a foreign dignitary."

Adam frowned at her. "I live for my God and my kin, Gudrid."

Thorfinn hadn't thought that the Ragnarök would begin so soon and so close, let alone so blatantly that he saw its effects in front of him. The coming chaos began where it always began—in the human mind. Thorfinn feared that the journey from denial to hysteria would soon follow. And then, finally, the human mind, sensing its own destruction, would destroy its world.

"I will not take orders from you, Gudrid—or you, Thorfinn," Adam yelled. Then he sneered at Thorfinn, "Your authority on this trip is dwindling to nothingness."

Before Adam said another word, Thorfinn's dagger was out of its sheath, its point touching the skin under Adam's chin; a tiny drop of blood trickled down the side of the blade. "Don't think that, after all you've done, I won't kill you."

"Go ahead, Thorfinn," Adam dared.

"Stop," Odin bellowed, capturing the wind with one breath

and shaking the branches of the trees; Thorfinn didn't know if he'd been thrown off balance by the suddenly trembling ground or by Odin's repelling force as the old man extended his arms toward Adam and Thorfinn. They stumbled back from one another as if invisible hands forced them apart. "Behave yourselves," he scolded in a quiet but serious tone—then staggered himself. He steadied himself against the nearest tree as his knees buckled.

Thorfinn stepped toward Odin, ready to help, but Odin's raised hand stopped him. Thorfinn glanced at Adam. For the first time on their trip, he noticed fear—or reverence—on Adam's face; he couldn't tell which.

"Adam, look out!" Thorfinn yelled, raising his dagger and pulling Adam out of the way of—

"I . . . I thought I saw something," Thorfinn said, freezing the dagger in mid-thrust. It had been as if a white apparition in the shape of Adam stood behind him.

Odin walked between them and touched Thorfinn's blade, lowering it. "No one move," he said, looking around the forest glen.

The wind rustled the leaves, as if signalling the beginning of something—then there was movement all around them, translucent apparitions whizzing pass them at the speed of thought, only briefly stopping before they moved out of sight again. Thorfinn felt a touch, but he wasn't sure if it was the wind tickling the hairs on his arms or something brushing past him.

"Where are they?" Elsu asked, craning his neck back and forth. "I—I can't see anything."

"Calm yourself, Elsu. You cannot see them because you are not Norse. Do not worry; they have no influence over you." Odin closed his eye and raised his hand to the wind. His lips moved. The movement stopped and the wind slowly died. Odin lowered his hand and opened his eye. "We've been allowed to join the symposium," he announced.

"Whose symposium?" Thorfinn asked.

"The Ljósálfar —the light elves. They've agreed to show themselves to us." Odin beckoned them to follow and led the way to a clearing within the dense underbrush, walking as if he already knew the way. He entered a circle of five cylindrical rocks that jutted up from the mossy ground on a slant, arranged so that one flat surface on each faced the centre of the circle. Within that circle was another grouping of five rocks, equidistant from the outer rocks.

"Sit down," Odin instructed his companions. "Do not speak unless they speak to you."

All but Adam quietly sat down on the rocks in the outer circle. Adam remained outside the circle, leaning against a tree, arms crossed. Odin sat and placed his hands on his knees. He stared into the centre of the circle, then closed his eyes.

"How long will we have to wait?" Gudrid asked no one in particular.

"The Ljósálfar will not show themselves until they're ready; be patient," Odin said, his eyes still closed. "The álfars were forced to leave Midgard when the Christians arrived; occasionally they return. We must wait till the forest light reaches its optimal point, then we will be able to see them."

Thorfinn breathed a long sigh and lowered his eyes to the mossy ground, letting his thoughts drift. A voice inside his head, just above his consciousness, spoke to him, questioning the reason for their journey—or was it his own inner voice speaking? Thorfinn couldn't tell.

"Welcome, Alfather," a voice whispered, riding on the currents of the wind. Odin lifted his head and opened his eyes. The breeze vibrated on the air around Thorfinn's ear and he raised his head and looked to the skies, seeking the source.

"Welcome, all," the voice continued. "I am Eöl. What do you need from me?"

Five translucent images flickered and warped the air around the rocks at the centre of what was now a pentagram, the points of which were formed by the inner rocks and those in the outer circle.

"I seek your counsel, Eöl," Odin answered. "We're seeking the child of one of our own."

"Yes. It was taken by a wolf with eyes of black pearls. The wolf still roams Midgard."

"Do you know where my child is?" Gudrid blurted.

"Silence!" a voice shrieked. Everyone slapped their palms over their ears, trying to silence the scream echoing through their heads. The echo trailed off into silence once again.

"Odin is the only one permitted to speak in the circle," Eöl said, pausing before saying, "Alfather, you must traverse the realm of the Dökkálfar—the dark elves."

"Yes," another voice interjected. "And as you travel through the caves you will pass close to Muspellheim, realm of the fire giants, and Niflheim, home of the ice giant; you'll no doubt encounter more dark elves in the service of Sutr and the Jötunn." The voice paused. "I am Elerösse, and I know your journey well. I have lost friends to the influence and the power of the Jötunn."

Thorfinn glanced at his companions for their reaction. Elsu sat rigid, eyes wide and jaw tense. "Elsu, are you alright?" he whispered.

"Thorfinn, I know this god. He is the father of the elves, Glooskap," Elsu said without taking his eyes off the energy fluctuations in the centre of the circle. "Do you understand him? He is talking in my language."

Thorfinn wasn't sure how, but the voices of the Ljósálfars that were in his head—or in his ears—spoke in his language; whatever Elsu saw, Thorfinn had no doubt that it was speaking in his native tongue, as well. The Ljósálfar's presence seemed to encompass the entire glade, but if Thorfinn moved, they disappeared altogether.

"We understand your need," Eöl was saying.

"But how are we supposed to—"

"You will know."

Confused and frustrated by the course of the conversation, Thorfinn scowled. He rarely liked surprises and had no patience for mysteries. If it could be avoided, he preferred the brute force of the blade or physical combat; mysticism was for the sages and people with the sight, like Gudrid.

"Eöl, can you tell us about the Dökkálfar, the dark elves?" Odin asked.

"You must take great care," Elerösse answered. "Just as they can come to you in nightmares, when you are in their realm, they can control your waking life as well, with their visions. They will use all of their powers to try to defeat you."

A new voice spoke. "You do have one advantage; unlike us, the Dökkálfar are beings of darkness. You only need to bring the light of the sun to their darkness."

The fourth energy entity in the circle brightened as still another voice spoke in Thorfinn's head. "When all is dark, there will be three that will see."

"The entrance lies suðr," a final voice said. "That is all you need to know."

The light beaming through the trees shifted and the Ljósálfars faded into nothing. Silence followed for several moments as everyone digested what they'd just heard.

"Alfather, what are your thoughts?" Thorfinn finally asked.

Odin lowered his voice. "We must take care not to fully trust the elves. With the destruction of the pantheon, Freyr's influence is dwindling. The elves are aligned with no one unless forced to it by greater magic than their own. For all we know, their advice may be useless."

"Are you saying that we shouldn't trust the Ljósálfars?"

"No, what I am saying is that we must only trust ourselves and each other. Don't put all your faith into one place."

Thorfinn nodded, understanding the alfather's trepidation.

"Come, we must leave Myrkwood and get to the native camp," Odin said as he pushed himself to his feet.

Thorfinn was happy to follow. Myrkwood was unsettling; the dark forest gave him strange dreams and confusing visions where nothing made sense, and the dense foliage made him feel claustrophobic. He longed for open spaces.

5

Gudrid sat alone, waiting for Elsu to return with the hide clothing. She'd asked Thorfinn and the others in the party to leave her so she could prepare herself mentally for what she was about to do. Her heart raced when she thought about walking into Elsu's camp disguised as his dead wife. She didn't know what she would encounter or what she had to do to maintain the illusion of being Yakima. It would be a combination of many things, she knew; not only the application of her makeup and costume, but her acting the part of a previous member of their community.

What was at stake far outweighed the risk involved. Gudrid was getting her son back—or, at the very least, finding out where to start her search, where to find the bread crumbs that would lead her to him so that he'd grow up with his family and take his place among them.

She looked across the forest in the direction Thorfinn and the others had gone. She'd chosen her husband well. Thorfinn was a wonderful, kind, honest man who accepted her faults and demands, so much so that he risked his profits on the trip so that Gudrid could resolve her past and feel comfortable in her present. Gudrid would never forget that expression of his love for her. And she was certain he would do the same for their son, and make a fine father. Some would say that any father would do that, but Gudrid knew that Thorfinn wasn't *any* father; he had a deep respect for her and her feelings and that would extend to Snorri. She smiled, and waited for Elsu with renewed calm.

She could just barely see Thorfinn through the trees; he was whittling something from a piece of wood, and she strained to see what it was. As he moved the object around in his hands, she realized that it was a toy knarr. He was carefully hollowing out the inside of the boat, making it lighter so that it would float, his movements as gentle as if he were handling a newborn baby. He paused and blew away the shavings, then continued, unaware of Gudrid's scrutiny.

Hearing rustling, Gudrid turned to see Elsu emerging from the trees with a bundle in his arms. He returned Gudrid's smile. "Your clothes," he said, handing the bundle to Gudrid. "I'm sure they will fit you."

She unwrapped the bundle and admired the intricate beadwork around the collar and the cuffs of the hide dress. "Were these Yakima's clothes?" she asked.

"Yes. I snuck into my camp and took them from my wigwam."

Thorfinn walked over to them and stood quietly nearby. Gudrid flashed him a reassuring smile.

"I also have some ochre to cover your face, arms, hands, and legs. It is very important that your white skin is completely covered. The ochre must stain your skin, not look as if it's been applied like war paint. We'll have to mix it with water so that it seeps into your skin."

Gudrid nodded and walked behind a bush to change into her new clothes. She heard the concern in Thorfinn's voice when he asked, "Elsu, will your people not suspect that something is up when they notice that Gudrid is not acting like Yakima?"

"I did think of that, but I think the fear of seeing Yakima will distract them long enough for us to talk with Bantam," Elsu replied. "I don't think they'll expect her to be as they once knew her."

"Will Bantam help you?"

"Yes. But she will not be fooled; she's too intelligent not to see through our ruse. I'm hoping that she'll know the importance of our deception, that we only want to find out what happened to Snorri."

Thorfinn nodded once, quickly, and left. As she tugged the dress down over her knees, Gudrid wondered what he was thinking.

ЖЖ

Thorfinn's thoughts dangled on Elsu's last words as he returned to the others and sat down in the circle of shavings where he'd been sitting previously. He was so caught up with Gudrid's vision that he didn't or couldn't consider the possibility that she was wrong. He didn't know how to prepare himself for that eventuality. His mind had to believe that Snorri was alive, for both their sakes.

Shaking his head to clear those thoughts, Thorfinn turned to check on the alfather, seated on the ground nearby, just as Adam approached and stood over the old man.

"I don't know who you are," Adam said, "but I don't believe that you're the alfather or the Norse god Odin."

"But do you recognize the possibility that I *could* be him?" Odin asked.

Adam crossed his arms. "No, I can't."

Odin cocked his head. "I don't see how you can acknowledge Thorfinn and the others' beliefs and not see me as real. Either you see their beliefs as delusional and not believe in me, or you acknowledge their beliefs as true and you believe in me."

Adam hesitated, brows pinched as if he were a little stumped. Thorfinn waited, unsure how he would respond to such reasoning.

"I think I can believe both, and that doesn't contradict the other. I can see that Thorfinn and Gudrid's belief doesn't negate or devalue what I believe in. The truth of your existence does."

Odin shrugged. "I suppose it really has to do with your expectations of a god. We really aren't much different from you. We're a little more aware, a little more sensitive to our surroundings, and much more intuitive, but that has more to do with how we spend our time and what we allow to occupy our minds."

"You don't have answers to any of Gudrid's or Thorfinn's

questions," Adam pointed out.

"You do not have the answers either, nor does your god. Why would I need to answer their questions when they can answer their own questions? They only need to search within themselves. Gods aren't here to live your life for you—that's why you have free will. We listen, but we don't have to always answer; you only have to hear the echo of your own voice. Gudrid is a prime example—she has the sight and she knows the answers that are all around her. She may not know how or where they are, but she listens and hears the reply. It's like knowing the bird by its call: you don't have to see it, you know that it's there by listening to what it's telling you."

Adam sighed in understanding, but resisted agreeing with Odin; by Odin's expression, Thorfinn suspected that he'd expected this. Thorfinn understood that Adam's belief offered to take him and others who followed it outside of themselves to something greater, whereas Odin knew that the greatness everyone sought was within themselves; they only needed to focus on it for it to manifest itself in the world.

"It wasn't my intention to take part in an intellectual or theological debate," Adam admitted.

"What was your intention?" Odin asked. "You engaged me."

"I only wanted to tell you that I don't believe that you're the alfather and that I will protect Gudrid and Thorfinn from you if I see that you're hurting them in any way; they've been through enough."

Odin smiled. "It's so wonderful that they have a friend like you, Adam. I feel comforted that my children are taken care of in such a concerned manner. If only everyone were like that for their kin and friends, we wouldn't have as much killing and destruction as we do."

Thorfinn looked away to hide a smile, impressed by Odin's diplomacy and strength of presence as he easily deflected Adam's accusations. Odin's answers were exactly how a god would reply to such a subjective viewpoint.

Rustling in the bushes drew Thorfinn's attention and he turned to see Gudrid stepping out.

"Gudrid! I didn't realize . . . how much you look like Yakima," Elsu stuttered. Recovering himself, he gestured for

Gudrid to sit down on a rock, then he mixed powdered ochre with some of their drinking water. "There are a few things that I need to tell you, Gudrid," he said as he began applying the mixture to her face. "As we enter the encampment, you must not speak to anyone. Your voice cannot be disguised enough to totally remove your Norse accent. And if Yakima's mother sees us, you must not let her touch you; she was our seer before Bantam and will know that you're not Yakima."

Gudrid nodded, then held still as Elsu applied the liquid to Gudrid's face and neck, following her hairline. Thorfinn lifted Gudrid's hair so that Elsu could cover as much exposed skin as possible. "If we're discovered, you must make your escape while I try to distract my people," Elsu said as he sat back to observe his handiwork.

"How will you do that?" Thorfinn asked.

Elsu looked up at him. "I don't know. But I'll think of something. The important thing is that we get you safely out of the camp. If I must, I'll fight for your escape."

"You will do that for us, Elsu?" Gudrid asked, looking into his eyes.

"Of course I will."

"What will they do to you?"

"They will probably torture me, but they will not kill me," he said. "Return here; my people won't follow you into the Dark Forest. I'll follow you back here when I can."

Thorfinn came around to look at Gudrid's face, and Elsu handed the bowl of ochre stain to him. " I'll let you put it on Gudrid's arms and legs."

"It itches," Gudrid said, grimacing.

"Don't scratch or rub it until it dries," Elsu warned, then turned and walked over to Odin and Adam.

Thorfinn rolled up one of Gudrid's sleeves and began rubbing the ochre onto her skin. "Gudrid, I know why we're doing this, but I wanted to say that it's not worth risking your life over. We can find another way to find Snorri; it doesn't have to be by walking into a wolves' den."

"What did you say?" Gudrid asked.

"I said that I think we can find our baby without having to resort to putting your life at risk."

Gudrid rose and walked over to Odin. Confused, Thorfinn followed her, the ochre paste dripping onto his coat.

"Elsu and Adam, leave us," Gudrid ordered. "I need to talk to the alfather." She waited while the two men rose and moved across the clearing, then asked, "Alfather, will you tell me more about the wolf?"

"I had that dream too," Thorfinn added, curious now. "A wolf was on your chest; you yelled out Fenrir's name."

"It appears that we all had that same vision," Odin said.

"What does it mean?" Gudrid asked.

Odin looked at Thorfinn. "Have you told Gudrid?"

Thorfinn shook his head. "No, I haven't."

"Told me what?"

"Gudrid, you must keep this to yourself," Thorfinn said, gripping her shoulders. "The alfather is here to usher in the Ragnarök."

Gudrid's shoulders immediately tensed, but before she spoke, she relaxed, and the alarm left her face like sand pushed by an ocean wave. "I know," she said, her voice heavy. "I guess I've always known. But somehow I didn't believe it."

Quietly, Odin walked away. Thorfinn and Gudrid watched him go, then Gudrid turned to Thorfinn, who nodded. Taking his hand, she led him behind a tree and he helped her spread the ochre on her legs up to her thighs.

"Thorfinn," Gudrid said, dropping her dress back over her legs, "I know that everything will be alright. We'll find Snorri and we'll survive the Ragnarök. I know because I've seen us together with our baby."

Thorfinn remained quiet, not knowing whether she was being intuitive or delusional. He wished that he could fully believe her this time, but if the alfather didn't know, then how could Gudrid? He decided to smile and nod, trying not to upset her before her mission. He applied the last of the ochre paste and pulled Gudrid's sleeves down to her wrists.

"I hardly recognize you," he said, looking at her in the morning light. "And yet I do. It's a strange feeling, to look at someone you know and also to see that you don't know that person." He chuckled, then turned and yelled, "Elsu, we're ready."

Elsu approached, then stopped abruptly in front of Gudrid,

staring into her eyes as if his brain were struggling over whether Yakima was really dead or really standing in front of him.

"Elsu, we *must* go," Gudrid prompted.

"Yes," Elsu replied, snapping out of his internal struggle. He became businesslike as he looked around at the men. "You must all remain in the Dark Forest. If you're seen by just one member of my tribe, you'll be putting Gudrid and me at risk."

"Can I walk with you to the edge of the forest?" Thorfinn asked.

"Yes," Elsu answered.

"Won't your people be scared out of their wits, seeing their dead kin walking toward them?" Gudrid asked.

"Maybe, but their reaction will be a desire to touch you to confirm that they're really seeing you. I'll try to keep them away by telling them that they must respect your spirit. But as you know, believing that a dead child will never come back home is a very hard thing to deny."

Gudrid gave Thorfinn an acknowledging glance.

"When we enter the camp, we must head directly to Bantam's wigwam."

"How should I behave?" Gudrid asked anxiously.

"I don't know; look dead, I guess," Elsu said, smiling.

"I'll try to be expressionless," she decided as they reached the edge of the forest. She turned to Thorfinn. "Well, this is where I must leave you, my love."

"I feel the same way I did when you left me to head for Markland. It seems that you're always leaving me, Gudrid," Thorfinn said with a wry smile. "When will I get the chance to leave you, so *you* can stay behind and worry?"

Gudrid chuckled sympathetically, then held Thorfinn head in her hands and gently kissed his lips. "I'll see you soon, my love," she said, brushing away some of the ochre makeup that had clung to Thorfinn's beard. She turned and walked away.

Thorfinn watched her go, remembering the day she'd left for Markland, feeling again the ocean breeze on his cheeks and the salt air stinging his nostrils. He wanted to follow and watch Gudrid from a hidden location, but he dared not indulge in his own fears and put her life at risk.

Instead he headed back to Odin and Adam. He expected them

to be at each other's throat over their differing beliefs; instead he heard them talking civilly to one another as he stepped into the clearing.

"Adam," Odin was saying, "I don't understand how one god can rule over humans in an equitable manner. Where are the opposing voices that counter that one voice?"

"It's the one voice of God; there *is* no other voice."

"But how do you know that it's the right voice? Nature doesn't speak with one voice, it speaks with many voices, each in harmony with all the other voices; I see the simplicity of a one-god world, but I don't understand how it's possible to manage such a world."

"But when that voice is the truth, it creates the harmony within," Adam insisted, "and that's when the world harmonizes with us."

Odin nodded his understanding. "You see, as gods, we have our own lives, and what we do in Asgard affects the world of Midgard," he said. "The humans' world is affected by us and we control their world, and ultimately humans, by what we do. Our primary motivation for what we do is based on how it affects Midgard. What is your god's primary motivation?"

Adam smiled. "It's love; he loves his children and everything he does is because of love."

"Yes, we love our children as well, but we leave them alone so that they can make their own decisions," Odin replied. "We've found that it makes stronger people and that we become better leaders of men."

༄ ༅

Gudrid knew what Thorfinn meant, and she felt pangs of maudlin guilt. Thorfinn was right; she was always leaving him. She had to remind herself that this time she left for both of them, so that she could put her family back together again. She refused to think that a storm at sea or an attack might take him away from her. She liked to think that they'd have a lifetime together, but she didn't know for sure. Bringing Snorri home would give them a life together.

Her thoughts turned to what lay ahead as she and Elsu

approached the native camp. They had to see Bantam to find out as much as they could about what happened to Snorri, then get out of the camp as soon as possible, and back to the safety of the Dark Forest. The longer they remained in Elsu's camp, the greater the risk that she'd be discovered; Gudrid had no doubt that, as Elsu said, she'd be tortured and put to death if caught.

She heard native voices up ahead and looked at Elsu. He stared back with an inquiring expression, as if asking her for confirmation that she was ready. Gudrid nodded.

They walked steadily into the camp, looking neither left nor right. A woman looked at them and paused as if she were trying to sort out in her mind what didn't look right; she suddenly screamed as she realized who Elsu carried on his arm. She ran away screaming, her voice escalating into an alarm for the rest of the native community.

They continued their calm walk through the community, knowing that at any moment, upon hearing about Yakima's ghost walking through the camp, more members would converge on them. They remained focused on Bantam's wigwam; Gudrid tried not to let her gaze waver when a shaman approached and shook a stick in front of them, as if he'd detected evil spirits and wanted to scare them away.

A contingent of warriors, spears at the ready, intercepted them just short of Bantam's wigwam. They stood in front of them like statues, blocking their path.

"Do not touch them," Bantam yelled, bursting through her door flap. "Let them pass!"

The warriors jumped, their tension heightened, then slowly backed away. Bantam beckoned Gudrid and Elsu into her wigwam.

Gudrid wasn't sure if Bantam was fooled by her disguise; if she wasn't fooled, she seemed willing to go along with their ruse—and if she knew, then Bantam must have an ulterior reason for playing along with them.

As they entered the wigwam and the flap door closed behind them, Gudrid both smelled and felt the smoke thickening inside her nostrils; it moved to the back of her throat and filled her head with a thickening cloud.

Bantam sat down across from them and, as the cloud of smoke swirled around them, went into a trance. Her head tipped back, her stare not wavering from the opening at the apex of the wigwam. "I see the sky; the approaching surf hitting the shore beyond the undulating surface of the great body of water and sky," she said calmly . . .

ꝏ ꝏ

But she wasn't calm. Bantam felt agitation within her soul and mind; she quivered not from fear, but from the uncontrolled state of the inner world that she inhabited in her moments of inner seeking.

Her thoughts immediately retracted to the shore of human consciousness; as she traversed farther and farther out, moving beyond the familiar world, the journey began as it always had, moving first through the clear skies of human thought, then submerging into the murky water where she needed to use her other senses to understand what she saw—to smell and touch the images in her mind, to actually feel their presence on her skin. Finally, she was always pulled back—back to her ignorant and three-dimensional world where she had only her consciousness as sole interpreter. She usually recognized the inhabitants in her visions, was given a sense of who she was channelling.

"I see a traveller aboard a ship that is crashing through the waves. The man is all-powerful and all-seeing," she said. "My mind can't merge with his; his consciousness lives among the lights in the night sky." She lifted her eyebrows almost instinctively. "For all of his power, he is just and fair, bound by the rules of his calling.

"He comes to rescue," she continued, "not to correct. There is another already here who comes to deceive, corrupt, and destroy. They are brothers and yet they are apart; one is a shape-shifter. The other holds the two together with his strength while the first pulls them apart.

"Gudrid, daughter of Hallveig and Thorbjörn, once married to Austrmaðr—a hidden and secret association, hidden from the family and hidden from the gods. I see a secret place at Straumfjörðr, the Fjord of Currents. There are passageways made by the waters, the walls smooth and contoured as the human body. The water flowing through them is the lifeblood moving through the arteries of the great mother Earth; the tunnels too, with one great, heaving inward flow of ocean water, fill up. At the centre of the connected network of passageways, a sword resides in the base of a great tree holding up the worlds, its steel neither tarnished nor worn."

Bantam was pulled once again to the approach of her kin—he had a white face and his head burned with the fire of the setting sun. There was a missing child.

"Gudrid, you are the woman without a child; the child of the daughter of Thorbjörn."

Uncrossing her legs, Bantam leaned forward and threw more sweet grass on the fire. As the smoke swirled into their noses and the burning grass crackled in their ears, Bantam blew out the small flame. The grass continued to smoulder, the tendrils combining to form a cloud of swirling smoke that rose and filled the empty space between them.

"Gudrid, this great figure," she said through the hanging smoke, "your alfather . . . he is here with the other."

The image disappeared into the grey cloud of swirling smoke and heat.

Bantam's head dropped as if all the muscles in her neck had been pulled by the strength of the retreating vision. She threw her arms up, pushing against the empty air, trying to protect herself by keeping the image from touching her again. At last she closed her mind and sat in silence. "That is all," she breathed.

꧁ ꧂

The hazy air changed from red-hot sunset to the calming hues of night as the embers in the fire fell into grey ash.

Gudrid felt as if her head were cooled by a cloth dipped in an icy stream; a fog bank moving past her consciousness slowly dissipated as it reached the back of her mind.

"Gudrid," Bantam said, looking directly at her. "I see your son . . ."

Gudrid stiffened, ready to jump across the hearth and wrestle the vision out of her if the seer delayed too long.

" . . . he is not here, but there is a large black wolf with eyes like black pearls—"

"Is my son in danger?" Gudrid asked.

Bantam lifted a knife and drew it across her palm, allowing her blood to drip into a bowl. "I do not see him in any danger; the wolf is protecting him as a mother would a baby. He is sleeping, calm and at peace."

Her head jerked up and she shouted, "You must go, *Gudrid*!" Reaching over, she touched the spot where some of the ochre makeup had rubbed off on Thorfinn's chin.

"Go where?" Gudrid asked.

"You must find your baby."

"I don't know where he is; where would I look for him?" she pleaded.

"Go to the cave where the great tree stands." The smoke from the smouldering grass was clearing; Gudrid could see Bantam's face now as she shook her head. "The vision is dissipating; my eyes are going dark."

"Get it back!" Gudrid demanded.

Elsu laid his hand on Gudrid's shoulder to calm her—or perhaps to remind Gudrid to respect Bantam's efforts to help them.

"I cannot tell you anything further. I'm given only what you need to know right now," Bantam said with a sigh. "The spirits of my ancestors can only guide us; they cannot dictate the outcome of our lives. They do influence and advise, but within their limitations. You must accept what they give, when they give it. That is your choice. If you don't, that is also your choice. Gudrid, do you understand?"

Suddenly, in the last of the swirling smoke, Gudrid saw another figure—Yakima. She smiled, then disappeared as the swirling smoke reshaped itself. Turning, Gudrid stared into Bantam's eyes for the first time since she entered the wigwam. She understood. She felt the same way, but was unable to articulate her feelings on a conscious level.

Bantam expressed the relationship between herself and the spiritual realm.

"Yes," Gudrid slowly said, "I do understand. You are a wise seer."

"I knew you would, Gudrid. We are woven with the same thread, you and I. I knew of our meeting before we knew that your people were on our land. I saw your great ship crossing the water."

Gudrid remained attentive.

"Your people and my people are intertwined. It was no accident that you found our land, it was meant to be when the world was new. Not only have our lives mingled on the physical plane, our destinies are connected on the spirit plane. Elsu's lost Yakima visiting you was the event that brought our two separate peoples together onto one path; the two paths are now parting." She crossed her hands in front of Gudrid.

"Yes, we spoke," Gudrid said. "But she disappeared before I could ask her why she was visiting me."

"Our relationship was never supposed to be that of two warring nations. But the course of events has put a schism between us that cannot be rejoined. It is unfortunate that both our cultures listen to our heads and not our hearts; that is where our connection lies, in the world of spirit, not in the world of the physical."

Bantam closed her eyes and took a deep breath. "There is one who is risking all; I see destruction and death for all of us. But I cannot see this one . . . I just know."

Bantam abruptly rose from her fur-covered pedestal. "You must go back to where you belong. You must never return to this land again; we must never speak again."

"Can you tell us in which direction the wolf left?"

Bantam remained silent. Elsu and Gudrid stared at her. Although still emotional, Gudrid found some relief in Bantam's revelations, even though they left her uncertain what to do next.

"I guess there's nothing to do but to go to Hóp," Elsu said.

"But what of Snorri?" Gudrid whined.

"We won't leave him behind," Elsu assured her. "We'll find him."

"Follow me," Bantam instructed, moving to lift the wigwam's door flap.

Gudrid and Elsu followed Bantam out into the morning light, then beyond the edge of the camp and to the base of a mountain pass cut by a dirt and gravel trail that disappeared in the underbrush at the bottom of the slope.

"This is where the beast carried your baby," Bantam said, pointing to the trail. "He was wrapped in a blanket."

"Who wrapped him in a blanket?" Gudrid asked, looking at her and then at Elsu. "The wolf couldn't have done it; someone else must have."

Frustrated when neither answered, Gudrid pushed past them and started along the trail to the other side of the mountain.

"Gudrid, wait," Elsu yelled, running after her. "You don't know where you're going." Gudrid ignored him. "Gudrid, please slow down; you're going to fall," Elsu pleaded, catching up with her.

"My son is down here somewhere," she said. "I have to find him, or find out where he is. Do you see any footprints on the ground?"

"Gudrid, we will find the wolf," Elsu reassured her. "But Snorri is not here; remember the cave and the fjord of currents."

"Alright, but I want to look around here for any evidence of his whereabouts," she said, not taking her eyes off the ground. "Where's Tostig when I need his tracking skills?"

"Gudrid, I'll follow you so far, but we have to turn back and meet up with Thorfinn and Odin. Do you agree?"

"Yes, yes, just help me find wolf tracks."

"It will be hard to pick up the trail; it's days old."

"Bantam said that it's a large wolf, so the paw prints will be larger than normal."

They followed the trail till it branched into several directions. They'd found no sign of a wolf. "Let's split up," Gudrid suggested, taking the path to her right.

"That leads to the river," Elsu said.

"Good, we'll eliminate the shortest routes." Gudrid pushed into the foliage, barely looking up, not noticing where she was headed. She lifted every branch of every low-hanging tree, seeking evidence of the wolf. When she heard rushing water up ahead, she knew she would soon have to turn back.

She walked out of the forest onto the river's edge, where a young native woman was beating clothes against the rocks and rinsing them in the rushing water. She continued her work without noticing that she was being watched. Gudrid moved closer and the girl looked up. Her eyes widened and her face froze in a terrorized mask, but only for a moment before she released a blood-curdling scream that rose above the sound of the rushing water.

Gudrid waved her hands in front her to try to calm the girl, but she backed away, and fell backward on the rocks, her basket of clothes falling into the river.

"Please, please, I'm not going to hurt you," Gudrid yelled to be heard above the rush of the river and the girl's screams. Half fearing that the girl would slip into the river and drown, or be heard by the rest of the native community on top of the hill, Gudrid slowly backed away.

"Amaguq! Amaguq!" the girl continued to scream.

Gudrid hoped that Elsu could hear the ruckus and was on his way to help. She turned to see him bolting through the bushes, running past Gudrid to try to calm the girl down. After a moment her screams faded to panting as she repeated the same words over and over again.

"What's she saying?"

"She thinks you are the Amaguq; an Inuit shape-shifter whose true form is a wolf. She thinks you're coming back to hurt her by taking the shape of Yakima. She keeps saying that she didn't want to do it."

"Ask her, where is the wolf?" Gudrid said.

"She said that he made her do it," Elsu translated.

"Do what?" Gudrid screamed.

Elsu spoke rapidly to the girl, who responded with a short answer. Elsu turned to Gudrid, his expression ominous. "Give him the baby."

"You gave him my baby?" Gudrid screamed, lunging at the frightened girl.

Elsu translated word for word as she gibbered: "I had to, I had to. He said that he'd kill my tribe if I didn't do what he asked."

"It's my baby," Gudrid whimpered, dropping to her knees. "I want my son."

Elsu again spoke rapidly to the girl, then translated: "It waited, pacing at the outskirts of the camp while you were giving birth. Bantam knew too. It was she who invited the wolf into our camp."

Gudrid turned, not knowing why, and looked up to the top of the hill. Bantam stood on the apex of the trail, looking down at them.

"Gudrid," Elsu said. "I had no knowledge of this."

"Did the wolf say why he wanted the baby?" Gudrid asked,

turning back to the young girl.

She shook her head.

"I think I know who may know the answer," Gudrid said, jumping to her feet and starting back toward the hill.

"Gudrid, never mind," Elsu said. "The knife that Bantam cut her hand with had poison on the blade."

Before Gudrid could turn to him, Bantam teetered and fell, tumbling down the rocky slope and disappearing amongst the trees at its base. Gudrid turned back to Elsu in defeat. She walked to the river.

"If Fenrir, Loki's son, is responsible for taking my baby, what could he possibly want with him?" she wondered. The answer felt as if it was on the edge of Gudrid's consciousness, but she couldn't shed light on the meaning of the symbols she saw. They were right in front of her, but she couldn't arrange them into a meaningful pattern. "Could it be because Odin and Loki are brothers, and Loki is his shadow? We must go to Hóp," she concluded.

"What about tracking the wolf?" Elsu asked.

"If I'm right," Gudrid said, "the wolf will find us."

༺ ༻

Gudrid and Elsu walked back into Myrkwood. The sky retained an orange hue from the haze covering the sun, as it had since Odin's arrival. Gudrid thought that she could smell an odour like burning sulphur in the air.

It started to rain as they approached the forest edge, and Gudrid kept wiping the dripping ochre from her eyes and tasting it in her mouth; streams of red ran down her forehead, staining her dress. She was eager to return to Odin and tell him what she had found out, in the hope that he could help her understand what was happening.

"Elsu," Gudrid said as they walked into the cover of the forest, "Yakima came to me in Bantam's wigwam. She's glad that you helped; it was an honour for her to be remembered in this way. She said that both of you will be together soon."

"I'm happy that my time to make the journey across the water will come soon," he replied, smiling and blinking away tears. "I've waited a long time to know that I'm nearing the end of my journey."

Gudrid put her hand on his shoulder, happy that she could give him some comfort after the risk he had taken to help her get closer to her baby. For herself, she would be glad to finally leave oppressive and mystical Myrkwood and the strange visions it induced. Since Odin's contact with the light elves, Gudrid swore she heard voices on each errant breeze that ruffled the treetops.

Ahead, through the trees, Gudrid spied Thorfinn, Odin, and Adam sitting across from one another; sensing or hearing their approach, Thorfinn turned and smiled, rising to walk over and hug her. When they parted, some of the ochre now smeared his tunic and cheek. "What did you find out?" he asked.

"A large black wolf kidnapped Snorri," she said immediately, her eyes on Odin.

"That would make sense," Odin muttered. "A large wolf with huge paws and eyes of black pearls." Gudrid, with Thorfinn, merely waited for Odin to continue. "So, he's here on Midgard . . . for me. It's Fenrir," Odin said, looking up at them, "Loki's son, and my nephew. Once I'm gone, unless Loki is stopped, his power will be boundless."

"What does he plan to do with my son?" Gudrid asked, her voice edged with hysteria.

"I don't know," Odin admitted. "You aren't a threat to him. Attacking you and abducting your son will have no effect on the events of the Ragnarök."

Is this the final battle? Gudrid wondered. *Not a battle of strength and might, but one that creates a future of subservience to the Jötunn for humans?* She shuddered. It would be a world of hybrids, where the Jötunn had political dominance. She felt the weight of the sky and the heavens settling over her body, and only longed to cradle Snorri in the security of her arms.

Driven by her thoughts, her eyes lifted, and she realized that the clouds were again scudding normally across the sky, driven by the norðr wind that blew across the fine blonde hairs on her arms, scooping up the warmth from her body and carrying it away with the day. *We will go to Hóp*, she decided, *and enter the caves as we've been told to do.*

ꙮ ꙮ

Thorfinn waited with Gudrid, Odin, and Elsu on the shore of Leifsbúrðir, seeking any sign of the *Mimir II* on the water, but all they saw was the dark ocean crashing against the rocky shore under a dark and clouded sky. Scanning the water for the familiar glow of the knarr's swaying deck lanterns, he was a little concerned that the gusting wind might prevent the knarr from travelling up the strait; it blew cold air from the norðr and Thorfinn felt a few snowflakes on his cheeks.

"There's something strange on the wind," Odin said, as if sensing his thoughts. "I think we have some people approaching."

Elsu turned and called for their attention; Thorfinn saw a group of tiny lights crossing the meadow, heading in their direction. "They're my people and they're planning to attack," Elsu said.

"We have to hide," Adam said, his tone urgent.

"That won't help, they've already seen us," Elsu replied. "Besides, we don't have any place to hide."

"Can we return to Myrkwood Forest?" Gudrid suggested. "Outflank them?"

"No, it's blocked," Thorfinn replied, pointing to another group of lights approaching from that direction. "Elsu, can we negotiate with them, tell them that we're waiting for our ship to take us off of Vinland?"

"No, my people are ready to attack," Elsu replied firmly, eyes on the approaching formation. "There's nothing we can do. They will attack with their spears once they locate us, then they'll capture us and kill us, or throw us into the water to perish."

"We'll have to run for it," Thorfinn said, taking Gudrid's arm.

Figuring they had the darkness on their side, that the night would conceal them, if only temporarily, Thorfinn led them along the shoreline in an attempt to outflank the native attack force. As they passed a grassy dune, Thorfinn saw the deck lanterns of the *Mimir II*, bobbing on the water not too far offshore. "There's the knarr," he yelled. As soon as the words left his mouth, he noticed the native attack force moving to intercept them; it was obvious that they also saw the knarr. His heart sank. "I don't think we're going to make it to the ship."

"All of you, go on ahead," Odin said.

"Alfather—" Thorfinn began.

"Do as I say, Thorfinn," the old man said.

Thorfinn looked toward the meadow, where the grey shadows of natives ran toward them. "Alfather, come—we don't have any time to waste," he yelled.

"Trust me, my son."

"Thorfinn, hurry," Elsu called from behind him.

"Go on without us; we'll catch up," Thorfinn yelled, his eyes on the native force. They were raising their spears, preparing to hurl them into the air.

Odin raised the spear that he used for a staff and shook it at the night sky, then closed his eyes and whispered words from the old language into the night breeze.

Thorfinn heard the war cries of the natives as they released their spears into the air toward Elsu, Adam, and Gudrid. Knowing it was useless to protect them, he drew his sword.

Suddenly the earth shook beneath their feet and the wind gusted with such strength that it bent the tops of the trees. It collided with the spears, hurtling them off their intended course. Thorfinn turned toward the thunder of thousands of fluttering wings, heading toward them from the norðr, and saw a massive black shadow flying overhead, toward the attacking force.

The charcoal mass descended on the natives. Thorfinn thought at times that he glimpsed ravens; at other times, winged valkyries. The natives scattered in terror, swinging their torches into the night and hitting nothing, unable to see what they were fighting.

As the winged creatures pushed the warriors back into the forest, Odin lowered his arms and turned to Thorfinn. "Let's go."

Thorfinn grabbed the alfather's arm and ran down the rocky shoreline to catch up with the others, glancing behind him periodically to make sure that whatever force attacked the natives wasn't heading in their direction. He wasn't positive, but Thorfinn thought he saw the indistinct outline of women with large wings flapping and swords drawn, hovering in the night sky. They were still focused on the natives, driving them away rather than attacking them.

A familiar figure ran forward to meet Odin and Thorfinn. "Snorri," Thorfinn yelled, recognizing the crewman who had saved Gudrid's life in Markland—their baby's namesake.

"Thorfinn," Snorri greeted him. "We couldn't get the *Mimir II* up the strait—the current was too strong and the waves too high for the few rowers that we could bring with us. We saw the torches in the distance and prepared to surprise them with an attack from behind, but it looks like you have everything under control."

"Thorfinn," Elsu cut in, his tone urgent, "we'd better go, in case there's a reprisal."

With a short nod, Thorfinn led the way to the *Mimir II* and escape.

4

Tostig closed his eyes, feeling the strain of reading by the candlelight dancing across the parchment. The light show continued to make shapes on the inside of his eyelids. He watched the movement of light jumping on his inner eyelids and played with the thoughts they created, witnessing worlds being formed and reformed in his imagination.

His group's relegation to the lake, far from Leif's Hóp camp, was a slap in the face that Tostig didn't mind taking. He knew that the slap would be returned tenfold when he and his men took what was rightfully theirs. He just had to bide his time and wait. One thing that did concern him, though, was that he didn't know how far Freydis's betrayal would go. It was a dangerous game of hawk and field mouse, one that Tostig knew could end in bloodshed. He wanted to avoid that, if he could.

His group had received Freydis's olive branch—a keg of mead—with suspicion. Tostig had warned them not to accept it, but the men wouldn't have it; they took the keg and started drinking anyway. Not wanting to participate in the drinking, he'd returned to the longhouse to review the plan in his head. Being that this was Tostig's first time as leader, he was unsure of himself and questioned every decision he made. But he knew that he'd eventually find the part of himself that turned the *weary* into the *warrior*.

Outside, the sun was giving way to stars and the birds, to night insects. The wind stilled and the lapping lake slowed to gurgles; the whole earth seemed to have paused at the end of a long exhalation. Tostig's thoughts drifted as his body grew more and more relaxed.

Then he heard footsteps approaching outside; a moment later the door, already slightly ajar, rattled as fingers wrapped around its edge and slowly pushed it open, its bottom dragging across the earthen floor, the dust-filled sliver of light widening, bathing Tostig's entire body where he lay on the bed in the last wan vestiges of daylight.

It wasn't until the door had fully opened that Tostig recognized the backlit shape of a female figure—Freydis. She stood silently staring into the interior of the longhouse, her arms at her sides. Tostig stared back. His hand slid between his body and the sod wall to touch the hilt of his dagger. He'd quickly learned that she was an extremely complex person, capable of many layers of deceit and violence. *She's probably waiting for me to make the first move*, he thought. *She's a dangerous serpent from a murderous and violent family.*

Aloud he said, "Freydis, what do you want?"

"I noticed that your door is ajar. Are you alone?" she asked, ignoring his question. Her speech was jerky, as if she were drunk, but she didn't move as if she were drunk; in fact, she looked composed and in control.

"Yes," Tostig answered. "The others are partaking of your generous gift of mead."

Freydis hesitated. Then, "Tostig, I'd like to talk to you."

"In here?" he asked.

"No," she answered abruptly. "Come outside."

Tostig thought for a moment, not sure what to expect. He didn't hear other footsteps approaching the longhouse so he felt confident that an ambush wasn't waiting outside for him. Still . . . he could've missed their approach while talking to Freydis. Finally, seeing no other option, he sat up on the bench and tucked the rolled-up parchment in his belt, then reached behind him for his sword.

"You won't need that," Freydis said. "I've come unarmed." She opened her cloak.

Despite that, Tostig couldn't trust the words of a woman who broke long-standing agreements. For all he knew, Freydis had concealed a weapon within the layers of her clothing. He slipped his dagger into his belt and rose.

The cool, damp fog clung to the treetops, slowly descending, swirling around the boughs of the coniferous trees, caressing the trunks of the spruce trees and the low-lying bushes, dripping dew onto the mossy ground. Tostig looked down as he followed Freydis and noticed that she was walking over the mossy ground in her bare feet. "You will catch your death, walking in your bare feet," he commented, without any real concern for her health.

The descending fog couldn't fully conceal the brightness of the rising moon; it shone through the misty veil like a candle shearing through a cobweb. Tostig sensed a strange stillness with the coming of the fog; an instinctive, lonely silence had descended over the rest of the camp. The cold, moisture-laden air would dampen any words spoken between Freydis and himself; he wondered if they would weigh just as heavy in the days and weeks to come. Their relationship up to now demanded that one misspoken or misinterpreted word between them could trap them in a battle of pride and swords that escalated beyond the confines of their groups to encompass their families and their clans.

Tostig could almost feel hidden hands reaching through the fog, clutching his clothes, pulling him in various directions, reaching for his throat. He clasped his weapon as the fantasy threatened to overtake his conscious senses. Fear gripped Tostig, threatening not to let go. He couldn't tell if the drops of water on his face were the sweat of fear or something from the unknown entities circling around him, concealed in the fog.

For one brief second Tostig felt victimized by the woman he followed, but he dug his fingers into the present and hung on, resisting the pull until he was able to gain a foothold on the cliffs towering above everything he knew. He looked at Freydis from this perspective and knew that, like most outward expressions of strength and dominance, hers was in opposition to her internal condition. Freydis remained small and scared within herself.

She partnered herself in fairness when she needed something, but when she got what she wanted or she felt that she was falling behind, agreements seemed to get buried under the stacks of hewn logs and baskets of grapes on their knarrs. It was an all too common occurrence; powerful families inbred their power into their children rather than instilling the idea that real and lasting power was always shared among the people.

Freydis stopped beside a tree stump and turned to face him. Tostig felt as if he was being led to the tree stump like a goat to the slaughter. “Please, sit down,” Freydis said in an almost authoritarian tone.

“I prefer to stand,” Tostig replied, not wanting to appear biddable in his own camp.

“I don’t like this tension between us,” she began. “It doesn’t make for a trustworthy alliance and a productive voyage.”

“I agree, Freydis,” he said, momentarily letting his guard down.

“If we’re to prosper on this land with so many challenges facing us all, then we must stick together. Our goal and direction must be a common one; we will fail unless we work together.”

Tostig stared at Freydis, trying to decide if she was speaking honestly or whether her meaning was as changeable as the meaning that the Jötunn gave to fairness and equanimity. “How dare you speak of common goals and being distressed over our current relationship when you have been plotting behind my back,” Tostig said, trying to be as direct and calm as possible. “You begin by throwing our people out of what you call your father’s camp for your own secret and devious purposes. You brought five more people on this voyage than we agreed without consulting me. I discovered that they’ve disappeared two dægur ago and no one has heard from them since. Where are they and what plot are you hatching in that brain of yours, Freydis?”

“You are hatching plots in your own head, Tostig. I fear that you’ve become unstable and paranoid,” Freydis calmly replied. “How do you know that we brought five more people aboard our knarr? Did you do a head count?”

“Just like you, we have people watching you, Freydis. When we were thrown out of your camp, I realized that you couldn’t be trusted. But rather than abandon the voyage, I decided to remain here and fulfill our side of the bargain."

Freydis remained silent, standing motionless, her black eyes flicking back and forth in the light from the flame of her torch before settling back on him. Tostig wagered that her stare could burn a hole through his chest. "You insult me and my family," Freydis snapped, her tone hard as ice.

Tostig sensed that her attitude had more to do with her ego, fed by her false sense of importance. Whether that was from what she believed she was entitled to or from an inner, deep-seated fear, Tostig wasn't willing to guess. He did know that he couldn't get caught up a battle of egos with Freydis, wasting time and energy when his primary focus was on accomplishing their mission.

He knew their alliance was much more self-serving than Freydis let on. She wanted to dominate the voyage, using deceit and heavy-handedness to take the profits for herself. Tostig remembered when she changed; he didn't know how far she would go to get what she wanted. He feared that she was maneuvering a plan into action.

"Freydis, I don't fully blame you for wanting to be a strong representative for your people," he said, "but we're on the same side—we're with you. We both could return to our home very wealthy."

"Tostig, how much timber and grapes did you harvest?" Freydis asked in a commanding voice that lingered in the air, poisoning the white fog.

"I think we have almost a quarter-ship load of timber and thirty baskets of grapes."

"Excellent," she said. "We are getting close to matching your amount. You and your group have done well, considering that you also had to build a camp for yourselves."

Tostig's sarcastic reply dripped down to the tip of his tongue like venom, but he sensed that she was baiting him and decided to clench his teeth. Freydis was the sole reason that they were evicted from Eirik's camp, forcing Tostig's crew to redouble their efforts to catch up with Freydis's crew. "Thank you," he finally said. "We wanted to honour our part of the agreement that you laid out, so we could in the future be partners, Freydis." He spat her name back in her face with hidden mockery, hoping that his controversial meaning was apparent.

"How are you getting on?" Freydis casually asked.

"We're enjoying this country very much. It's filled with abundance. We'd like to make future trips to Vinland and Hóp, perhaps even establish a colony on the mainland. We've encountered none of the native resistance we did at Leifsbúrðir. What do you think, Freydis?"

She stood with an uncomfortably blank stare. Her eyes looked drugged, even possessed. Her lips parted slightly, then shut again. Finally she replied, "I think that may be a possibility for future discussions, Tostig. Other than the skræling and the Christian monks on Markland, we have not encountered any persons from our side of the world."

"There is one thing that I don't like, Freydis," he said. "How our business relationship has degraded; it's hard on our people. They feel uncertain and they fear what it may do to our profits. I think you and I can agree right now to end this tension between us, thus ending the tension between our crews; as their leaders, we should bring our crews together in celebration after the harvesting is over and before the winter comes, to compete in exhibition games. If nothing else, it will allow the two crews to let off some pent-up steam and dispel some of the fear that's been building up over the last Mánuðir."

"Yes, I agree," Freydis replied, the life returning to her eyes. "It was a risk for us to bring your shipbuilding group and my people together without fully involving them in the preparations and the full weight of their roles as members in the larger group. We can begin organizing the games tomorrow, once the dægur's work is over." She paused. "Before I go, Tostig, there is one last thing that I wanted to talk to you about. I've been hearing rumours of a network of tunnels here at Hóp, and a central cavern with a tree at its centre. Some say that it's Barnstokkr. Have you heard anything about this?"

"I don't know what you're talking about, Freydis. This is news to me," Tostig said.

"Yggdrasil and Barnstokkr: the tree of life and Gram, the sword of power. Yggdrasil connects all the nine worlds," Freydis said, her pupils growing to twice their original size.

Tostig looked into her eyes and saw the black madness in Freydis's soul. It was an evil told about in stories and myths that warned of the evil trapped in the souls of men and women—the evil in the heart that, if unchecked, could and would destroy them. "Freydis, where did you get this information about the caves and Barnstokkr?" he asked carefully.

"I can't say," she replied, her tone becoming defensive. "But I know that it's somewhere below us; it may be at Straumfjörðr."

Tostig tried to hide his fear. Freydis had somehow found out why he wanted to partner with her. The legend of the cave told to him by Odin was why—to take the sword from Yggdrasil and destroy Nidhogg, before he destroyed the tree. Tostig knew that he had to protect his men from the likes of Freydis, and those who would take by force, without thought.

"Freydis, I have no knowledge of what you speak about," he said in a voice as sincere as he could make it. "But if you would like to take your people on this quest that you speak of, then please do so. We will remain here to continue loading up our ships with as many supplies as we can harvest."

A protracted silence followed, as Tostig and Freydis stared at one another, instinctively waiting for the other to strike—physically or verbally.

"I have one final request," Freydis said. "I'd like to take your ship, Tostig. I will loan you mine in its place; your ship is much larger."

And you want to take the wood and the grapes we worked so hard to harvest and leave us with the smaller cargo, he thought. With every request that Freydis dared to make, her web of deceit was easier and easier to tear apart. "If we unload our cargo and load it into your knarr, that will waste valuable time," Tostig said, baiting Freydis to reveal her true intent.

"Keep the cargo on the ship," Freydis replied. "We'll add to it."

"If that will make you happy," he replied, trying to keep focus on the real purpose of their trip to Hóp.

"Thank you; I will not forget your generosity," Freydis replied, then yawned. "I'm afraid that I must leave. It's late and I must get home."

"Safe travels home, Freydis. We can talk more tomorrow."

As Freydis disappeared into the thickening white fog, a chill moved through Tostig's body; caused not so much by fear as the realization that his purpose had somehow been revealed to him during their conversation. He read the words that she was not speaking and saw the meaning as easily as the sun rising in the morning sky; as if Odin's pantheon had written the future on her body for him to find and read.

Tostig turned and walked the short trip back to his longhouse. The full moon remained partially obscured by the blanket of fog, and within, the fire was reduced to embers. Its transient glow moved across the skeletal remains of once-living branches. The rise of the full moon and the dying fire marked the end of the eventful day. Frustration made Tostig throw another log onto the fire more forcefully than necessary, smashing the glowing log apart and releasing millions of tiny lights into the air to drift toward the smoke hole atop the grass house.

ꟸ ꟹ

Confidence made Freydis walk without fear through the dark forest toward her camp, where fading hearths and lamps glowed through the fog. She crossed her arms over her chest against the night air, and her fingernail dug into her skin. Blood trickled down her forearm, staining the outside of her cloak.

She felt another consciousness within her; one that was a part of her, but also apart from her. It influenced and controlled her actions and directed her thoughts. She remembered the conversation with Tostig, but she couldn't remember what they'd talked about. Thoughts drifted in and out of her head like a weaving shuttle through the loom, but she wasn't able to see the pattern they were creating. She neither consciously influenced them nor consciously controlled them; her body moved independently from her thoughts.

She looked around to make sure no one else had left the tents for a nocturnal meander as she approached a tree. Grabbing onto the trunk, she slammed the side of her face against it, paused to steady herself, then slammed her cheek into the trunk again. She lowered her head and breathed in the pain, imagining that the tree was Tostig and that the attack was real.

She hunched over, the crown of her head resting against the tree until the disorientation passed. Ready for the next surge of pain and dizziness she raised her head, all the while forcing her consciousness to believe that the attack originated from Tostig and that she was the victim.

Finished, she turned and staggered to her sod house, creeping up to push the door open only wide enough to squeeze her body through the gap. She didn't want the creak of a swinging door to awaken Thorvald. She removed her cloak inside the warm house and rubbed her hands up and down her arms, brushing off the chill of the night air.

Thorvald lay on his stomach, sprawled diagonally across the bed, the fur covers and woven blanket partially covering his lean and tight muscular body, his long, sandy blond ringlets covering half his face. Freydis could smell his body odour from a day spent working in the field, felling trees and carrying the thick trunks to piles that would eventually make their way to the knarr beached at the water's edge.

She tried navigating into the bed as stealthily as she had the doorway, slowly lifting the covers just far enough so that her body could slip under them. She carefully slid one of her cold legs between the warm covers, but her damp foot snagged the dry blanket, and she ended up trying to balance on her other leg.

Thorvald's body suddenly jerked as Freydis accidentally touched his leg with her cold, wet foot. With a grunt, he lifted his head and looked at Freydis, still balancing. "Freydis, where have you been?" he asked.

"Outside," she said.

Thorvald squirmed underneath the covers to make more room for Freydis, then lifted the fur bedspread and helped her between the warm coverings. He wrapped his legs around hers, using his body heat to warm up her cold feet. He snuggled her within the blanket as a valkyrie would wrap her wing around a fallen warrior on his journey to Valhalla. Then he opened his eyes and leaned forward to give Freydis a kiss good night. Whatever he saw in the waning glow from the hearth made him recoil, then frown, peering at her face. Touching her chin, he slowly turned her head so that the firelight illuminated her full face. Freydis lifted her hand to her cheek, swollen and misshapen. Thorvald gently pulled her hand away. Freydis met his concerned eyes with her own.

"Freydis, what has happened to your face?" Thorvald asked.

"I . . . I don't want to talk about it," she lied. "It's nothing that I can't resolve on my own."

"I am your husband; I have a right to know!"

"Please Thorvald, my love, I do not want to burden your already busy mind with a matter that I can handle myself."

Thorvald sat up. "Freydis, I demand that you tell me what happened to you. It looks like someone struck you."

Freydis tensed her face up as if she were trying to relive the fabricated moment when Tostig struck her. As she actually began reliving the memory, her expression contorted, accentuating the swollen red mark on her face. "I went to Tostig's camp to offer to buy their ship, because I thought we'd be harvesting more resources on this trip, to make the most of our time left on this voyage." Freydis paused to measure his reaction to her story on his face. "This made him angry, so much so that some of his men held onto me while Tostig struck me repeatedly. I tried to defend myself and fight back, but their combined strength was just too much for me; some of Tostig's punches landed on my face and did the damage to my cheek that you see."

Thorvald's expression ranged from shock to horror as he tried to take in all the details of her story. Frowning again, he examined her wounds in the flickering light. "Did you say anything to him, threaten or insult him in any way?" he asked. His tone was a little too submissive for Freydis's liking; it was not the reaction that she had hoped to provoke.

"Thorvald, it's sounding like you have no intention of avenging this assault on me," she said, her swollen cheek almost slurring her words. "I come home battered like a beaten wolf, and you don't want to do anything."

"What has changed, woman?" he exclaimed. "You come home and coyly ask me to not get involved in what happened to you; you didn't want to tell me—I had to drag it out of you."

"Well, I didn't want to get into it tonight." Freydis scowled. "I'm tired and sore. I want to sleep and deal with this matter tomorrow."

Thorvald huffed in frustration, turning over in the bed. "I think we should wait till we've completed harvesting all the wood, grapes, and other resources for the trip home. And then, like the fox, we should strike and avenge this violation."

"You wretch!" Freydis yelled, jumping out of the bed. "You will never avenge my humiliation, or your own, for that matter. I now realize just how far away I am from my home and my family in Grœnlandia. Unless you avenge this, I will divorce you. You will no longer have a tie to my family; their riches and influence will not touch you."

Her final words appeared to cut deep into Thorvald's ego, damaging his self-image of a provider and family head who aspired to become a powerful patriarch in the future, leading one branch of the Eiriksson family empire.

"If we show signs of weakness now," Freydis pressed, "we will not be able to control our people; we will appear weak in the hearts and minds of our crew. Our group will fracture into smaller, weaker groups who will either move off on their own or ally themselves with Tostig. Our common goal will shatter and we will lose all that we've gained on this trip."

Thorvald had no response. Freydis continued. "My family's reputation will suffer, all because you couldn't move your honour to a place where courage feeds and nurtures it."

"Woman," Thorvald yelled, surging from the bed to stand naked before her, "I can't stand your taunts any longer." Without another word, Thorvald put on his clothes as fast as he could and stomped out of the longhouse.

Freydis ran to the door and watched him as he continued to dress while walking through the camp to gather his men. If the situation weren't so dire, she would've found the scene funny. Moments later she heard Thorvald's shouts in the distance as he tried to raise his men out of their drunken sleep.

Unable to remain in the house, Freydis quickly dressed, slid her sword into her belt, and followed Thorvald into the foggy night.

ꟷ ꟷ

Freydis heard murmur of voices in the distance, the words obscured by the lake's lapping waves. She crept through the bushes, then crouched and carefully bent branches aside to peer toward the orange flame of a flickering fire. Bobbing lights flickered in the distance as the men moved through Tostig's camp.

There were sounds of scuffling and muted thuds.

As she approached the centre of Tostig's camp where the fog wasn't as thick, she saw dark shadows moving through the houses and rickety shacks hastily built by Tostig's crew. They moved though the night from house to house like a moon moving through the daylight sky, almost unnoticeable in their agility and quickness. Their swords penetrated the sod walls of buildings, piercing whatever was on the other side, meeting no resistance. The mead laced with mandrake seemed to have worked perfectly to either kill Tostig's crew or induce such a motionless slumber that striking them with the bluntest sword or club would finish the job and ensure no witnesses.

She couldn't help feeling proud of herself; her plan couldn't have been better executed if she'd done it herself. She'd fooled everyone, including her husband. Once her enemies were destroyed on Hóp, her crimes would remain hidden. She could return to Grœnlandia with any story that suited her needs. It would be her word and her family's authority and reputation against a few contradicting stories and controversial hearsay. And, when she returned with two knarrs full of supplies, she'd be welcomed as a heroine and her voyage marked as a success by all who saw those two boats sailing into the fjord at Brattahlid. The events at Hóp would soon be forgotten in the planning of future voyages.

She skulked toward Tostig's house in time to see Thorvald and two armed men drag Tostig from his house and thrust him to his knees in front of them.

"You will pay for striking my wife—with your life," Thorvald growled.

"Thorvald, we've been friends since childhood, I was a witness at your wedding!" Tostig protested. "I spoke on your behalf to get you onto this voyage; we fought side by side. I would not strike your wife, nor insult you in this manner."

"Are you calling my wife a liar?"

"Yes, he is," Freydis answered, stepping forward. "Look at how Tostig defines friendship and partners in commerce," she said, turning her cheek toward the torchlight to display her swollen face.

"Freydis, you lying snake," Tostig spat at her.

"Don't you say another word," Thorvald growled,

backhanding Tostig.

"We cannot trust Tostig and his crew as honourable partners and friends; they must be eliminated—all of them," Freydis yelled to the group returning to the centre of the camp.

As the men approached from the lake, she noticed that they surrounded and escorted a group of women. The armed escort stopped and parted to reveal three women—one very young and the other two pregnant; they looked like sisters. "Thorvald, these are the only three left alive," one of the escorts said.

Tostig lowered his head, ashamed and tormented by how blind and stupid he'd been to trust Freydis, despite his gut feeling. He would go to Hel for the crime he'd committed against his crew and their families.

"It was strange, Freydis," another said, looking at her. "The men didn't move as we struck them; some were either so still that they may have been dead already, while others were breathing but didn't wake as we approached."

"And what of these women?" Freydis barked, twisting his comment in her own direction. "Why are they not as dead as their husbands?"

"Please, Freydis; we cannot kill women bearing children in cold blood," the first man protested, pointing to the two pregnant sisters.

"Yes, Freydis," Tostig pleaded, "let them live; what harm could they do to you?"

Freydis turned to Thorvald. His eyes met hers, full of fear for the social repercussions of murdering unborn children. "Freydis," he said, "I don't see what can be gained by killing these women; we will take them back with us."

"Take them *back*?" Freydis yelled in angry consternation. "So they can tell all what's taken place here, tonight? Or to have their kin and their descendants seek retribution on us and our families?" She stomped over to the three women. "Thorvald, bring me the axe."

Thorvald hesitated, looking around at the others, no doubt hoping to hear a counter-order or that she would reconsider what she was about to do. Finally his shoulders slumped and he walked over and lifted an axe from the base of a tree. He handed it to her without looking at her or the women.

The three women clutched one another, screaming in terror. "Odin, come to our rescue and stop this madness!" one of the sisters shrieked. The other two women recoiled back against the chests of the men holding them as Freydis hefted the axe.

"Freydis, please think of what you're about to do—you're murdering the unborn," the man heading the escort pleaded one last time.

Ignoring him and the silent protests of the other men, Freydis walked over to the kneeling Tostig. Leaning over, she put her face nose to nose with his. "Now you will see what happens to those who do not yield to the authority of the Eiriksson family," she whispered, spitting her final words into his face.

"You mean who don't yield to *you*," Tostig hissed. "You should be a leader of your people, instead of using them for your shield."

Freydis screamed in anger and slapped Tostig across the face with her fist, where Thorvald had initially struck him. "You must've stood by the pantry shelves discussing cooking with your mother and sisters more often than you went to horse fights," she growled. "Or that's how it seems, from your little blond beard."

She turned on her heel and walked over to the three women, holding the axe in the air. "Hold her," Freydis ordered, indicating one of the pregnant women.

The lead escort took two steps back from the group, shaking his head, wanting no part in the senseless slaughter.

"Hold her, I say, or you forfeit your share from this trip, and return home in humiliation," she threatened, caring only that her plan succeed.

Two younger men hastily stepped forward and held onto the woman's arms.

"Please, Freydis," the woman sobbed, "for the life of my child, I will strike a bargain with y—"

The double-headed axe came down, splitting her esophagus in two. Her eyes rolled to the back of her head and her limp body collapsed to the ground.

Not flinching, and in an almost reverent silence, Freydis moved over to the older pregnant sister, who stared in shock at her dead sister lying on the ground beside her. Then, as if jolted to consciousness, she began struggling in the grip of her captors, trying to get away from the axe. She stopped as she saw a reflection of the flame flickering in its metal blade, held over Freydis's head. Raising her face to the starry heavens, she closed her eyes, meeting Freydis's death blow head on.

Freydis struck a second time, without hesitation, blood splattering over her hands and forearms. Then she approached her final victim, feeling as if the blood of the previous two pulsated through her veins. Grinning, she stared into her victim's blank eyes and saw her deformed cheek reflected in the woman's fear-enlarged iris—or was it the face of a Jötunn staring back at her? Taken aback, she stared at the enlarged nose, the heavy brow, the widely spaced eyes and elongated forehead, all masking her gender. She stared harder and harder into the reflection, leaning forward then arching her back to put distance between her and the image—which gave the illusion of a hump protruding from between her shoulder blades.

She raised the axe, shutting down all emotion, using all of the darkness within her to swing the blade down onto her last victim—but paused. A flicker of humanity gripped and held her arms as she considered a different course, like the whiff of a new scent passing in front of her nose . . . Then thoughtless darkness seized her again and the axe fell across her final victim's chest.

Freydis lowered the axe and turned away as easily as a wolf turning from a carcass to scan the terrain for challengers of her dominance. Her chest throbbed and her breaths came in pants.

Her crew stood around her in a fearful trance, unable to fully fathom what had just taken place in front of them. They stood rigid, as if prepared to defend themselves. Thorvald stood watching Freydis as her breathing slowly returned to normal, his expression one of shocked disapproval.

Her blood frenzy evaporated and she dropped the blood-splattered axe to the ground. She turned and walked away, her only badge of honour the blood of her victims splattered on the front of her smock and dripping from her hands and wrists.

༄ ༄

Coyotes howled in the distance, smelling the blood from

the freshly slaughtered bodies. Thorvald watched his wife leave, remembering what she'd told them when they'd first arrived, and the *Mimir II* crew disappeared into the forest while Freydis stepped back onto *Hringhorni*: "Tostig's group will set up their own camp away from ours," she'd announced, ignoring their questioning stares. "It's what he's decided to do."

Had he? This act of barbarism cast Freydis's behaviour and motives into doubt. Only retribution demanded such a response, and this was not such an occasion. He looked around at the faces of the crew and knew that they agreed with him. They too were unable to find a compelling enough reason to justify Freydis's actions—their actions. How could they justify killing thirty-three of their fellows? Until tonight, they had all seemed to be one cohesive force in the service of the entire community. Tonight had split it forever into unwilling victors and undeserving victims.

ꟾ ꟾ

Freydis cast a glance at Tostig, still kneeling in the flickering light, as she left. No one else moved.

Taking advantage of the group's shock, Tostig struck the nearest of his captors in the groin, knocking him into the other one; as they stumbled together, he jumped to his feet and fled into the woods.

"After him," he heard Freydis yelling to her crew behind him. "We'll lose him in the fog."

Moments later, Tostig heard them crashing through the underbrush. He knew their chain mail and heavy weapons would slow the men down, while he, being unequipped, could run faster and would be able to go farther. Sure enough, his pursuers gradually slowed, hindered by armour and fog, until the sound of their pursuit gave way to the silence of the forest night; another moment, and the night animals resumed their calls.

Still, Tostig didn't want to go too far; now that he was out of immediate danger, he had to figure out how to find Thorfinn and warn him of Freydis's madness, before he too fell victim to her deception.

"Spread out, men," he heard one of his pursuers call, the sound muffled by both fog and distance; "go alone if you have to. An unarmed man won't be a challenge for the weakest of us."

Tostig dropped and rolled under the heavy lower branches of a cedar tree and peered through the boughs, trying to figure out how to get away from his pursuers. Finally he crawled from his hiding place, preferring to fight his way out rather than wait to be found and slaughtered. Even if one of his pursuers heard him, the fog would disorient him enough for Tostig to get away.

The slaughter of the women haunted him; the images of them falling under Freydis's axe replaying in his mind. He was determined to stay alive and avenge their deaths on Freydis and her clan. He wouldn't stop till he mounted Freydis's head on the bow of his ship, her rotting flesh a constant reminder and a testament to the brave and honourable people who lost their lives at the hands of those butchers. Tostig would not let anyone forget the sacrifice that they had to make with their lives for trusting a monster like Freydis Eiriksdóttir.

ꙮ ꙮ

Freydis paced the clearing like an agitated wolf, worried that Tostig would escape into the night with the knowledge of what had happened tonight; it would mean certain destruction for her and her family's authority and reputation.

She feared the restrictions that her family would impose on her, Thorvald, and every man in their group if they found out what had taken place tonight. And what that would mean in matters of commerce and trade agreements with her family in the future. She remained determined that her actions on this trip would be buried in the shallow grave of Tostig and anyone else who threatened to expose her deeds.

First she needed to find Tostig. And with his tracking skills, finding him would be difficult. If there was any way for her to lure Tostig back to her, she had to find it.

ꙮ ꙮ

The fog was both Eir's blessing and Rindr's curse. It concealed Tostig's pursuers from him, but it also made pursuing him just as challenging. He wasn't sure in which direction to head;

even though the fog allowed him to escape, it trapped him as well. He decided to keep walking. It was harder for his pursuers to find him if he didn't remain still. He ran away from the veiled moon, using it as an indicator of his general direction.

Hearing rustling close by, Tostig stopped dead. The thick fog swirled a concealing wall around him.

"Moði, is that you?" a hushed voice called. Tostig crouched, ready to jump his pursuer. The man stopped in front of Tostig, not seeing his crouched form, waiting for a reply from the silent fog.

Noticing an unsheathed dagger dangling from the man's belt, Tostig reached up and with one motion, snatched the weapon and sprang to his feet. Reaching up, he pushed the point into the nape of his victim's neck. He held onto the dagger's handle, feeling the warm blood flowing through his fingers and down his arm as he waited for the convulsing body to subside and allow death to take over.

When the momentary shock of a brother's blood on his hands subsided, Tostig rolled the body over to scavenge through the clothing for anything he could use. Only then did he recognize his victim: Magni, who had fought by Tostig's side many times, even protecting him in several battles when they'd been overrun. Rage rose up in Tostig. *Freydis's evil cannot be allowed to go unchecked; she must be destroyed,* he thought.

࿇ ࿇

Screams and shouts interrupted by the moans of wounded and the grunts of warriors heaving swords and axes pierced Tostig's brain as easily as a sharp knife might pierce his flesh; the memories repeated themselves over and over again, growing in intensity with each cycle. There was nothing that Tostig could do to save his comrades; the screams that he heard were the echoes of the dead, torturing his mind into thinking that it was happening in the moment. With each repeat of their tortured screams, his life force leaked out of him more and more, diverting the energy from his muscles that he needed to escape.

The thoughts chased him as he ran through the forest night with owls hooting in the sky overhead and the fog trapping him in its cloak. He ran through the white curtain to escape both the memories and Freydis's men, pushing through the pain of his cold, bruised feet, feeling the fear of a hunted and disoriented animal.

At last Tostig stumbled to a stop and collapsed at the base of a tree. His world stopped with him and the silence hit him hard. He didn't know what was worse, the screams and moans of the night before or the haunting silence afterward. The absence of life hollowed out his heart and left emptiness.

He'd been running so hard for so long that he didn't feel his strained chest muscles until he'd stopped and finally tried drawing in the abundance of air that his lungs craved—only to find himself unable to breathe deeply. His head throbbed and he felt the sting of his bleeding feet. He swayed, and grabbed a pine bough to steady himself; the pricking jab of its needles distracted him from his thoughts and for the first time since his escape from the Hóp camp, his mind calmed and his thoughts became coherent.

He pulled out his dagger, looked at the blade, and carefully slid it into his belt, imagining gripping the handle so tightly his fingers went white, and staring into Freydis's eyes as he slid the blade into her throat. He wondered if Freydis's betrayal was what Odin meant when he said that he couldn't tell Tostig anything about his family and his past. Perhaps the beginnings of the slaughter would be a part of that past.

Tostig slowly rose to his feet, steadying himself against the tree. If he was to go on, he'd have to leave the slaughter of his men behind him in the lake camp. The screams finally diminished into the darkness at the back of his brain as he walked through the night, hoping that the heavens would guide him. A loud silence penetrated his consciousness, one that almost overtook the glimmer of courage that he felt.

Ahead, the forest opened into a meadow, blanketed by low-lying fog. Tostig looked around him at the lightening forest and felt as if he was moving in a trance that he couldn't fully shake. He felt a strange sense of calm entering his soul, as if he'd inhaled the fog around him and the whiteness penetrated him and made him invisible. It left as the fog slowly dissipated. He looked to the sky and saw faint pinks and oranges. Soon he would no longer have the night and the fog concealing his escape route from Freydis and the rest of his pursuers.

As he watched the sky, it was if a presence were tugging at

his coat, pulling him away from what was once a living camp, one that now had the rotten stench of a cemetery hanging over it that not even the coming winter storms could quell. Fiery orange crept through the uncertain pinks, reflecting off the wispy clouds; as the sky burst into light and the fog slowly rose from the forest floor, he saw farther and farther into the distance.

He closed his eyes and imagined he heard the hiss of frothing white sea water as waves hit the dark greenish rocks of the cliffs; salty ocean air tickled his nostrils and the cool spray riding the ocean wind gently misted his face.

When Tostig opened his eyes, he found himself lying on a mossy bed. A woman leaned over him, her golden hair hanging down around her smiling face. Dawn light shone behind her, illuminating the back of her head and sending shimmering light down the strands of her hair. Tostig thought that he saw the shadow of folding wings behind her as he squinted, trying to focus on her.

"Good morning, my love," she whispered as a lover would to her rising companion. She stroked his hair. "I came to remind you that you're not alone."

Tostig slowly raised himself to his elbows, his cheek lightly touching the sheer cloth covering her breast. He smelled fresh morning air and the warmth of the rising sun on her body. Her presence enveloped him, and he forgot about his troubles, everything except the beautiful presence leaning over him. "What's your name?" he asked.

"My name is Sváfa."

"Sváfa, are you really here?"

"Yes, I am. Can't you believe your own eyes?" She smiled.

"I—I'm not sure," Tostig said. His insides quivered.

"I have a gift for you," she whispered.

"What is it?" Tostig asked, entranced by the aqua blue in her eyes.

"I know the location of a great sword. You will see your friends again. You must go with them into the caves."

"How will I find—"

"Shh, no more questions," Sváfa whispered, touching the side of her finger to Tostig's lips. "I want you to commit what I'm about to say to memory." And she recited:

Swords I know, lying in the Isle of Sigars,
Fifty there are, save only four;
One there is that is best of all—
The shield-destroyer; with gold it shines.

In the hilt is fame; in the haft is courage;
In the point is fear, for its owner's foes;
On the blade there lies a blood-flecked snake,
And a serpent's tail round the flat is twisted.

"I will always be with you, shielding you from danger," she said in her calm voice, which seemed to echo. "I will not break my word to you."

"I believe you," Tostig said.

Sváfa lightly touched her lips to his; he inhaled her sweet breath of daffodils, felt the satin smoothness of honey as the tip of her tongue brushed the supple flesh of his inside lip, tasted sweet berries where her lips touched his. He opened his mouth wider, eager to return her oral embrace, but a wind rose, and Tostig heard the flutter of wings. He fought to escape from the trance before she disappeared, but he opened his eyes too late.

Sváfa backed away from Tostig and unfurled black raven wings. "You're a valkyrie," Tostig said as she flapped her wings and rose to hover in the air.

"Keep moving. You will find the caves. I will see you soon," she called down to him as she caught the next gust of wind and flew over the trees to the heavens.

3

"I want to go with you into the caves," Gudrid said as they walked up the beach of Straumfjörðr.

"No, Gudrid," Thorfinn said firmly. "I want you to go with Adam to the camp. I don't want to risk losing you. It's a dangerous journey."

"So I'm supposed to sit and wait for your return, wondering if you're safe or if I'll ever see you again."

Thorfinn stared into Gudrid's tear-filled eyes. "Gudrid, I can't do my job if I'm worrying about you."

"There's a storm approaching," Odin said, interrupting them. "Gudrid, your job is to get your people to safety. There is a cave up there, at Hóp, where you will be safe; your survival depends on it. We will bring your baby back to you; you have my word."

For the first time since Odin's arrival, Gudrid didn't know whether she believed Odin's promise. When it came to the safety of her son and her husband, she wasn't so sure that her faith could provide her with the same comfort as having her baby in her arms or her husband at her side.

The cold Atlantic wind blew across Thorfinn's face, lifting his curls. The scene was all so surreal; it was happening in front of her, but it could've been a dream.

"We don't have much time," Odin said. "There's a wall of water heading in this direction; it will soon hit the coast of Hóp."

"Where is it coming from?" Gudrid asked.

"Far beneath Jörmungandr; the water's being pushed in this direction by an event that's pushing Iceland farther and farther away. I don't know how far the water is from us; we must go and you must lead your people to safety, as you did at Markland."

"How did you—" Gudrid stopped her question in mid-sentence, expecting his reply to be as enigmatic as he was himself.

"I will take care of Thorfinn and Elsu," Odin concluded. "You and Adam return to your camp."

Odin looked to the austr and Gudrid followed his gaze to see what looked like an ominous grey and black cloud forming over the ocean. It moved in their direction, churning the heavens into unbelievably strange and alien shapes and pushing their deadline closer and closer. Even the stars moved in irregular cycles and patterns, changing their familiar shape as if Asgard were moving to make space for another heavenly presence.

Gudrid and Adam stood on the beach and watched Thorfinn, Elsu, and Odin disappear into the foliage at the edge of the forest. She looked at Adam and without a word headed toward Leif's suðr encampment.

"Adam, I don't like this at all," Gudrid said as she stomped toward the grassy hill below the field where the camp was located.

"Don't like what?" Adam asked.

"Not being in control of our destiny. That's why we sought out lands in the first place—so we could create our own life and build it for future generations, be the creators of our own future."

"That doesn't seem possible," Adam replied.

As they scaled the hill, Gudrid noticed the smoke rising from two camps: one to norðr of their location and the other suðr of their location. "That's odd," she said. "Why is there smoke coming from two locations? Something doesn't seem right."

She detoured from the footpath, almost striding over Adam's feet, and pushed her way through the coniferous boughs, releasing them to slap Adam in the chest as he followed her into the forest.

Gudrid emerged from the woods near a sapphire-blue lake that reflected the mountains in the background. To the left of its beach stood a field of hastily assembled lean-tos and a large, recently constructed longhouse. She hesitated, sensing death all around her, and confused by the contrast of beauty and devastation.

The dead silence gripped her as she walked into the camp; the stillness of death moved through her mind like the wind moved through the still camp, disturbing nothing except the ash from the hearths that it picked up and pushed into funnel-shaped dust-devils. The smoke came from the dying fires.

The ground felt strange as Gudrid stepped across it; she felt as if she were drugged and her legs were rubber. Gudrid knew she wasn't drugged; she was taking on the feelings of the people in the camp—they knew they'd somehow been drugged. Her eye landed on a tipped barrel in the distance and she smelled the sweet honey scent of mead spilled on the ground. She stopped.

"What's wrong, Gudrid?" Adam asked, staring suspiciously at Gudrid.

"Oh Adam," she said, grabbing his hooded cloak, "I feel death all around me—betrayal and death."

Adam walked into one of the lean-tos and turned around; he stared silently back at Gudrid wearing a grim expression that could only mean that her suspicions had been appallingly confirmed.

"Oh Adam, what happened here is inconceivable," she moaned. "There's an enemy in our midst who did this; they're walking free among us, posing as a friend and as kin." Gudrid walked toward the longhouse, toward a pile of bodies where hawks walked over the carcasses, feeding.

She turned away, unable to look at the dead anymore. The reality of her comrades lying dead on Hóp earth, rotting beneath the Vinland sky, was too much emotional devastation; so much so that the faces of the victims dimmed as she struggled to fathom the motive for the crime. "Adam, the victims and the perpetrators are a blank in my mind. I know that the bodies are our people and I know that they're dead—killed—but I can't see them up here, nor can I see who did this." Gudrid said, touching her forehead and starting to cry.

"Try to calm yourself," Adam said. "There's nothing that you could've done; it's already been done."

Gudrid blinked back tears and looked at Adam. She felt that she was the mother to the group; now she felt the loss that a mother feels, as well. Her emotions walked through a second devastation: the severing of the emotional connections of her community.

They silently headed for Leif's suðr camp. Gudrid's pace quickened as unformed fears began taking shape in her mind of what she and Adam might find there. She hadn't seen any traces of whoever attacked the first community; neither had she seen signs of struggle, which confused her. It was as if the group either couldn't or wouldn't fight to defend themselves. Perhaps they hadn't seen the attack coming. But that was highly unusual; once the attack had begun, the rest of the camp should've been alerted.

What disturbed her most was why the two groups were separated in the first place. There wasn't any sign of harvesting in the dead camp, so why would part of the camp be there? She needed to find Freydis, if she wanted to find the answer to the riddle.

The camp they approached was active, but there was a morbidity pervading the group. The faces that did meet Gudrid's stare neither smiled nor seemed happy to see her; they turned away as if ashamed and returned to their work. A dark cloud of guilt hung over the camp she and Adam moved through, looking for Freydis.

"What is going on here, Adam?" she asked quietly, noticing a Vinlander scurrying away from them as they approached him.

"It's very unusual, like we're walking amongst strangers," Adam noted.

"Snorri," Gudrid yelled, noticing him up ahead. "Where's Freydis?"

"Freydis and Thorvald are in custody," Snorri said, joining her and Adam, "for the murder of half of our people."

Gudrid lowered her head and stumbled backward as a wave of dizziness overtook her. She felt as though the ground were undulating like the world serpent's back. Adam grabbed her just before she toppled to the ground.

"By Thor, how did this happen to us?" she gasped.

"We're unsure why; Freydis ordered mead be given to Tostig's group as a peace offering. Unbeknownst to us, she'd laced it with hemlock, which either killed or drugged his people. Then she and Thorvald took a group of warriors to their camp and slaughtered them," Snorri said.

"This is all so unbelievable," Gudrid announced, looking at Adam. "These things do not happen except for reasons of vengeance, and those unusually occur under conditions of misunderstanding or greed."

"Freydis claimed that, being the only direct relation to Eirik the Red at Hóp, she had the right to take possession of the camp in your and Thorfinn's absence, and that Tostig had no right to occupy it alongside her group," Snorri said.

"Where is Tostig?" Gudrid asked, determined to get to the bottom of the mystery.

"No one has seen him," Snorri replied. "We assume that he was killed with the others."

"Take me to see Freydis," Gudrid ordered.

Snorri turned and led the way to a small group of men armed with swords and spears. As they approached, the men parted to allow them through.

Freydis and Thorvald, hands bound, had been tied to a tree. As Gudrid stood over her, Freydis looked up at her sister-in-law and long-time friend, the skin around her eyes puffy and rimmed by fiery red rings, her eyelids drooping as if she hadn't slept in days. Thorvald's head remained hanging down in shame. There was only one word that Gudrid could force through the shame and despair that blurred her vision like the tears that filled her eyes. "Why?"

Freydis stared numbly back as if unable to think; as if she'd drunk the poisoned mead herself. Now faced with the reality of what she'd done, no longer hidden by the darkness and the fog, she seemed overpowered by the light of truth and the honesty of Gudrid's question. "Because . . . " Freydis mumbled, "because I could do it."

Her words struck Gudrid as if she'd been struck across her cheek by the hard edge of a battle shield. Freydis had summed up their entire reason for landing on Vinland and occupying another people's continent: *because they could.*

They had crossed over from exploration to exploitation. Gudrid finally understood Thorfinn and what he'd tried to avoid. She finally understood what Elsu and his people were trying to protect, just as she and Thorfinn were trying to save their world from the ravages of the Ragnarök and the Jötunn, as the gods moved to take Midgard and exploit it for their own desires.

It was an unavoidable truth of existence that without a governance mechanism in place, humanity's natural tendency was an inability to distinguish between exploitation and coexistence. Elsu's people were able to grasp that basic human difference and work it into a practical system.

"What do you want us to do with Freydis and Thorvald?" Snorri asked.

"I don't know," Gudrid mumbled. She turned and walked away, removing herself physically and emotionally from the responsibility. "We must get our people farther inland," she said without looking back. "There is a great wave heading in this direction. It threatens to sweep away everything, including us, unless we can get to safety."

"What about the knarrs, out in the water?" Snorri asked.

"There's no time to get them to a safe port; we'll have to leave them where they are."

༺ ༻

Tostig heard feet shuffling through leaves and snapping twigs up ahead; the pine forest was still too dense to see who it was, but it was definitely people walking. *Could Freydis and her killing mob have somehow circled around and ended up in front of me?* he thought. That was unlikely, but Tostig couldn't take chances. He crept forward through the dense foliage, making use of the natural camouflage as much as possible.

He spied three figures walking through the bushes—Tostig could just make out their heads. The foliage was still too thick to identify them, but they seemed not to be members of the same race; there was a disjointed quality about the group. Something wasn't right about them; it was like walking into a familiar room and knowing that one object had been removed, but not which one.

As he watched them, he noticed that one was a cloaked elderly figure who shuffled his feet and stumbled over undergrowth. *Odin*, he thought, *thank Thor*. A moment later he recognized Thorfinn and Elsu, following him. When they stopped in a clearing, he calmly walked forward to join his friends, yelling Thorfinn's name as he approached the trio.

"Tostig, hello! What brings you here?" Thorfinn asked in surprise, his eyebrows held high in confusion. "Is everything okay at Hóp?"

"I'll need to talk to you about that," Tostig said, keeping his eyes on Odin, who swayed, trying to maintain his balance. "It may take some time to explain. Could I walk with you?"

"Of course," Thorfinn answered. "I thought you and Freydis were off harvesting grapes."

"Yes, we were, but something happened, Thorfinn. I think that we should talk about it—in private." Tostig still stared at Odin and kept Elsu in his peripheral vision.

"I sense deceit on the part of Freydis," Odin said in his crackling voice. "Why has she betrayed me, you are asking yourself."

"Yes, you're correct," Tostig replied, surprised. He turned directly to Thorfinn and whispered, "Freydis is pursuing me along with a group of her men; I don't know how close they are, but I know her intention is to kill me."

"It is not she who's doing the betraying, it's my deceitful sibling, Loki," Odin said, turning his hooded face toward Tostig. "Loki has taken possession of Freydis."

Tostig stared into the dark cavern of the hood. He could barely make out the features of Odin's face but he did see the studded leather patch over his left eye, and his wrinkled chin and mouth.

"Don't stare too close into the face of power, boy," Odin warned; "many have gone mad."

Tostig recoiled, not knowing how to take Odin's statement.

"Isn't Loki bound for killing Baldur?" Thorfinn asked.

"He's escaped—that was the tremor we felt. The hound Garmr has been set free; he is at the cave, Gnipahellir."

"Is there anything we can do to shape-shift Loki back into his original form?" Thorfinn asked. "If Freydis's people see that it's not her, then they will no longer follow the impostor."

Odin shook his head. "Until Loki is in my presence, it will be hard for me to know more than what I already know now; where we've been and who we've seen lingers like the scent of rosewater on a woman—I can sense it when it's in my presence as clearly as I see the nose on your face, but it's hard for me to see what is beyond my immediate sphere."

The alfather's voice hardened. "It's that impertinent hybrid, both Æsir and Jötunn. It was a mistake to keep him with us for so long. We should've cast him out with his Jötunn offspring when we had the chance. We've put up with him long enough." His vehemence knocked his hood back on his head.

Tostig widened his eyes in comprehension as the implications sank in. Odin saw his dismay and said calmly, as if he had been giving the same reply since the beginning of time, "I know the question on your mind. Even though Freydis's deeds are not her own, will she suffer for them? Unfortunately, Freydis's reputation and her descendants will bear the brunt of Loki's deception. Once the deeds are done in her guise, it will be difficult for others to trust Freydis ever again. It is a very sad affair," Odin mumbled. "There are many things that are occupying my mind right now and I'm finding it a little difficult to focus . . ." His voice faded into an inner monologue.

"Where's my völva?" Odin suddenly demanded of no one in particular.

Tostig looked to Thorfinn, who recovered from his own confusion to say, "Alfather, your völva isn't here."

Odin looked at their faces, staring at each as if he were trying to match each with the face of his völva. "Of course she isn't here," he stammered. "Why would you say that?" He looked at their faces again, this time looking embarrassed. "What was I thinking?" His weak laugh couldn't mask his confusion.

Tostig saw Thorfinn frown at Odin's attempt at a cover-up, for cover-up it was; Tostig had also noticed small indications that Odin was confused or seemed unable to concentrate. "Alfather, do you know what is happening?" Tostig asked respectfully.

Odin smiled knowingly, focused once again. "Yes, of course I do. It was I who put these events into motion," he proudly stated. "Loki is seeking the Gram, the sword that I thrust into what you know as Barnstokkr, but it now resides in the base of Yggdrasil, the great tree that connects the nine worlds. The sword is just one of many magical artifacts that that evil bastard Loki is collecting so he can take control of Midgard. Like all of us, he knows that his own death is upon him; this is his attempt to stop it. Once we're gone, the only thing left of us will be the magical items that the

Jötunn had forged for us and that Loki has stolen back for them."

"How do you know that, Alfather?" Tostig asked.

"Because I put it in Yggdrasil," Odin blurted. "It was originally in Barnstokkr, at the centre of King Völsung's hall; the king's son, Sigmund, pulled it out, and Sigmund's son, Sigurd, abused its power by using it to slay a dragon." Odin snorted. "As if that was the sword's purpose, to kill dragons for the vanity of a petulant youth! Sigmund was given the Gram to lead. So I took it from Sigurd and thrust it with my last bit of strength into the tree at the centre of the cave—a chamber at the centre of a network of tunnels where the base of the great tree, Yggdrasil, rests.

"Its roots extend across the floor of the cave," Odin continued. "It is there that the sword resides. Loki cannot pull the sword out of the tree because the rightful owner of the sword and its power is you, Tostig—you are the heir to the throne of Völuspa. That's why Loki possesses Freydis, to try to get you to do it for him."

"But something went wrong," Thorfinn guessed.

"Yes. Loki didn't expect my arrival, so he needed a diversion. He stole away and created chaos amongst the humans, so he could hide among them." Odin looked to Tostig. "Even Loki, with all of his power, cannot subvert the power of the Gram. I held the information from you because I couldn't risk Loki finding out. He has more information about the coming end than he should; Loki doesn't need anymore. But Loki will be present when you pull the sword from the base of the tree, you can be assured of that. He will try to take it from you."

"But I won't pass the sword over to Freydis," Tostig protested.

"Loki is a shape-shifter, my boy," Odin reminded him. "He'll become whoever he needs to be so he can take the sword from you."

"Alfather," Thorfinn asked, "isn't Loki's power dwindling too?"

"Yes, but he's half Jötunn and has the power of that race as well. The elementals have their own magical source that is different from ours." Again he looked back to Tostig. "Gram is a powerful sword, but more importantly, it's a symbol of power."

"What must I do with the sword when I have it?" Tostig asked.

"Fight the serpent Nidhogg in a chamber below the cave."

"Nidhogg?" Tostig squeaked. "I'm a navigator, not a warrior! I don't have the training to fight a serpent!"

"Don't worry, Tostig," Odin said. "I'll be at your side, fighting along with you."

"Are you sure you can defeat him?" Thorfinn asked, failing to mask his doubt.

"The universe will unfold as it was always destined to unfold," Odin answered. "All of us, gods and men, must play the roles that we've been given, Thorfinn." He paused. "I wish you could hear the music that is playing in my head; it's the melody of all beings in harmony with one another, one sound complimenting the other. All we need to do is play our part within the larger group. We all know what our role is; it followed us into this realm at birth. It's only when we arrive here that we try to undermine that role. Do you understand what I mean?"

"I think I do, Alfather," Thorfinn replied.

"Good, because once I'm gone, you must look within for your answers," Odin said, tapping Thorfinn's chest with a forefinger.

"I don't know if I'm ready to face that reality," Thorfinn said. Tostig nodded wryly.

"Ending has many meanings," Odin said. "Don't take its obvious meaning as the only meaning."

They walked in silence alongside Odin, each trying to find some relevance and meaning to the alfather's words. They didn't sound like words from a man suffering from senility, but thoughts that weighed heavily on the alfather's mind. They couldn't ignore Odin's words; regardless of its state, Odin's mind was still powerful, containing infinite wisdom and knowledge that expanded the history of the nine worlds.

"Tostig," Thorfinn asked, "are you sure you are still being followed?"

"I assume that Freydis and her band of people are tracking me. I think I have at least a dægur lead on them, but I lost track of the time—for all I know, they could be right behind me."

"Not to worry, my boy," Odin interjected. "If Loki is your true nemesis, once he sees me, he will not attack. He may still have his shape-shifting abilities, but I can assure you that he forfeited something to keep them. I still have the ability to counter whatever Loki has to throw at us."

Tostig felt his tense face muscles relax a little; for the first time, the creases in his forehead eased as he found comfort in the alfather's words. But he wasn't convinced that everything Odin had to say could be trusted; Odin's mind seemed to waver between lucid and confused.

"Thorfinn, Freydis drugged our mead and she, along with her men, walked through our camp as easily as you and I are walking now," Tostig said. "They slit the throat of every man and woman—thirty-two people, dead . . . her own people," Tostig managed to say. His voice cracked as he recalled the horrifying devastation of human life.

"Half of my group . . . dead," Thorfinn lamented, his expression shifting as he struggled to accept what Tostig was telling him.

"*Slaughtered* is more to the point," Tostig grated, forcing the sentence through his teeth. "Freydis gave us drugged mead and they were murdered while they slept—pregnant women, as well."

"It is terrible; Loki has violated one of our most basic and sacred tenets: to do no harm and to take no human life without provocation or purpose," Odin said. "Even then, rules still must be obeyed; life is far too difficult to create, only to turn around and destroy it." A tear trickled down Odin's cheek.

"Loki has no appreciation for life," he continued, "neither gods' nor human lives. To him you are all chattel, fit only for his amusement, or slaughter—again, for sport. He thinks we will not harm him or punish him for fear of prematurely initiating the twilight. But Loki doesn't understand that by interrupting events, he has in fact brought into question whether providence will dominate and the Ragnarök will go ahead as previously ordained, or if it can be stopped. That shows his ignorance and his lack of understanding; he is living only for his selfish means.

"*I will not* stand for it!" Odin banged his staff on the ground, and his voice rose. "Now that the Jötunn have control of Asgard, Loki thinks he can do whatever he likes and get away with it. I will not have a subservient being like Loki think that he has power over me because of his Jötunn ancestry."

Odin faded back into unintelligible mumbling, punctuated by exclamations of anger. He finally fell quiet, shuffling through the damp leaves on the forest floor, and the three men walked in silence behind him, each trying to digest the information. Changes were coming at them so fast that it was tiring, trying to keep up with the rapid shifts.

Tostig's mind drifted back to his waking dream that morning. As he recalled the golden-haired woman, he gasped in sudden comprehension. "The sword—the cave—these were told to me by the valkyrie, Sváfa."

Odin looked over his shoulder. The old god's grin confirmed the truth. "You were visited by King Eylimi's daughter; she told you about the swords."

Tostig nodded. "Perhaps Sváfa was told the location of the sword by one of the gods," he said, not taking his eyes off of Odin.

"I suspect she visited you in a dream state," Odin surmised.

"Yes," Tostig replied, "as I was escaping Loki."

Odin stopped and turned to look at them, brow puckered in confusion. "What has Loki done now?" He leaned forward, grasping his staff with both hands to prop himself up as he lowered his head toward the ground. "What have we become?" Odin mumbled to himself. "How can we sit in judgement when we can't even govern ourselves?"

His words trailed off to a solemn, silent part of his mind. The birds chirped; the branches overhead knocked together, clacking like hollow reeds as the wind shook the treetops. Thorfinn grabbed Odin's arm, almost pulling it away from the staff. He gently prodded the alfather forward.

"Alfather, what are the caves like?" Tostig asked after a while.

"Like everything else—twists and turns; darkness and illumination for the heart and mind," he replied.

Odin's answer confused Tostig. It was always difficult to interpret the mind of a god, even when he stood beside you. They were so self-involved and self-centred that they failed to see a reality outside of themselves, except for very brief moments when the gods' interests overlapped human matters and directly affected them. Even then, they spoke in metaphor.

Tostig sighed. Thorfinn gestured to Tostig to let the topic drop, and he readily complied.

ꕤ ꕤ

Thorfinn was thinking of Gudrid, worried about her safety. As far as Thorfinn knew, one camp may have initiated all-out war against the other. Who knew what was and wasn't possible in these chaotic and uncertain times? What other deeds was Loki responsible for initiating? How deep did he thrust his tainted stinger into the hearts of all of them?

"We can't predict the safety of anyone or anything now that the Jötunn have control over Asgard," Odin said suddenly, as if reading his thoughts. "This is Loki's desperate attempt to maintain a semblance of power here on Midgard—by coveting and acquiring objects that are magical in nature. He fears for his end—or rather, the unknown that his end entails. And like a criminal facing his executioners, he regrets his misdemeanours and longs for the chance to prolong his sad existence, to find that place within himself that doesn't shift and change. It's a fool's temptation and proof that he can't control his Jötunn side; he will not see that until he jumps out of his pond and discovers where he is and how he lives.

"It's the beginning of a new empire that will sweep Midgard. It will take you out of the Dark Age and move your people forward," Odin continued.

"Tostig will lead us?" Thorfinn asked.

"He'll begin the new age. We must stop all this chit-chat about the future and focus on the present," Odin snapped, suddenly impatient. "The future will come when it comes. We must secure our situation right now by sticking to the issues at hand."

Odin was right, Thorfinn thought. They had to live in the moment, to not only see what was happening but to be ready for future changes and deal with them. It was like fighting a hidden enemy that could strike at any moment. Thorfinn sighed. Life was changing so much and so unpredictably that the weather was easier to predict than what was happening dægur to dægur.

It was difficult to understand the gods' view of time in their realm. Perhaps they ignored it, just as humans ignored something as unseen as the air that they walked through. Since time previously had no influence over the gods, they wouldn't see it as something that affected them in any way. Perhaps time was in the moment and their experience of it was different than how humans experienced the moment, never fleeting and always present. Or all these thoughts could just be the result of the differences that they shared. Any questions would be like asking a fish about the water that he swam through.

They journeyed in silence, the mood shifting to a solemn march to an unknown place.

Thorfinn allowed the sounds of the forest to mingle with his thoughts, until he remembered the story of Loki's binding marking the beginning of Ragnarök. He wasn't sure of Loki's full involvement, but he knew that his involvement must mean something. They needed a plan to deal with this eventual circumstance.

Odin hadn't divulged the limit to Loki's power, but if he still had the ability to shape-shift, there was no telling what other abilities he possessed. "Alfather," he asked, "why does Loki still have the ability to shape-shift?"

Odin gave him a wry glance. "Yes, that would seem inconsistent with what I told you, wouldn't it. Loki is also part Jötunn, remember; it seems that his Jötunn abilities are still with him. It is hard to know hybrids' abilities; it's not always clear which side of the lineage they favour. I suspect Loki's shape-shifting abilities come from his mother Laufey's side; her very name means 'kenning,' two separate words combined to create a new meaning; it would fit with Loki's nature."

The power inherent in the gods didn't lie entirely in their lineage but also in the power of their words. Thorfinn wondered if he and the others who inhabited Midgard also possessed this ability. Could they manifest the world around them just by creating words from their thoughts? He supposed that to a certain extent, that was what they were doing as they rode over the waterways of Midgard.

The air felt heavier and Thorfinn guessed that they were getting close to the ocean. The group's mood changed once again as they felt the breeze and heard the sound of the breakers up ahead. The salt air tickled the openings of his nostrils and provided the impetus he needed to push forward. Even Odin seemed to walk on the current of the offshore wind with more vigour.

Tostig and Elsu walked ahead, stopping at the edge of the cliff to scan the rock face for a path down to the ocean. "There's a path farther down the coast, but to get to it and to return will take us much closer to miðnœtti," Tostig said as Thorfinn joined them, pointing to a faint line in the distance that marked a trail to the water. Thorfinn could barely see it but he trusted the accuracy of Tostig's eyesight. "It will be too late. The tide will have returned and the caves will be filled with water once again. We'd be trapped in there," Tostig added.

"There is a trail down the rock, here," Elsu said, pointing below them. "But the rocks are narrow and it will be dangerous for the elder."

"We have no choice—we take the direct route," Thorfinn decided, unslinging the coiled rope from his shoulder.

2

Odin stared across the ocean, reminded of the expanse of time and space that he'd crossed to be on Midgard. Despite the ease of his transportation, it was probably as hard for him as it was for the humans who travelled to Vinland from their home on Grœnlandia.

His thoughts returned to the day of his arrival and how the liquid surface felt like being mired in time. He sighed. The longer he stayed on Midgard, the slower his thoughts moved and the more effort it took to move his joints and limbs.

Odin saw it on the horizon, where the sky met the water—a wave so high that even with his one eye he saw the depth and the magnitude of it; not so much a wall as a gargantuan, rolling cloud moving toward the land, a massive avalanche of water that would reshape wherever and whatever it hit.

Pushing the water were two fleets of ships heading toward one another, the vessels carrying hundreds of thousands of fearless warriors who had been waiting a millennium to fight once more; they'd been fearless in life and were now impervious to mortal weapons in death. The famous and infamous men and women of history would be fighting alongside one another, drawing on accumulated lifetimes of knowledge and experience. A force to be reckoned with when alive, now that they were beyond the constraints of the physical world, they were indomitable.

Odin stood on the shore of Straumfjörðr, staring into the oceanic abyss . . . waiting. The Vinlanders stood behind him, also waiting, but for the slightest move from their aging leader.

If the war between the Æsir and the Vanir taught the gods anything, it was that neither side could defeat the other, which was why the war ended peacefully with an exchange of members to the other house.

Odin knew what they were up against. It was he who took the warriors' mortal talents in Valhalla and imbued them with supernatural power, to shape them into a fighting force that could defeat the armies of the Jötunn. He expected no less from the leaders of the Jötunn.

"I will make a killing force of you that will end the fighting forever, and usher in a new world where we all will taste the honey-sweet mead on our lips and feel its intoxicants pulsing through our bodies and our minds," Odin had told his warriors.

He looked and knew that he had lost his fighting force to the Jötunn, who were now the leaders of Asgard. He wondered what they'd promised the warriors—no, Odin didn't have to wonder. He knew that they'd offered control of Midgard. Riches were of no interest to spirits; that was a mortal concern. They could only have promised one thing that would interest the Jötunn—to rule over Midgard and to claim what they had created for the gods of Asgard. But it couldn't work, because the stage was being set for the final war. Just like the war between the Æsir and the Vanir, this battle would shape the post-Ragnarök world.

Odin knew what would happen if he were captured. His steadily draining powers would reduce him to a marionette for his captors, with strings reaching up as far as the halls of Valhalla. He envisioned a future of a fugitive on the run, living his days out in the nocturnal world, scurrying from cave to cave as a rat does, existing in a hidden world away from all other species of Midgard for fear of agents of the Jötunn everywhere.

He almost welcomed that change from his previous existence, a life in which he could inhale the breath of life and feel the bite of the cold wind hitting his face and smell the salt wind of the great ocean, as he did now for the first time. *Was this what it's like to be mortal?* he wondered; t*o live in a world of the senses?* Odin couldn't breathe in this reality without feeling the cold air as a wonderful and magnificent sensation, touching the inside of his nostrils and warming as he pulled it into his airways. He felt as if today was his first day of life—what a magical thing it was, to exist in a world where every moment could feel like the first one!

Odin started to question his previous existence. Was what he experienced now life? If so, what had he been experiencing before? Seeing his life in a whole new way made him uncertain of who he was before and what he was now.

The ships disappeared below the horizon line, obscured by the ethereal light. Even though it appeared to be a straight line separating the water from the sky, Odin could see the actual curvature of the phenomenon and he knew what was on the other side: the Hel fury of thousands of years of existence. But once again the blowing wind and the smell of the air released him from the burden of that thought and even the responsibility.

This has all happened before, he thought, *and it will all happen again*. The idea of eternal recurrence wasn't unfamiliar to Odin; he was the one, after all, who threw Loki's child, the great serpent Midgard, into the ocean; it encircled the world and bit into its tail, creating the ouroboros linking the beginning and the end. It was he who was responsible for creating the world as it was; Jörmungandr kept them all in time and framed the recurring events to come.

Somewhere in the cave up ahead—or perhaps below his feet—Odin saw his future and his past converging into a whirling cyclone.

The more he used his limited mortal mind, the more he wondered why he didn't design a mind that could not only imagine the world as it might be, but one that could also live in that imagined future. If only he could do it all over again . . . Perhaps he would get that chance again.

Without turning around, Odin heard Thorfinn's approach—or maybe it was the new-found sense that Odin had just experienced.

ꝏ ꝏ

"Alfather," Thorfinn said.

"Yes, Thorfinn, what is it?" the old man asked absently, his eye on the ocean.

"We've found a way into the water caverns below us. We're ready to go in. I think we'll be alright," Thorfinn assured him.

Odin turned to him. "Yes, I agree with your optimism. I've observed while walking with you that you're magical—your creativity makes you so."

Thorfinn couldn't help but smile with a sense of pride that he rarely showed. He instinctively clutched Odin's arm to lead him to the precipice overlooking the lagoon where the waters had previously covered the ocean floor and the entrances to the underwater catacombs.

He'd felt himself pulled into the role of father and caregiver to the alfather on their journey to the Fjord of Currents; it was hard to see Odin as the alfather when Thorfinn only saw a frail old man who needed constant attention, not some distant figure watching over him and his race. Thorfinn felt obligated to care for him just like he would a young child, which produced a strange duality. When he held onto Odin's frail bicep, feeling his frail bones, his sinewy muscles, and flabby, wrinkled flesh, Thorfinn realized that the god that he aspired to emulate was deteriorating just like the rest of them.

They stepped closer to the edge and Odin stopped.

"Alfather, what's the matter?" Thorfinn asked.

"Thorfinn, I cannot see," the old man stammered. "The world has turned black."

Thorfinn looked at Odin's face, confused and lost. It was as if the father-son role had flipped once again, and he was the lost child, helpless and directionless. He looked over the edge of the cliff to the sea below, wondering how he would lead a frail old man down the steep and narrow incline to the shore below. In places the rock ledge looked loose and gravelly, as if it would give way under a misplaced foot; in other places tufts of grass thrust through the rock, a dangerous obstacle for a misplaced foot that might slip or stumble over it. Without sight, there was no way the alfather could traverse the cliff.

"Alfather, I don't think you'll be able to make it down the rock face," he said. "We'll have to take you the long way around."

"But there's no time for that," Odin snapped. "We've wasted too much time already. The sun has reached undorn dagmark; we don't have much time before the waters return."

Thorfinn stared blankly, wondering what to do.

"Thorfinn, you must leave me," Odin said, interrupting Thorfinn's thoughts. "You cannot sacrifice the mission for me. I am no longer that important to the world of men. You must save yourselves—leave me here."

"No, Alfather, you're the key to all of this; we must take you."

Odin looked as if he was about to argue; then he clamped his mouth shut, almost as if he heard a voice confirming Thorfinn's truth. The old man's self-assured smile faded, replaced by a pained expression, and Thorfinn realized that the gods, too, would endure much as they came to terms with living in a permanently changed world.

And without the pantheon, with the Jötunn controlling Asgard and Midgard, who would humans look to? They'd live in an unknown world, but one that was familiar to them; one where the sun rose and set, but without an explanation, where the moon rose in the sky without a reason. Who would they turn to when they feared the world?

Thorfinn knew these were concerns that Odin could no longer attend to. They'd have to recreate their world once again, possibly finding refuge with the one god. For now, that seemed to be the only choice.

Thorfinn gently tugged Odin away from the cliff. "Where are we headed?" Odin asked in an almost childlike manner. "We're returning to the other side of this embankment," Thorfinn told him. There's a footpath that will take us down to the water. We'll have to swim and climb over the rocks to reach the sea bed below, but it will be much safer for you."

"Couldn't you lower me down to the seabed from here?" Odin suggested.

Thorfinn wasn't sure whether he was willing to risk the alfather's life, when the path on the other side of the cliff would provide a safer, though longer, route down to the sea. Once they reached sea level, it would be difficult to help the alfather over the algae-slicked rocks and through the crashing waves back to the lagoon. Odin's idea would allow them to keep to their schedule.

Once the alfather was safely down on the sand, Thorfinn and the others could walk down the path and join him.

"Alfather, I don't like either option," Thorfinn said, "but I agree with your wisdom. We'll lower you down the rock face." He removed the pack he'd been hauling up the mountain and threw the coiled rope on the ground. "Alfather, I'll tie one end around your upper chest," he said, matching actions to words.

"Thorfinn, my son," Odin whispered, beckoning with his bony finger. "I must tell you . . ." Odin paused, waiting for Thorfinn's ear to move closer to his mouth. "There's an armada of ships approaching, filled with your dead brethren. Once they reach your shores, the battle between the Æsir and the Vanir will begin. It will start with separating the allegiance of our people and then the razing of the earth. I tell you this because I do not know who are aboard those ships."

"What do you want me to do, Alfather?"

"You will know what to do," Odin said.

Thorfinn pulled his head back as he would from a lover's sour breath. He remained lost in the truth of Odin's words, struggling with frustration over the gods' seeming refusal to impart information. Was it an attempt to keep the power within a closed community? There were many stories about the selfishness of the gods and how they made decisions or acted for their self-interest and self-preservation. He felt that despite the Ragnarök, the gods still didn't want to trust humanity with certain bits of wisdom. On the other hand, he had to admit, he could also see that part of the responsibility of being all-knowing and all-seeing was making decisions over what could or should be imparted to those who experienced and lived through time.

Thorfinn himself had discovered an unfortunate side effect of knowing about the Ragnarök: his fear was giving birth to cynicism, regret, anger, and despair.

"Take the other end of the rope," Thorfinn instructed Tostig and Elsu, "and wrap it twice around that beechwood tree."

They secured what was left of the rope to themselves by wrapping it around their waists; the three men would use their weight to counterbalance the weight of the alfather.

"Alfather, before we lower you to the shore, you will need to sit down and slowly slide your body off the edge, "Thorfinn said, carefully escorting Odin to the edge of the cliff.

"Thorfinn, if you apply the confidence in your abilities that I know you have, you'll accomplish great things," Odin said as he settled carefully on the rocky precipice. "I fully put my faith in you." Then he pushed himself over the edge, taking a scatter of gravel and dirt with him. His cloak fluttered in the wind before a crosswind caught it. As he swung back and forth, the rope tightened around the tree trunk, rubbing and creaking.

"Steady . . . steady," Thorfinn called back to his men as he watched Odin dangling in mid-air, moving farther and farther away from them. "Alfather, how are you feeling?" he yelled down, the wind carrying his voice out somewhere above the ocean.

"Like a valkyrie! I can't believe that I've never flown on my own before; Sleipner will be so jealous," he yelled back with childlike glee. "Thorfinn, I can now see much more than I ever could with my own eyes."

Thorfinn couldn't contain his laughter any longer; it pushed the fear for Odin's safety out of his mind. He watched Odin spread his arms as the wind caught him and his body began spinning one way, then slowing as the rope coiled, and spinning in the opposite direction.

"Alfather, how old are you?" Thorfinn yelled, suddenly curious, amusement deepening his voice.

"I've lost track. Even if I did know, the real meaning of the number would be meaningless to you."

Thorfinn looked back at Tostig and Elsu behind him to make sure that they were alright; their faces indicated no strain from countering Odin's weight. "Alfather," he yelled, "you're almost at the bottom."

When Odin had safely reached the shore and was groping for the knot to untie it, Thorfinn yelled back to Tostig and Elsu, "Ready . . . stop." Then he peered over the cliff and shouted, "Alfather, stay where you are; we're on our way down."

When the men felt the rope slacken, they pulled it up and secured one end to the tree, knotting it securely.

"Tostig, you go first, then Elsu; I'll follow behind."

Tostig grabbed the rope and stepped onto the narrow ledge angling down the face of the cliff. He descended slowly, pausing in places to probe the ledge in front of him with a foot before putting his weight on it, and using rocks jutting out of the rock wall to get past unstable spots. Some of the rocks were close enough together that they provided what appeared to be a horizontal path across the wall. On these he carefully examined the surface of the ledge with his toes while his other foot shuffled along behind him, pivoting and bending his body as he carefully moved on the balls of his feet.

Elsu waited till Tostig was most of the way down before stepping down onto the steeply sloping ledge. Like Tostig, he carefully probed the ledges with his toes, making sure a section would hold his weight without collapsing.

Thorfinn followed close behind, holding onto the rope to steady it both for the others and for his own descent down the cliff. The wind blew across their bodies in gusts that made it difficult to maintain their balance. Suddenly Thorfinn's foot slipped out from under him; he managed to regain his balance, although he showered stones and dirt on the men below.

He paused and looked down to see where the others were. Tostig was nearing the bottom and Elsu was halfway down the cliff; their smaller sizes assisted them in scaling the wall much faster than Thorfinn, with his powerful but awkwardly inflexible frame. There were only a limited number of ways that he could twist and contort his body to safely remain on the ledge. The most comfortable position was hugging the wall, walking his hands across its rough surface, probing for a natural handhold as his feet side-shuffled along the ledge.

He realized the effort it took to maintain his balance on the narrow ledge when a bead of sweat crawled down the ridge of his nose and dripped off its end. His hands burned on the rope as he tried to control his descent. When he next looked down, he was happy to see that despite his bulk, he was catching up to Elsu, who was having problems getting to a lower ledge where the winding ledges abruptly changed into vertical steps.

Thorfinn felt a pull on the rope that almost tugged it from his grip. He heard a yell below him and looked in time to see a moccasin tumbling through the air; Elsu's legs dangled in mid-air and his body swung slowly from side to side in the ocean breeze. Both his hands grasped the rope, and his upturned face was red with effort as his body slid jerkily down the rope.

"I'm losing my grip!" Elsu yelled, the wind carrying his desperate words up to Thorfinn.

"Elsu, hang on—I'm coming!" Thorfinn yelled.

Without thinking, Thorfinn stepped from one rock to the next, quickening his descent, until he finally landed on the ledge just above Elsu's dangling body. "Can you reach up and grab my hand?" Thorfinn yelled down, extending his hand toward the native, who swung in wider and wider arcs.

"Yes," Elsu grunted. He tried to swing his body, closing the gap between Thorfinn and himself.

Thorfinn grabbed Elsu's arm when it came within reach and pulled the smaller man up to him. He struggled to balance on the ledge that accommodated only his toes. With the rope wrapped around his wrist and using a jutting rock as a handhold, Thorfinn held onto Elsu while he scrambled to get a foothold.

As Elsu struggled to regain the ledge, Thorfinn felt the rope slacken—the knot holding it around the tree was loosening! "Elsu!" Thorfinn shouted.

"I know—I felt it too."

Their cautious and measured descent now became a reckless race to the ground as the other end of the rope continued to slip. Thorfinn looked down to make sure that if the rope gave out, he wouldn't hit Elsu on the way down.

The rope jerked as the knot slipped again. Thorfinn looked down to the shore, gauging if he could safely jump and land on the soggy sand without breaking any bones. He decided to risk the jump rather than fall uncontrollably and risk a fatal injury when the rope gave way. Pushing himself away from the wall, he let go of the rope and leaped out into the air, head down and knees flexed, ready to bend once his feet hit the soft sand. All thought ceased; all feelings froze in anticipation of what would happen when he hit the ground. The only sensation was the air rushing up from below, hitting his hands and his face, and weightlessness. He enjoyed that, and wished the feeling could last only one moment longer as he watched the ground speeding toward him.

Thorfinn landed hard, grunting as his feet sank into the wet sand up to his ankles. For a brief second he felt the force of the impact shooting up his legs to his torso, as if his insides were being pushed down to his feet; then his body rebounded off the ground and he landed on the sandy seabed with a thud.

"Thorfinn, are you hurt?" Tostig yelled, running over to him.

Thorfinn slowly pushed himself up, feeling as if he were mired in the sand. He looked down at his feet and rotated his ankle, grimacing through the pain, but nothing was broken.

"At least your ankle isn't broken," Tostig noted, watching it rotate. "Can you walk on it?"

"Yeah, I think so," Thorfinn replied, accepting Tostig and Elsu's hands to be heaved to his feet.

Balancing on one foot, suffering only minor pain in that leg, he slowly applied weight to his injured foot. "Put me back on the ground," Thorfinn barked as pain shot through his injured foot. They settled him back on the ground.

Thorfinn looked toward the cave entrances. "Tostig, did you see the alfather when you touched down?"

"As a matter of fact, I didn't," he replied, frowning. "I was too focused on you."

"He may have wandered into the cave. Could you check?" Thorfinn asked Tostig.

Tostig nodded and ran toward the cave, yelling, "Alfather."

Thorfinn sat looking at the wall of cave openings; some were the size of a doorway but most were too small for a full-grown man. Green ooze leaked out of some of the entrances, staining the chalky white rock wall below their threshold. *I wonder how we'll find Barnstokkr before undorn,* he thought. The day was getting away from them and the ocean was moving into the lagoon. The wall of water heading toward them would push more water into the tunnels and fill up the network of caves much more rapidly, destroying any chance for them to get out alive and save their people.

Thorfinn and Elsu sat on the sand waiting for a sign of Tostig or Odin; when none came, Thorfinn decided to struggle to his feet and follow them, despite his pain. Elsu picked up their gear and helped Thorfinn to his feet. Thorfinn leaned on him, limping toward the cave entrance.

They stepped into the cave and were hit by the stench of rotting seaweed and decaying fish that was so potent, it was like walking into a wall. Green slime oozed from crevices in the walls. Thorfinn used his sleeve to cover his mouth and nose so he wouldn't throw up.

Soft light found its way through openings higher up on the rock face to filter down into the cave, highlighting the dark gaps of human-sized cracks in the rock walls; Thorfinn wondered if some might be entrances to tunnels leading to other parts of the underground network. The floor was covered with sodden sea plants.

"Tostig," Thorfinn yelled, his voice echoing.

"I'm over here," the navigator replied, stepping into the light. "I couldn't find the alfather. I think we'll need some light."

Elsu ran back outside and returned with a long piece of driftwood to use as a torch. Tostig reached into his sack and produced a tar-soaked rag and two flints. While Elsu wrapped the rag around the wood, Tostig struck the two rocks together until a big enough spark jumped onto the rag. His gentle breaths coaxed the ember smouldering on the rag into an orange flame that engulfed the end of the torch. He leaned back, saying, "This should burn long enough."

"If we're still in here when the flame goes out, I don't think it will matter. We won't be coming out alive," Thorfinn said.

Tostig passed the torch to Thorfinn and they cautiously made their way farther into the cave, the torch pushing the darkness deeper and deeper back with each step they took. The firelight glistened on the slimy walls, turning the interior of the cave into an abstract depiction of the starry heavens moving around them; Thorfinn felt as if they were stepping across a star-filled sky.

"Where could Odin have walked off to?" Thorfinn asked, looking around. "He's blind."

Tostig bent closer to the ground, then beckoned Thorfinn over. In the thin layer of moisture and congealed ocean detritus, he noticed a scuffed set of footprints, as if left by someone whose gait was unsteady, shuffling across the cave floor.

Thorfinn followed the footprints until the cave branched off into three different directions. The floor here was free of detritus and anything that might hold tracks. As Thorfinn gazed at the three possible paths, his imagination jumped and leaped; which path had the alfather taken?

"We could split up," Tostig suggested.

"No, I lack your and Elsu's tracking skills. Remember what

the elves said in Myrkwood: *When all is dark, there will be three that will see.*"

As they contemplated the three passages before them, Thorfinn thought of the nearly forgotten journey through Myrkwood Forest. Suddenly an enigmatic phrase had become a meaningful and relevant statement.

Tostig lowered himself to the rock floor and examined it, crawling on his hands and knees. Then he looked up. "Thorfinn, I think the alfather headed in this direction." He pointed at the centre tunnel. "Odin's steps disappear through this entrance."

"Thank the gods for your tracking skills, Tostig," Thorfinn said, relieved. Holding the torch before him, he cautiously entered the centre tunnel. Its floor sloped downward to a sharp turn at the bottom. Somewhere beyond their sight, a low and constant rumble echoed off the walls.

Thorfinn reminded himself that the caves were truly water caves. Somewhere within the network of tunnels, there must be rivers of water flowing, fed by water from surface pools and waterways that seeped through cracks into a natural aqueduct system that likely stretched into the interior of Hóp.

He stepped carefully onto the slick slope, relegating the low rumble to the back of his mind to merge with his other thoughts. Here, too, the tunnel walls glistened and sparkled as the flame hovered over them. Thorfinn treated the glass-like surface of the floor as he would a gleaming lake of ice.

"I will show you a gait that my people perfected when chasing caribou onto a frozen lake," Elsu said, moving forward to demonstrate a simple yet effective way to walk across the slippery floor. Thorfinn and Tostig imitated him, and soon they were moving with less risk of their feet slipping out from under them.

Thorfinn noticed a waterline running along the tunnel wall just above his head. His hand moved along the wall, feeling where the water had polished the jagged rock to a smooth surface, rounding sharp edges and giving the cave an almost organic atmosphere; Thorfinn felt as if he travelled through a birth canal, and thought of Gudrid, hoping she was safe. He missed Iceland and couldn't wait for Gudrid to travel home with him to see the land of simmering volcanoes and glaciers. A land that inspired stories of gods in the country's great skalds, who translated the land's passion into word and song.

Most importantly, Thorfinn wanted his son to grow up in that land, to take over his business and carry on the family name and the family influence, but also to grow and prosper and make his own mark in the world, and help shape it for future generations of Karlsefnis.

He saw a flickering light up ahead, its dancing casting elongated shadows across the uneven surface of the cave wall. Was it the alfather? Thorfinn was still perplexed, wondering how Odin could have gotten this deep into the cave system without the use of his eyes. Why had he left them to travel on his own?

As they drew closer to what Thorfinn realized was a lit chamber, the shadows moved up their legs and fell across their chests. He rounded the corner and stopped, Elsu and Tostig peering around his large frame at the many torches pushed into cracks all around the chamber walls.

"How can this be?" Tostig asked. "These passages are normally filled with water. Who lit the torches?"

"Spirits . . . perhaps," Thorfinn answered, gazing at the ceiling of the chamber.

"Or perhaps humans," Elsu said. "I've heard of ancient tribes who lived in these caves after their cities were destroyed and they abandoned living on the surface. It is said that they still worship here and care for the caves, awaiting the return of the Owners. No one has seen them; nor do we understand them. They live in the darkness and are not part of the world of light."

Maybe the dark elves, Thorfinn thought.

"Maybe not all the tunnels fill with water," Tostig suggested.

Thorfinn looked at the walls of the chamber and noticed that it had five sides. The room itself was in the shape of a pentacle and three of the five vertices had a flaming torch stuck into a crack in the wall. There were four other openings besides the one they stood in. At the centre of the room, a massive white limestone rock had been carved into the shape of a mushroom; its surface etching had been worn by centuries of water smoothing across the design, but it was unmistakably a pentagram. Thorfinn dragged his hand across the tabletop's surface as he passed; it was as smooth as polished marble.

They stopped for a moment and looked at one another, each

waiting for the other to recommend a new direction.

Tostig moved away, peering intently at the mucky floor. “There are footprints,” he murmured, “but not the prints of the alfather . . .” He stopped and turned. “Thorfinn, the alfather’s trail ends here.”

Elsu looked from him to Thorfinn. “Which way? We have four openings in front of us.”

Tostig shrugged, also watching Thorfinn for a decision. “It seems to be a gamble.”

Thorfinn felt their stares as he studied the openings. “Maybe the question is not which doorway the alfather might take, but which doorway might a blind man take?” He had to believe that not only did the alfather know where he was going, but he wanted them to follow him. Yet, Thorfinn saw no clues. Why hadn’t Odin waited for them so they could all go together?

The maze Thorfinn’s indecision was creating in his mind seemed harder to navigate than the maze-like network of the cave system. The only way to shatter the walls of the maze within his mind was to take action. “I think Odin wanted to be followed,” he stated, moving forward to examine the walls of the chamber.

There were torches between three of the four openings; there was a hole in the rock where one should have been beside the third opening and, when Thorfinn turned around, one missing torch next to the opening they’d used to enter the chamber. “We go this way,” Thorfinn said, pointing to the third opening.

“What makes you think Odin meant for us to go through the third opening?” Tostig asked.

“I’m assuming that Odin wouldn’t have wandered off unless he knows where he’s going, and that he’s trying to lead us through the network of caves and chambers; there are two empty places where a torch should go. Since each torch doesn’t correspond to a door in any way, I take that as meaning we should take the third opening.”

“What if one absent torch meant to go through the first entry?” Tostig asked.

“A lit torch is a beacon; it must indicate the direction to head to and not the other way around. Removing one torch to indicate the direction wouldn’t be in Odin’s nature,” Thorfinn answered.

“I agree with Thorfinn,” Elsu interjected. “Gods direct us by signs, not by the lack of them."

"I see your point now," Tostig answered, smiling.

They now had an idea of what to look for as they travelled through the tunnels, and felt a little less lost than when they'd entered the cave system. Thorfinn felt confident that they were headed in the right direction, although he wondered if events were happening in accordance with some divine plan, or if their course was charted with a beginning and an end, but no established route between the two points, similar to the journey from birth and death.

"How is your foot, Thorfinn?" Elsu asked.

"It hurts a little less than it did," Thorfinn replied. "I'm trying not to think about it." He paused. "Elsu, I didn't ask you, but why did you want to accompany us on this trip? We don't plan on returning to Vinland."

"I know. Since losing my wife, I have not felt a part of my tribe; there isn't a place for me within that group anymore. I want to leave all of that behind and start new someplace else."

"Is that why you came empty-handed?" Thorfinn asked.

Elsu smiled gently. "Our people are so different. We don't carry our world with us because our world is all around us. We do not live in two separate worlds—indoor and outdoor. It's all one and the same."

Thorfinn understood the wisdom of Elsu's philosophy. He noticed that his people did have a mentality that distanced them from the natural world. In fact, they sought to tame the natural world and alter it for their use, rather than Elsu's peaceful coexistence with the natural world. They were a part of it and followed its rules, not forcing themselves upon it, but merging with it.

Of course, the Norse people wouldn't go back to that way of living; it was counter to what they valued as growth and advancement, both culturally and commercially. But could there not be a meeting somewhere along that scale, a balance somewhere between the two extremes that would benefit his people? It would be a forced change, though. His people created their world—that was what came when a higher self was needed to communicate with the pantheon of gods.

Thorfinn had always maintained that his people had something to learn from every person and country they encountered. He liked to keep an open mind and welcome alternate ways of doing things. He felt that this openness was the basis for his success as a merchant and explorer. Conquering was easier than diplomacy, though, and it was why the Viking era began. It was easier for them to steal from undefended settlements and monasteries rather than work for themselves, but it came with higher costs. This was not a sustainable way for his people to grow and prosper. Conquest took its own toll; not only did it destroy lives, it also created two separate sides: the aggressors and the victims. Their growth and prosperity depended on alliances and harmony for both sides, for all involved. Conflict was an unfortunate occupational hazard and not an end in itself.

Tostig, leading the way, slowed as the torchlight revealed that the tunnel narrowed to a large crack in the wall up ahead. He glanced back at Thorfinn, who knew what he was thinking: he and Elsu could squeeze through it, could Thorfinn? Thorfinn studied the gap as Tostig stuck his head through the opening.

Thorfinn moved forward to thrust the torch through so Tostig could see, but stumbled as the ground suddenly shook beneath their feet.

"What was that?" Elsu gasped when it had stilled.

Tostig yanked his head back from the opening and looked around wildly. "Is that Nidhogg chewing on the roots of Yggdrasil?"

Thorfinn nodded, almost afraid to answer.

Tostig waved his hand toward Thorfinn. "Pass me the torch."

Thorfinn complied and the smaller man passed the torch through the crack, then pushed his body through. Thorfinn peered through the opening behind him. He heard the dripping of condensation, saw sheets of it glittering in the torchlight as it trickled down the wall from the ceiling, feeding a pool of water in the centre of the chamber. The torch sizzled as drops of water landed on it. Tostig turned inside the chamber and the torch illuminated a dim submarine light rising from the pool to fill the chamber with a ghostly aquamarine glow.

"This may be a dead end," Tostig called back. "I don't see another tunnel connected to this chamber."

Thorfinn pulled back and turned to look back along the tunnel they'd travelled through, wondering if he'd misinterpreted their direction back at the pentagonal junction. But no; his decision felt right.

"It looks like there is a tunnel through the pool," Tostig called, drawing Thorfinn's gaze back to the crack. Tostig was standing beside the pool, torch held high, peering into the water. "I could swim through it to see where the cave ends up."

Elsu stepped past Thorfinn, traversed the crack, and took the torch from Tostig, holding it up while the dwarf removed some of his clothing and equipment.

"Tostig," Thorfinn yelled through the opening, "Don't go too far into the tunnel and run out of air before you can get back to us; you don't know where the tunnel ends."

Frustrated that he had to act the spectator, Thorfinn squeezed his large frame into the crack, contorting his body in an attempt to fit through. He managed to get his upper body through along with one leg, then he had to stop and rest. Finally, using his hands and arms as leverage, he pushed the rest of his body in, managing to slip past the jagged edge of the opening without injuring himself. With one last, bone-popping push, Thorfinn managed to pull himself through the crack to stumble out the other side.

Tostig was pulling a rope from his pack. He tied one end around his waist and handed the other end to Thorfinn and Elsu. "Two tugs on the rope mean to pull me back," Tostig instructed. Then he turned and waded knee-deep into the pool, shuddering as the frigid water touched his skin.

He stopped at the centre of the small pool and drew a couple of deep breaths, slowly exhaling each to prepare his lungs. Holding his third inhalation, Tostig dove, disappearing below the glassy translucence of the blue pool.

Thorfinn and Elsu fell to their knees and watched Tostig kicking his feet, moving into the tunnel. He used the walls to push himself farther and farther away from them, until he was obscured by depth. They continued to slowly feed him rope, waiting silently for the slightest tug on the lifeline that would signal them to pull him back.

Only the distant rush of water and the drip of the condensation hitting the still surface of the pool measured the minutes as they waited for something to happen. Thorfinn didn't know what was worse, the waiting itself or the tricks that his mind played on his consciousness as he waited; his mind wandered to problems to solve and emergencies to attend to, the thoughts knotting his shoulders with tension. Each emergency dissipated into nothingness, but then reshaped itself into something else. Flashes of light and shadow from the torchlight on the pool also diverted his attention away from Tostig's lifeline.

So when Thorfinn looked down and noticed that the rope, Tostig's lifeline, had gone limp, he looked wide-eyed at Elsu, then at the rope floating on the surface of the pool, and began pulling the rope toward him, hand over hand, as fast as he could.

"Thorfinn," Elsu yelled. "There's no drag on the rope. I don't think Tostig is still—"

As the other end of the rope whipped through the air, spraying water over them, Thorfinn's internal world became a sad reality—his navigator and friend was gone.

Thorfinn quickly pushed the contents inside his knapsack down, compressing them as tightly as possible. He extinguished the torch in the water and tied it around his waist, hoping that the flint and the tar-soaked cloths he carried would remain dry during the journey through the tunnel, and that he'd be able to light the torch once he was on the other side. Then he prepared his lungs with a few inhales and exhales and, with his cheeks full of air, he slipped into the water and pushed himself toward the underwater cave.

Elsu dove into the pool a few seconds after Thorfinn, giving Thorfinn enough of a lead that he wouldn't be blocked from reaching the surface if he ran out of air.

Kicking through the murky water, Thorfinn entered the tunnel, grabbing onto jutting rocks to help propel him along. His chest tightened, fighting for air; his heart pounded harder as it tried to extract oxygen from his lungs to feed his blood, and his muscles became sluggish. A warm current flowed across his body. Then the dim light in the tunnel brightened, and Thorfinn hoped it was a sign that he was reaching the other end.

There was a hazy, dark mass in the water up ahead. Thorfinn squinted, struggling to identify it; it didn't appear to be moving.

He emerged from the tunnel, pushing off from its bottom with his feet and kicking upward. He broke the surface of the pool like a whale breaching in the ocean, sucking in a great lungful of air, and whipping his head around to drive the water and hair from his eyes. Then he took his first look around this new cavern.

The chamber that he surfaced in was darker and slightly larger than the one he had left. He heard the sound of a waterfall in the distance, the rush of water much louder than before.

Thorfinn spun his body around and saw Tostig tottering out of the water onto a sandy beach. The dwarf collapsed to his knees, then toppled forward to lie on the sand. Elsu surfaced seconds later.

"Tostig, are you alright?" Thorfinn yelled, feeling a surge of panic.

Without moving his body, Tostig raised his thumb up in the air, his torso heaving as he caught his breath.

Thorfinn swam toward Tostig till he felt the pool floor sloping upward beneath him. He stood and waded toward the shore, holding his backpack above his head. Water poured out a hole in the bottom. He felt the weight of his water-soaked clothes as the water level fell around him.

"I don't know about either of you, but I'm not convinced that this is the route that Odin took," Thorfinn said as he reached the shore.

"I was thinking about that too," Tostig commented, sitting up. "He must've taken a different route. He couldn't have swum through that tunnel." He looked at Thorfinn. "Where are we headed?"

Thorfinn drew a breath and looked around for inspiration. All he saw was the waterfall in the distance.

"I think a good question to ask isn't whether Odin headed in this direction, but whether we should head in this direction," Elsu suggested.

Thorfinn unfolded his knapsack and rooted through it for the rags and the flints to light them, exhaling in relief to find that the water hadn't penetrated to those. After wrapping the rags around the piece of driftwood he'd carried through the water with him, he struck the flints against one another and in seconds the tar-soaked cloth burst into flames. The wet driftwood crackled and spat as the flame grew in strength, engulfing the end of the torch. He raised the torch into the air. It illuminated a faint rainbow arching over the waterfall, disappearing behind the wall of falling water.

"Is that bifrost?" Tostig asked, looking at the multicoloured lights in wonder.

"It could be," Thorfinn answered.

"What is bifrost?" Elsu asked.

"It's a bridge that connects Midgard to Asgard," Thorfinn told him.

"Yes, and it will break when the sons of Muspel—the fire demons—ride over it," Tostig added.

"That mustn't have happened yet, because the bridge is still intact," Thorfinn said.

They headed toward the waterfall. Thorfinn noticed a narrow ledge protruding from the rock wall behind the falling water. Holding the torch before him, he led the others along it. The curtain of water roared over the rocks above them to crash into the pool of water below. The torch blew in the shifting eddies, but didn't go out. Thorfinn stopped, noticing movement up ahead, and indicated what he'd seen by pointing the torch toward it.

A frail hand reached around the rock wall, probing it. As Thorfinn saw more and more of the arm, it looked less and less threatening. He relaxed and walked over to the drenched and shivering alfather.

"Thorfinn, is that you?" Odin asked.

"Yes, Alfather, Thorfinn replied. "How did you get this far?"

"I got through the tunnel before the tide moved in; I must've got turned around. I'm so glad to find you. Tostig, are you still with us?" Odin called out.

"Yes I am, Alfather; it's nice to see you again."

"I wish I could say the same, but until I get my sight back I can't see any of you. Enough chit-chat; there is a doorway that I can't get through that I need your help with—come."

Thorfinn, Tostig, and Elsu followed Odin through a crack in the wall ahead to a stone staircase that descended into darkness. Holding the torch high, Thorfinn stepped onto the first step with trepidation; though it was chiselled from the same rock as the wall, he noticed in the torchlight that the steps were crumbled in places, and some looked ready to collapse, or were worn down by either the flow of water over time or decades of foot traffic; some of the treads were so worn away that he had to step sideways so his foot remained on them.

They descended carefully. "I hear scuffling somewhere down there," Thorfinn whispered at one point, not able to see beyond the light of the torch.

They finally reached another level of the cave system. In front of them was a slab of rock. "I can't get through this door," Odin said, lifting a hand to indicate the slab.

Tostig leaned over. "There's a hole—a vent, perhaps—at the bottom of the door. Or maybe drainage—it looks like water flows through it. I can fit through it." He dropped to his stomach and Thorfinn passed the torch to him. Thrusting it before him, Tostig squirmed through the hole.

"What's in there?" Thorfinn yelled through the hole.

There was silence for a moment, then, "Stand away from the door," Tostig yelled.

There was a loud creak as they backed up, as if a stiff lever were being pushed. Then the door itself creaked and fell forward with an earth-shuddering bang. When the dust cleared, Tostig was standing on the other side of the threshold. "The door was built to open from the inside," he said as he pulled his hand away from a wooden lever jutting from the wall. Behind him, a corridor sloped downward.

They silently walked down the tunnel. There were more noises up ahead, but nothing recognizable. Thorfinn's imagination kept him focused on the dim light at the end of the tunnel. "Alfather, do you know what that is?" he asked as they moved toward it. When he got no answer, he stopped and turned around. "Where did Odin go?" he asked, noticing for the first time that the alfather wasn't with them.

"I don't know," Elsu said from the rear. "I thought he was up there with you."

"Odin!" Thorfinn yelled, his voice echoing along the tunnel. "Why does he keep doing this?" he muttered in frustration.

After a moment Thorfinn turned and they continued their journey, arriving at the arched opening to another cavern. They stopped in the entrance, gazing in awe at the trunk of the great tree, Yggdrasil. Its massive root system covered the cavern floor, great roots pushing through cracks in the rock, smaller branchings weakening the floor in their persistence to spread. Yggdrasil's massive trunk rose up into an opening in the ceiling.

Thorfinn slowly stepped toward the sacred tree, unable to take his eyes from it. He could scarcely believe that he was actually seeing the tree that was responsible for their existence, the tree that gave him and the rest of the nine worlds life. He stopped before it and reverently reached out to press his palm against the rough bark, expecting to feel some sort of sensation. All he felt was the rough surface of the trunk. Nevertheless, it was still a thrill to be able to touch an object that his people held as sacred as the Christians regarded the crucifix.

As he stood there, Thorfinn felt a strange sensation, something that didn't feel quite right. He looked at Elsu and Tostig, wondering if they could see or feel it as well. They returned his stare with silent confusion.

Curious, Thorfinn walked around to the other side of the tree, and saw what could only have been the cause of the disturbance he sensed: a sword—the Gram—stuck in the side of Yggdrasil. Its hilt glistened in the torchlight. "This is it," he murmured, walking around it but hesitating to touch its hilt.

Tostig and Elsu had followed him. "What should I do?" Tostig asked nervously.

"You're the bearer of the sword," Thorfinn answered. "You should pull it out."

Tostig raised his hand, but hesitated before grasping the hilt. "Thorfinn, I don't know if I can do this," he said, retracting his hand.

"Why not?"

"I don't know; I'm not ready. I feel like things are moving too fast—my future is moving too fast. In a blink of an eye, it's here. How did we all get here so fast?"

Thorfinn offered a rueful smile. "If I knew the answer to that, I wouldn't be standing here talking to you right now."

"You're not alone, Tostig," Elsu said. "We're here with you."

Tostig managed a smile and looked back at the hilt. He wrapped his fingers around it and pulled. Nothing. "It's not moving," Tostig said.

"What?" Thorfinn replied, confused. "That's impossible. Try again."

Tostig pulled harder and the sword began to slide out of the tree. As he prepared to use his body weight to heave the sword out of the tree, they heard a sound coming from farther around the trunk; as they listened, it suddenly changed to a baby's cries.

Elsu and Thorfinn looked at one another. Then Thorfinn dashed toward the sound, and carefully scooped up the bundle he found at the base of the tree. He returned to the others, hardly daring to breathe. He needed confirmation; he didn't dare to hope without confirmation.

"It's my son?" he questioned as Tostig reached up and pulled the swaddling blankets aside. "This is my son?"

As Tostig removed the final layer of cloth, Thorfinn looked down and momentarily forgot to breathe. He was staring into his son's eyes for the first time. The rest of the world stopped as Thorfinn was pulled into the face of his son—Snorri's ocean-blue eyes framed by golden blonde curls. Snorri looked at Thorfinn and gurgled, as if he knew that he looked into the face of his father. Thorfinn stroked Snorri's porcelain-white cheek with his grimy finger, unable to express in thought or words what he felt in that moment.

"You're my son," Thorfinn finally said.

He looked up. "Tostig, pull out the sword so we can finish our job and leave Hóp."

Tostig grabbed the hilt, braced his foot against the trunk, and with one final pull, pulled on the sword with all of his strength. As Gram's blade came free, the trunk trembled. Then the ground, the entire cavern, violently shook.

As dirt and stones fell from the ceiling, Thorfinn clutched Snorri against his chest and ran toward the cave wall with Tostig and Elsu on his heels, all fearing that the ceiling would collapse on top of them. The safety of the wall proved false, however; a torrent of water burst through the cave wall behind them to rush into the cavern, the force of the deluge widening the opening until the torrent threw Elsu off balance, and pulled Snorri from Thorfinn's arms as he was caught in the onslaught of water.

"Thorfinn!" Elsu screamed over the roar of the water, reaching out to Thorfinn as he was pulled away by the current. Thorfinn jumped into the current to rescue his son and watched in anguish as his friend disappeared into the swirling funnel of water, tortured by the choice to save his son instead of his friend.

The rapidly flowing water picked up rocks in its path and forced them through the opening into the cavern. Dodging and ducking them, Thorfinn and Elsu waded through the shifting currents and the continually deepening water swirling around them.

"Where's Elsu?" Tostig yelled, clutching a boulder as he frantically looked around for the native.

Thorfinn's eyes fell on a growing whirlpool on the other side of the cavern. The water had risen above Thorfinn's chest; he felt its drag on his body, and he fought the current flowing into the whirlpool. "Where he wanted to be—with his wife," Thorfinn yelled, unsure if Tostig heard him over the rush of the water.

Thorfinn spotted Snorri, still wrapped in the blankets, wedged between two boulders and threatened by the rising water. He reached over, struggling not to be pulled into the whirlpool as well, as his feet left the cavern floor in the rising water.

"Hand Snorri to me," Tostig yelled from atop a chunk of rock that the rushing torrent had pushed into the chamber. He lay across the top of the boulder and reached out with one arm to grab the baby.

Thorfinn raised the wet bundle, but it went limp, only a wad of blankets pulled down by the weight of the water. In rising panic, Thorfinn looked frantically around him, looking for any sign of Snorri floating in the shifting eddies. Seeing nothing, he dove beneath the surface. Moments later he surfaced, yelling, "Tostig, I can't find him! Do you see Snorri from where you are?"

"No," Tostig shouted, desperation tightening his voice.

The current ebbed and churned, flowing around rocks and boulders and them, dragging anything in its path toward the whirlpool. Tostig and Thorfinn waded through the water to separate ends of the cavern, desperately looking for a pale object bobbing in the water.

Gradually the flow of water tapered off, and that in the cavern drained through the hole in the floor beneath the whirlpool faster than it was pouring into the cavern—Thorfinn could see it as the water level dropped below his knees.

"Thorfinn," Tostig yelled, pointing to some rocks. They stared for a moment in speechless horror at two small, limp legs jutting out from behind the jumble.

Thorfinn ran through the water, tripping and stumbling in his desperation to get to his son. He reached out for the limp body, hoping that he wasn't too late, that he could somehow save him. But as his hand grabbed Snorri's ankle, the white skin disintegrated into black soot that, as if carried by an unfelt wind, blew into the air in swirls of black smoke. Thorfinn watched in confusion as the plumes spread above his head, then drifted apart into nothingness.

Thorfinn looked up in terrified confusion, then collapsed to his knees and rolled over onto his back, screaming as loud as he could, trying to push the pain and anger out of his chest. He wished that he'd been swept away by the water, rather than having to live with losing his son a second time.

He didn't know how long he lay in the puddle of water, his beard plastered across his face like a mask, staring toward the cavern ceiling with empty eyes as his mind replayed again and again the vision of Snorri disappearing into the air. He lay on the cave floor wishing that the water would rush over him and drown him—better to die than live with the pain of Snorri dying, again. He didn't want to move; he didn't want to have to stand up and return to living.

He heard a drone in the distance that slowly changed to the sound of a voice, vanishing and returning as water tickled into his ears, and Thorfinn realized that his head lay half submerged in a puddle. He lifted it, and heard a voice calling his name.

Thorfinn turned his head and saw Tostig standing behind him. "Did you call me, Tostig?"

"No."

Thorfinn, can you hear me? the voice asked.

"Yes, I can hear you. Who are you?" Thorfinn replied, unable to tell whether the voice was male or female.

Bring me the Gram and I will give you the child.

"Tostig, did you hear the voice?" Thorfinn asked, his tone desperate.

Bring me the Gram and I will give you the child, the voice repeated, and Thorfinn swore that it echoed through the cavern as if carried on the wind.

"The voice wants me to give it the sword," Thorfinn said. "In return it will give me Snorri. Give me the sword, Tostig."

"No, Thorfinn; it's Loki. Remember what Odin told us."

Thorfinn didn't care if Tostig was right; his only concern was to get his son back by whatever means necessary. "Tostig, give me the sword," he ordered, reaching toward Tostig.

Tostig shook his head and instinctively turned aside, guarding the Gram with his body.

"Tostig, I must have the sword," Thorfinn said, standing up and tramping through the puddles toward his navigator, his boots sloshing through the water.

Tostig turned his head as another voice echoed somewhere in the cave: " . . . him the sword . . ."

"Did you hear that, Thorfinn? It sounds like the alfather; he's trying to speak to us."

Thorfinn peered at Tostig with desperate eyes, his hands outstretched to grab the sword from Tostig's hand.

"…give him the sword," the disembodied voice repeated.

Tostig stopped backing away, as if the voice lured him into a trance, controlling him with the sound of the words. "Thorfinn, please don't make me give the Gram to you," he pleaded.

"I want my son back," Thorfinn said, stalking Tostig like a wolf moving on his prey.

"Tostig, don't give him the sword," the voice said.

Tostig, about to surrender the sword, pulled it toward him and backed away.

Thorfinn loomed over Tostig. He reached out to grab the blade.

"Stop," a voice bellowed from the cave entrance above them. They looked up to see Odin standing in the doorway. "Loki, if I throw Gungnir, it will pierce through you and kill you. Leave his body."

"You will kill this mortal as well," the voice replied through Thorfinn's mouth.

"That is the price that I'm willing to pay to stop you; are you willing to take that as payment?"

Thorfinn felt his lip curl in a sneer. "You're blind, old man."

"Are you stupid?" Odin replied. "Gungnir will not miss; it will find its intended target and kill you." Odin raised his spear into the air, ready to hurl it.

The cavern shook with an ear-piercing scream; black smoke

appeared above Thorfinn's body and dissipated into the air above him.

"Tostig," Odin yelled. "Quickly—descend into the hole before Loki returns." He pointed to the hole created when the floor collapsed. "I'll take Thorfinn back to the surface."

ꙮ ꙮ

A wall of water pushed its way toward Hóp, so high and so wide that the wave brushed the sky, almost pushing the churning clouds with it as it headed toward the coast. As the survivors of the massacre gathered as much as they could, Gudrid decided to stay close to Freydis to make sure that she and Thorvald didn't escape in the chaos.

The Vinlanders were trying to take most of their personal effects, objects they wanted to take home with them. Gudrid feared that the number of items would weigh them down too much to outrun the water. Several people were wasting time negotiating with one another, seeking help in carrying what they couldn't.

"We have to leave," she shouted, eyeing the wave moving closer and closer. The roar of the water was deafening, and the ground began to shake—Gudrid wasn't sure if it was caused by the rumbling of the water or if the ground actually quaked.

Snorri ran up to her. "I was only able to secure *Mimir II* to the shore. We moved it as far as we could into a cove. We may have to make some repairs, but it should remain intact."

"Okay, let's get Freydis and Thorvald to safety," Gudrid ordered.

Snorri nodded and untied the ropes binding them to the tree. The ground shook once again, and the ground cracked and heaved. The large ash tree that held Freydis and Thorvald tilted as the shifting ground pushed up its root system; each successive tremor pushed the tree farther aslant. Thorvald took the opportunity to fight free of his captors. Snorri struggled to maintain a hold on him, as Thorvald swung his bound hands, attempting to hit Snorri.

Another tremor rocked the ground. Thorvald maintained his balance and quickly looped the rope around Snorri's neck, then tightened the loop and pulled with all his strength. Mouth gaping as he sought air, Snorri clutched at the rope around his throat, trying unsuccessfully to dig his fingers underneath to pull it away. As his eyelids fluttered and his knees buckled, Thorvald managed to twist his hands free as their struggling loosened the knot binding his wrists. He grabbed the rope and threw it over one of the limbs of the tipping tree, then pulled, further tightening the rope around Snorri's neck. As Snorri collapsed, struggling for breath, Thorvald fled.

As the guards looked from their fleeing prisoner to Snorri, trying to choose whether to save Snorri or recapture Thorvald, Gudrid ran forward and pulled at the rope around Snorri's neck. The movement freed the guards from their indecision and they dashed over and struggled to hold the other end of the rope that had become tangled in the tree branches, trying to prevent it from being pulled any tighter as the tree continued to tip. With the help of one of the other guards, Gudrid was able to loosen the rope around Snorri's neck and pull it over his head. Snorri collapsed wheezing to the ground, his chest heaving.

They all looked to see which direction Thorvald had gone, but he was nowhere to be seen. "Never mind him," Gudrid said, answering the guards' confused stares. "We need to get to the cave."

As if punctuating her order, the wall of water hit the land, spraying rock and earth and water up into the azure heavens. Gudrid grabbed Snorri and dragged him to his feet; he stumbled after her as she pulled him up the embankment. The water rushed across the land like a deluge from a broken dyke, only briefly slowed by trees and boulders, moving undaunted across the land, ripping up all in its path.

Gudrid looked up to the cave mouth, then took one last quick look around, making sure that no one was left behind. As the onslaught of water roared behind her, she plunged into the safety of the cave. Then she turned, and saw the water being diverted into a valley by the curvature of the land. They were safe for the moment. She sighed, thinking of Thorfinn, hoping that he was safe.

1

Tostig descended down the tunnel beneath the great tree, pushing aside the fibrous mats of roots that hung in his way. The Gram's hilt didn't seem to fit in his hand. It was too big and felt a little off-balance—and the responsibility was too large. Tostig feared that, with the first lunge at Nidhogg, the sword would fly out of his hand.

The encounter with Loki had left him a little shattered and scared. He stepped cautiously around curves, his eyes scanning all directions as he crept farther into the tunnel through the root system of Yggdrasil. He sensed that he descended into another realm beyond Midgard; perhaps he travelled through another part of his home that he knew nothing about. He could be in Ginnungagap, the place where everything began.

He felt the tree quivering as life pulsed through it, trying to counteract Nidhogg's attack on its roots. With each shake, Tostig steadied himself with a hand on the wall. The tunnel narrowed and he climbed over a mass of roots and through large gaps in the rocky floor where the roots had pushed through.

His clothes were drenched with perspiration that trickled down his skin just as condensation streamed down the walls of the tunnel. There was a heat source somewhere in the lower cave system, perhaps where Yggdrasil was getting its nourishment—it had to come from somewhere. The air was quickly becoming stifling and Tostig struggled to breathe. The farther he descended, the more suffocating the air seemed; his lungs felt as if they had shrunk until they were too small for his body. His tongue was pasted to the roof of his mouth and he longed for a drink of water, but there was a sulphurous smell coming from the water dripping down the tunnel walls that sickened Tostig and made him forget about quenching his thirst. Suddenly a whoosh of air pushed past him, blowing the dangling roots into his face and eyes. The air was hot and dry, but a welcome change from the uncomfortable humidity in the tunnel.

Each time Tostig approached another intersection in the tunnel system, he wished that Sváfa was with him to help guide him. He had nothing except himself and his faith in the power of the sword to pull him in the right direction—it quivered in his grip, guiding him into the unknown. Even Odin, without his sight, would've been a help to Tostig, whose fears made him question the power of the sword.

As Tostig descended farther and farther beneath the surface, the tree seemed more alive. It moaned each time it quivered—or was it the wind blowing through the tunnel, making strange, unearthly sounds? There were so many distractions criss-crossing in Tostig's mind that he wasn't sure what he saw and heard was real or imagined.

The tunnel levelled off. Tostig saw a red glow up ahead. He swore he could smell the acidic fumes of an active iron smelter, similar to those at Leifsbúrður. He slowed, moving with caution, the Gram held in front of him, ready.

As another tremor shook the tunnel, Tostig touched the wall to steady himself, then recoiled as a thin root pushed through a crack in the wall and touched his hand. He stared a moment, then placed his hand back on the wall and allowed the root to wrap itself around his palm; it was as if it sought another being's strength and support. He didn't feel threatened by what he could only describe as a gesture of comfort. In fact, his fear quickly transformed to sadness, and he suspected that the tree was transmitting this feeling to him via the root's touch. It was a strange sensation that started in Tostig's hand and moved to his brain, where it transformed to feelings of loss.

The feelings became nearly overwhelming and Tostig wanted to pull his hand away, but felt compelled to leave it where it was for the moment. He felt as if they were sharing their fear with one another, as if he were comforting a sick and dying family member. In a sense the great tree was part of his family—it bound all the species of the nine worlds together. As Odin had said, he and everyone else was made up of the same stuff.

The ground shook once again and the root retracted back into the crack in the rock wall. Tostig knew that, like the rest of them, the great tree was in its last days. Its foundations had become unstable and the rock walls were crumbling around him as the earth shifted and shook.

Tostig walked into a chamber containing a large well full of water that glowed azure blue. He stepped closer to the side of the well and peered into it, then stumbled backward and let the sword fall to the stone floor when a hand clutching an eye rose out of the water. As he straightened, Tostig heard a deep inhalation, then he saw Odin's head rising above the side of the well. Water had flattened his long hair and beard to his face, neck, and chest. Supporting himself on the side of the well, Odin took the eye from the hand, lifted the leather patch on his face, and put the eye back into its socket. He closed his eyelid, rubbed it, then opened it and blinked a few times.

"Oh, Tostig, it's good to see you again," Odin said with a chuckle. "I was just getting my eye back from Mimir. I'd forgotten how deep the well is." He pulled his naked body over the side of the well and dropped onto the cavern floor. Then he tiptoed over to a pile of clothes that Tostig just now noticed and started dressing. "Are you a little surprised to see me, my son?" Odin asked, interpreting Tostig's silence as uncomfortable surprise.

"A little," Tostig answered. "What are you doing here?"

"Retrieving my eye from Mimir. I exchanged it for knowledge . . . it seems like only yesterday. Now that the Ragnarök is upon us, I'm getting it back so I can die with it." Now dressed, he picked up his staff. "Shall we go?"

"Where are we going?" Tostig asked.

"To Nidhogg; you must defeat him before he completely destroys Yggdrasil."

.

.

Tostig had to double his pace to keep up with Odin's longer strides, his staff tapping with each step.

"Did you encounter any dark elves on your journey?" Odin asked.

"No, you're the first person I've encountered so far."

"Good. When Asgard fell I was worried that the absence of a divine authority would make them impossible to deal with, if not outright belligerent." The cave shook once again. "The tremor you're feeling is Nidhogg gnawing on Yggdrasil's roots. It's destroying the great tree and if it's successful, the destruction of Midgard is imminent."

"I'm still a little confused about my role in saving Midgard. Will I be the one who defeats Nidhogg?" Tostig asked.

Odin looked at him. "Yes, of course. Is that so hard for you to believe?"

"Well . . . uh . . . yes it is," Tostig replied. "I'm not a warrior, as you can see. In fact, I *don't* want to be a warrior."

"Great power can come in any size. Look at the ant: it can move a mountain, one grain of sand at a time. You must defeat Nidhogg for your people to survive and for all the worlds to survive."

"Odin, why was I chosen?"

"Why were any of us chosen?" Odin answered. "For all of my power, it really comes down to only one thing—my knowledge in exchange for my eye. We are what we are."

"Perhaps if I knew what kind of world I'm saving, it would help me," Tostig said.

"Before all of this is over, I think you'll know." Odin replied.

They approached an opening through which a fiery light cast shadows across the tunnel wall like the reflective colours of a sunset. Odin stopped in front of the opening and looked expectantly back at him. Tostig stepped up to the threshold and looked down at the sprawling and intertwined roots of Yggdrasil. It was an endless maze of twisting and looping patterns that reached high enough to touch the cavern ceiling and stretched far across the vast cavern. It was so dense that Tostig couldn't see how far below it the floor was, or even if there was a floor.

"The light you see is the fires of Ginnungagap," Odin told

him. "They are far enough away to not be a threat, but as Nidhogg chews on more and more roots, Yggdrasil's foundation is weakened even more. It will fall into and be consumed by the fires that helped create it."

"Odin, how am I going to get through all of this?" Tostig asked, gesturing toward the twisting mass of roots.

"You'll find a way. We all have a part to play in this drama. You will play your role as you're destined to play it."

"What if I refuse?" Tostig challenged.

Odin sighed, impatient with Tostig's stubbornness. "Remember when you asked me about your family and where you came from? To know that truth is also a part of who you are and how your destiny will unfold. When you're jumping from rock to rock across a brook, you won't know which rock will teeter, causing your fall into the water. You can't choose which rock to stand on. You must step on each rock to get to the other side. Tostig, if you choose not to cross the brook, the great tree will fall and our universe will disappear just as a single thought does when sleep overtakes us."

Tostig stared into Odin's face for a long moment. Then he stepped down onto the broad root that twisted up to the cave opening—it was wide enough for him to walk on, but he gasped when it bent under his full body weight. It rebounded, and Tostig relaxed, then shuffled slowly down its length, careful to maintain his balance as he approached a tangled mass of tentacle-like offshoots at its end.

"This is a maze, how can I navigate through this?" Tostig muttered in frustration.

"How would you navigate on land—or on the ocean, which has no landmarks?" Odin asked.

"I navigate using the sun and the wind currents, and sometimes the stars."

"And where does all of this measurement take place—is it already done for you?"

"No," Tostig answered. "It takes place in my head."

"So you think through your course by creating and following patterns in the sky—the wind patterns and the regular path of the sun as it moves across the sky," Odin said. "It seems to me that you have everything you need to navigate through the roots of Yggdrasil."

"I'm afraid, Alfather."

"You're doing wonderfully, my boy. Everything is moving forward as it should," Odin assured him.

Tostig crouched to sidle through the gap where another root looped around the one on which he walked. Whenever he approached an opening, the looping roots seemed to spread to allow him passage—or perhaps that was a trick of the light cast by the distant furnace, which made the roots seem to move and shift all around him in the dancing light. The strange and wonderful light display also lit his way through the maze underneath the great tree, for which he was grateful. He was able to look around for recognizable patterns in the tangle.

Grabbing an overhead branching to steady himself, Tostig looked up as he stepped onto a much thinner root, and saw thousands of roots converging on a gargantuan central trunk. "Is that the trunk of Yggdrasil?" he asked. When he didn't hear an answer, Tostig turned around. He was alone. "Odin!" Tostig yelled, hoping for a reply. None came. Having no other choice, he continued.

The way on the thinner root was more perilous, and Tostig moved with caution, pausing as the bough sagged momentarily with each step. Suddenly, instead of rebounding, it gave way, bending so far under his weight that he dropped. "Nyah!" Tostig grunted in terror, then gasped as his scrabbling hand found the root above him and he stopped, dangling in mid-air, one hand holding onto the root and the other hand gripping his sword. He looked down and saw a rock ledge—or the cave floor; he couldn't tell which, in the midst of his trauma and in the flickering light.

He swung his body toward another root that looked strong enough to support him and pulled himself onto it, then lay hugging it, panting. Tostig didn't know how long he lay there, trying to regain both the strength and the courage to stand and push on. A violent tremor that shook the root system reminded him of the need to continue.

About to push to his feet, Tostig paused as a gust of air, heavy with the stench of rot and putrefaction, rose from somewhere below him. He lay back down on the root and looked down into a rocky shaft. A walkway spiralled down its walls, affording access to dark openings that Tostig presumed were the tunnels that snaked beneath Hóp.

He looked to the roots nearby, and saw his target suspended amongst them. His tail snaking around one of Yggdrasil's primary roots, Nidhogg took massive bites from it, consuming some and allowing the rest to drop into the chasm. Moving slowly from that wound to another root, Nidhogg's massive clawed feet dug into the tendrils that provided Yggdrasil's sustenance, as the serpent consumed them one by one. It was hard to tell whether Nidhogg was actually eating the roots with the intention of destroying the great tree, or whether it was tangled in the snarl underneath Yggdrasil and was trying to chew himself free.

Tostig slipped the sword into his belt and used the meshed roots to descend toward the serpent, feeling the vibrations as the large serpent moved through the network of roots below him. As he got closer, he saw human corpses and bones as well as other remains tangled in the roots of the tree and scattered on the ledge. Tucked into a nook was a blanket-wrapped object. *Snorri*, he thought. *That must be Snorri!*

He climbed away from Nidhogg, unsheathing Gram and using it to hack at the roots that Nidhogg clung to below him, detaching each, trying to weaken Nidhogg's hold on Yggdrasil. The fewer roots supporting the serpent's weight, the more Nidhogg's weight would strain the roots holding him.

Tostig was close enough to see Nidhogg's flat head and the forked tongue flitting out of its mouth. Its claws sank deep into the larger roots, the body sitting low above them, as if the serpent was meant to crawl along the ground. Its slow but powerful movements could be a weakness that Tostig could use against it.

He pierced another large root with the tip of his sword, knowing that the damage he was doing would not be permanent. As he severed that root from the rest of the tree, Yggdrasil shook once again.

As Tostig weakened more and more of the roots, moving dangerously close to the serpent, he noticed Nidhogg's tail twisting tighter amongst the roots of Yggdrasil, further securing its place in the tree. Tostig slowly maneuvered away from Nidhogg's tail but, unable to discern the tip from the roots, he backed into it. The tail immediately closed around Tostig's torso and began squeezing, either mistaking him for part of the tree or sensing him as a threat.

Tostig wheezed and gasped for air, trying to turn his sword around before his constricted circulation numbed his hands. He managed to lift the sword up over the tail and thrust it through the serpent's scaly hide. The monster howled and released him. Tostig fell into a mesh of roots and scrambled to get away from Nidhogg's tail before it attacked him again.

Brittle roots creaked and snapped around Tostig as Nidhogg, thrown off balance, grabbed at those nearby, his injured tail flailing. Standing, Tostig began hacking at the mass of roots above his head, trying to deny Nidhogg as many handholds as possible. A mass of roots ripped free of Yggdrasil and dropped, Nidhogg falling with them. With an ear-numbing howl, he disappeared over the ledge into the rocky chasm. Its moans echoed up to Tostig, who watched, panting with effort.

Teetering along a root that descended to the ledge, Tostig paused near its end and used another root like a rope to swing down to the sand-strewn surface. He slowly reached out for the bundle, almost afraid to touch it, fearing what lay within may be dead. Gently lifting the bundle, he slowly unfolded the layers of cloth protecting the baby—yes, Snorri, and alive! Tostig smiled as, cradling Snorri in his arms, he clasped a tiny hand and rubbed the back with his thumb; Snorri slowly squirmed and gurgled. Relieved, Tostig drew his first breath since picking the baby up. Then he looked around for a way out, and noticed the corpses. This, he realized, was the fate that awaited Snorri if he hadn't been rescued.

He climbed to the edge of a rocky embankment and saw a crack in the rock wall—perhaps a potential way out. He moved quickly through the dead bodies lying around him, headed for the path to freedom.

A roar erupted behind him, starting low and rising as a clawed foot landed with a ground-shaking thud on the ledge. Tostig whirled to see Nidhogg pulling himself onto the ledge, maneuvering until the bloody tail landed on the ledge with another thud. The jaw gaped wide and the serpent tipped its head back to let out another deafening screech. His tail swished back and forth, raising clouds of dust and grit. Then the monster rose to its feet, its body swaying back and forth, and charged forward to trap its prey.

Tostig backed hastily away from the exit. Snorri began wailing in his arms. Ducking behind a boulder, Tostig gently concealed Snorri behind it, then unsheathed his sword and stepped out to stand between the baby and Nidhogg.

The serpent let out another roar; its damp, hot breath struck Tostig's face like a slap. Nidhogg's cheek muscles moved, and the serpent's forked tongue slid out, then quickly retracted. Nidhogg swished his tail around, catching Tostig off guard and tripping him; he fell to the ground and the sword flew out of his grip, stopping just beyond arm's reach. Tostig realized that the impact of the attack more than made up for Nidhogg's slow movements.

He jumped to his feet and grabbed his sword, pointing the Gram at Nidhogg, ready to swing at its tongue or its tail. Nidhogg spat his tongue out again; Tostig swung and missed. As Nidhogg swung his tail, Tostig leapt over it, managing to land on his feet, but when the tail swished back again, it caught Tostig and he fell across it, instinctively wrapping his arms around it. Nidhogg swished his tail from side to side, but he couldn't dislodge the dwarf.

Hugging the serpent's jerking tail, Tostig crawled up its length to the base of Nidhogg's spine. He managed to get to his feet and run up Nidhogg's scaled back, his low, stout body aiding him in remaining on top of the shifting serpent. He leaped and wrapped his legs as tight as he could around Nidhogg's neck, then raised his sword in the air, ready to plunge the blade into the base of its skull.

The serpent slammed its chin to the ground and Tostig tumbled forward, rolling across the ledge and landing on his stomach, the sword flying from his hand. As Tostig rolled over, Nidhogg's forked tongue struck his arm, breaking the skin; blood oozed out of the wound, mixing with the serpent's saliva, and Tostig screamed in pain, clutching his arm.

Nidhogg crept closer, its clawed feet scraping along the ledge. Nearly blinded by pain, Tostig looked up as Nidhogg's head loomed over him. He swore the serpent was smiling as it opened its mouth to chomp down on him.

Then a spear hurtled through the air and embedded itself in Nidhogg's flank. The serpent writhed and howled in pain, thrashing its head around.

"Run!" Odin yelled from the rock where he stood.

Tostig jumped to his feet, pressing his wounded arm against his stomach as he looked around for the Gram. Nidhogg's breath huffed behind him, the serpent seeming determined to finish off Tostig before attacking its second foe. Spotting the sword, Tostig sprinted for it, Nidhogg lumbering behind him, the ground shuddering with each step the serpent took. Snatching up the sword, Tostig swung around and pointed the tip at Nidhogg's snout.

The serpent stopped. Tostig noticed its cheek muscles moving as they had before, as the serpent prepared to strike. He hefted the sword over his shoulder and, as Nidhogg's tongue shot out, Tostig swung the Gram down, slicing through it.

It howled in pain, the stump of its tongue swinging wildly in the air, splattering blood on the rock walls and ledge. Tostig bolted toward Nidhogg's open mouth and used the momentum and the weight of his body to slam the blade into the roof of the serpent's mouth. It drove through into Nidhogg's brain, and its legs buckled instantly, slamming its tail and head to the ground, followed by the rest of its body.

Tostig sagged to his knees in front of Nidhogg, panting for breath. He stared at the lifeless head, then looked at his arm. The blood had clotted, but his arm was swollen and turning black and blue. Suddenly feeling tired, as if his life force were leeching from him, Tostig slumped.

"Gungnir has never failed me," Odin announced, walking up to Nidhogg's still body and pulling his magical spear from its side. He leaned on it, resuming its use as his walking staff.

Tostig tried standing, but he felt as if even the weight of the air held him down. The cavern spun and he stumbled back down to the ground.

Odin walked to Nidhogg's mouth and pulled out the sword.

"Alfather?" Tostig asked, confusion creeping into his mind.

"It's Nidhogg's sting; the poison is pulsating through your body. It will soon reach your heart."

"Can you do anything for me?" Tostig asked as he felt the

blood drain from his face, his skin becoming cold and clammy.

"I'm afraid not," Odin answered. "But you've performed a heroic feat here today—you saved Midgard."

Tostig couldn't find the right expression as he began losing muscle control. His chest heaved with effort, as if Odin were standing on it.

A point of light that looked like a reflection grew on the cavern wall. Tostig watched it get bigger and bigger until the air around it seemed to unfold, and a tunnel opened up. A winged figure flew through the opening—and the world went dark.

"Tostig, can you see me?" a female voice asked.

"No, but I can hear you," he replied.

"It's Sváfa."

"Oh Sváfa, I'm so glad you're here. I wish I could see you, but I'm blind," Tostig breathed. "Will you take me to Valhalla?"

"Valhalla doesn't exist anymore, my son," Odin answered. "But you and Sváfa are destined to be reborn together—she a princess and you a warrior."

"I will give you your name and we'll fall in love," Sváfa added.

"As I love you now," Tostig replied as he closed his eyes.

He felt Sváfa lift him into her arms, heard the rustle as her wings unfolded, felt the air move as they flapped. "Alfather, please don't forget Snorri," Tostig said, his last words trailing him into unconsciousness.

~~~

"I'll take him back to Thorfinn and Gudrid," Odin said quietly to the valkyrie.

As Sváfa and Tostig flew toward the portal, Odin felt a tear trickling down his cheek. He watched as they entered the tunnel and it closed up behind them, disappearing into the cave wall. Then he picked up Snorri.

As Odin pulled back the swaddling and looked into Snorri's deep blue eyes, it was hard to think of endings; all the alfather could think about were beginnings. He held the baby tightly, knowing that the bundle in his arms was more precious than all the gold in the nine worlds.
~~~

When he walked out of the cave of Straumfjörðr he saw the *Hringhorni* partially beached. Soon the tide would move in and fill the lagoon and the caves with water. The world beneath Hóp would be submerged and everything that had happened in there would be erased from time, as if it never took place, just as Odin's footprints that he made as he walked across the moist sand would no longer exist.

As he approached the knarr where the survivors were gathering at the bow, a woman jumped over the side and ran toward him across the sandy shelf, kicking up sand, her arms outstretched to grab her baby.

"My son," Gudrid screamed as she took Snorri from the alfather and held him to her breast for the first time.

Thorfinn came up behind her and unfolded the bundle, eager to see his son. He peered into Snorri's blue eyes and touched his blond hair. "He's the most beautiful thing I've ever seen," he said. "Thank you for bringing our son back to us, Alfather."

"It's not me that you should be thanking, it's Elsu and Tostig. They gave their lives so your son could be returned to you."

"Tostig is dead?" Gudrid said, bursting into tears.

"Gone, but *not gone*," Odin replied.

"Gone but not *forgotten*," Thorfinn corrected, looking at Odin.

"Alfather, your eye patch is gone," Gudrid observed, "and you have your eye."

"Yes. And I must leave you now, my children. We must go our separate ways. It's time that I fulfill my destiny and you must return home to fulfill yours. Be well."

Odin took a final look at the knarr and noticed Freydis tied to the figurehead on the front of the boat. He knew that paying for Loki's crimes was an unfair judgement on her, but there was nothing that he could do; this was a human matter that would have to be resolved by humans.

"I see that the *Hringhorni* survived the onslaught of water," he said. "I suppose it's fitting that Tostig died with the destruction of the ship that he built."

"Alfather, what about the battle between the Æsir and the Vanir?" Thorfinn asked.

"That is yet to come," Odin replied, turning and walking across the sand. "Take care of my knarr," he called as he walked away.

With Gudrid cradling Snorri, she and Thorfinn boarded the *Hringhorni* and the knarr was pushed off the sandy bank. As the rowers backed them out to the current, away from Straumfjörðr and Hóp, Thorfinn watched the alfather walk down the beach and clamber up the rocky path to the top of the cliff. He thought of Tostig and Elsu; they would be missed. He wished that he had a part of their bodies to be buried back home.

As the sail ballooned and snapped in the wind, Thorfinn saw a large black wolf moving toward the alfather. Noticing the animal, Odin threw his staff over the cliff. It cracked and splintered as it hit the rocks, then disappeared somewhere among the boulders, waiting for the tide to take it out to sea.

They stood for a moment, facing one another. Then the wolf leapt onto Odin, pushing him to the ground. The wolf's jaws opened so wide that it looked as if they'd unhinged. Then they closed around Odin's neck, and the wolf shook its head, sinking its teeth further and further into the alfather.

Thorfinn turned away. No one else had noticed the scene that he'd just witnessed. They were too busy trying to see the new baby. He walked into the crowd and escorted Gudrid away from them. They walked to the side of the ship and watched the orange glow of sunset breaking through the clouds that were parting for the first time since Odin's arrival.

As the *Hringhorni* sailed away from the evening sun, taking the survivors home, Thorfinn tried not to think of the friends and the beliefs he had lost, but rather what he had gained.

Glossary

Æsir is one tribe of Norse gods; though not in every case, they represent the reasoning part of human nature.

Alfather is what the name implies: "all father," or "father of all." Another name for Odin, the leader of the Norse pantheon.

Álfars are elves.

Asgard means "enclosure of the Æsir." It's one of the nine worlds and is home to the Norse gods and Valhalla, Odin's enormous hall.

Austr is east.

Baldur is the Norse god of light. It's said that he's so handsome, wise, and bright that light shines from him.

Dagmál: day-measure, a unit of time.

Dagsigling is a day's sailing

Dökkálfar are dark elves.

Dægur is defined in the ancient Icelandic work on chronometry called Rímbegla: “In the day there are two ‘dægurs;’ in the ‘dægurs’ twelve hours.”

Fótr is foot (measurement).

Hóp (pronounced Hop) is Eirik’s southern settlement.

Hustrulinet is a universal Scandinavian symbol of the wife, sometimes worn as a headband.

i-Viking is a term meaning to go raiding, this means that you are going to raid a specific place, most commonly on land or on ships.

Jötunn is a class that includes giants, elves (both light and dark), dwarves; a race of nature spirits with superhuman strength. They sometimes intermingle and intermarry with the tribes of the Æsir and the Vanir.

Kjalarness is the place name where Thorvald was buried.

Landvættir is land spirits.

Leifsbúrður is Leif’s (Eiriksson) Camp.

Ljósálfar are light elves.

Mánuðir is a month.

Midgard literally means the “middle world” inhabited by men.

Miðnœtti is midnight.

Misseri is actually a composite with an etymology corresponding directly to “half-year.”

Norðr means north.

Ouroboros is an ancient symbol depicting a serpent or dragon eating its own tail. In Norse mythology, it appears as the serpent Jörmungandr.

Óvitr means ignorant.

Ragnarök or ragna-rokkr literally means "the twilight of the gods."

Straumfjörðr means "Fjord of Currents," or tidal lagoon.

Suðr is south.

Sunnundægur means Sunday.

Túnlengd means "Homefield-long." It's the length of an enclosed homefield, or a short distance.

Tvö misseri literally means two semesters; two semesters is equal to one year.

Undorn dagmark is afternoon (eykt, although the direct translation is lost).

Vanir are another group of gods once separate from the Æsir, now a subgroup of them. They loosely represent the emotional side of human nature.

Vestr is west.

Viknatal means week; literally, counting of weeks.

Völva literally means "wand carrier"; they practised shamanism, sorcery, and prophecy.

Other Books by R.G. Johnston

so   cs

Vinland: The Beginning

ABOUT THE AUTHOR

༄ ༄

R.G. Johnston grew up in central Newfoundland. The province's cultural and natural beauty inspired him at an early age to write about humanity's association with the land. He won a bronze medal for Best Regional Fiction – Canada East for his first book, *Vinland: The Beginning*, and CBC Radio reviewed his book for their East Coast Morning show. He's talked about the Vikings and the Norse on local television stations and CJBQ Radio in Belleville, Ontario.

For more information visit
www.vinlandthebeginning.com & **www.vinlandragnarok.ca**.

Credit Front Cover Image
The Ash Yggdrasil
By Friedrich Wilhelm Heine

CPSIA information can be obtained at www.ICGtesting.com
235443LV00004B/6/P